C000170751

BEST GAY EROTICA 1996

WITHDRAWN FOR SALE

30127 0 4606 274 6

BEST GAY EROTICA 1996

Selected and Introduced by
SCOTT HEIM

Edited by
MICHAEL FORD

Suffolk County Council

Libraries & Heritage

JMLS	0896
	SHO		

CLEIS
PRESS

Copyright © 1996 by Michael Ford
Introduction © 1996 by Scott Heim
All rights reserved. Except for brief passages quoted in newspaper, magazine, radio or television reviews, no part of this book may be reproduced in any form or by any means, electronic or mechanical, including photocopying or recording, or by information storage or retrieval system, without permission in writing from the Publisher.
Published in the United States by Cleis Press Inc., P.O. Box 8933, Pittsburgh, Pennsylvania 15221, and P.O. Box 14684, San Francisco, California 94114.
Cover design: Scott Idleman
Interior design: Pete Ivey
Cleis logo art: Juana Alicia
First Edition.
Printed in the United States.
10 9 8 7 6 5 4 3 2 1

"Stroke the Fire" ©1995 by M. Christian. "Playing Solitaire" ©1995 by Mitch Cullin. Appeared in *Christopher Street,* Issue 226, June 1995. "First Shave" ©1995 by Jameson Currier. "Prime Real Estate" ©1995 by Mark David M. Fennell. Excerpted from *Rampant,* a work-in-progress. "The Last Blowjob" ©1995 by Stephen Greco. Appeared in *Flesh and the Word 3* (New York: Plume, 1995), edited by John Preston and Michael Lowenthal. "Whiskey Dicks" ©1995 by Rick Jackson. "The Voice of the Capon" ©1995 by Alex Jeffers. Excerpted from the forthcoming novel *Selected Letters: the Ethan stories.* "A Traveller's Relief" ©1995 by Owen Keehnen. Excerpted from the novel-in-progress *Doing Time in Bayetteville.* "Loveth Thou Me, Boy?" ©1995 by Miodrag Kojadinović. "The Yellow" ©1994 by Michael Lassell. Appeared in *Looking for Mr. Preston* (New York: Richard Kasak Books, 1995), edited by Laura Antoniou. "Good in Tension" ©1995 by Scott O'Hara. "Ganged" ©1994 by Carol Queen. Appeared in *Looking for Mr. Preston* (New York: Richard Kasak Books, 1995), edited by Laura Antoniou. "Pleasingly" ©1995 by Matthew Rettenmund. "What He Did" ©1995 by Thomas Roche. Appeared as "Adrienne" in Norway's *Cupido* Nr. 7/1995. "The Adored One" ©1995 by Michael Rowe. "Aegis" ©1995 by D. Travers Scott. "Hotter Than Hell" ©1995 by Simon Sheppard.

Contents

FOREWORD

Erotica. Pornography. Smut. The name changes depending upon who's reading it, publishing it, censoring it. But whatever it's called, writing and reading about sex—real or fantasized—is a vital part of gay male popular culture. Perhaps because what we do sexually is so often used to define who and what we are, we have made sexuality in all its varied forms something of a point of pride. More importantly, how we perceive ourselves and others sexually as gay men frequently reflects how we feel about other areas of our lives, and writing about our experiences not only provides unusually candid insight into what's happening in our community as a whole but can, in fact, shape our perceptions of what is possible in our lives.

When I was twelve or thirteen, I bought my first porn magazine. It was a Christmas issue of *Torso*, and it had a picture of beefy, hairy porn star Al Parker on the cover, wearing nothing but a Santa hat. I went home and fantasized endlessly to that magazine, first to the pictures of Al and the other models and then to the stories I found sandwiched in between the photo spreads. While the photographs most assuredly had some influence on my taste in men and what I visualized when I jerked off, in a far greater way, reading the stories expanded the possibilities for my own sexuality. While I read, I became both the top and the bottom, depending on my mood, both the cock sucker and the one getting sucked. I had never read about men doing these things before, and as a young queer, imagining the scenarios suggested in the stroke stories, tame as they were, was a new and welcome experience.

A decade later, long after I'd actually had sex with another man, I would sell my first porn story to *Torso* and begin my foray into the world of writing about gay desire. Like a number of people who write porn, at first I did it because I thought it would be fun, something to tell people at parties. I wrote up a locker room sex story based on life with my college roommate—who really was captain of the baseball team—and sent it off. A week later, I received an acceptance letter and a request for more material. I called a friend and laughed about it. "Me writing porn!" I said. "Can you imagine anything more ridiculous?" Writing porn seemed incongruous with my work as a writer of serious nonfiction.

Much to my surprise, however, I found myself writing another story. Then another, and another. I discovered that I had a lot to say about sex and what it meant to me, and that porn stories provided a perfect forum in which to do so. The first few early stories were just about the mechanics of sex—who did what to whom and what it felt like. But then I started to wonder why the characters were doing it, and what it meant to them. My stories got longer, more involved. And the more I explored, the more people seemed to like them. I got letters from readers. Editors asked for more. I published one book, then a second. One day while sitting at my computer and trying to come up with yet another way to describe some character's spectacular orgasm, I realized the truth: I had become a pornographer, at least part-time, and porn had become, to me, a serious literary pursuit.

Beginning in the late 1950s and early 1960s, the publishing of erotica for gay men was largely an underground business. Early erotic books were turned out by workers in what were effectively porn sweatshops: rooms full of typewriters and struggling writers (frequently women) who were paid by the page to sit day in and day out and churn out stories of beautiful, and often troubled, young men in lust. Dressed up in gaudy covers and featuring lurid titles that frequently had little to do with the actual content of the books (*The Gay Lords* is one of my personal favorites, conjuring up images of debauched royalty but in fact being about a marauding gang of oversexed queers), these torrid tales, purchased by men who hid them beneath mattresses and in closets, sold briskly. The plots were thin, and generally the gay characters were portrayed as confused, even delinquent types who used cunning and often drugs to seduce the innocent heroes. They inevitably met bad ends.

The 1970s saw a greater tolerance for writing openly about sex, and this included gay male sex, at least to some extent. For many gay men, the literary touchstones of the time are Gordon Merrick's string of pseudo-pornographic novels, the first gay-themed romance books to be published in the United States by a major publishing house. Unfortunately, the sex in Merrick's books was generally of the overdramatic, stereotype-riddled variety in which freshly-showered, pretty young men buggered one another with abandon without breaking a sweat or messing up their hair. Despite the books' flaws, gay men devoured them ravenously, eager for any validation of their sex lives and fantasies.

Also providing an outlet for erotic writing were small gay presses such as Alyson, Gay Sunshine, Alternate Publishing, and Fire Island Press, which beginning in the mid-1980s published some of the first titles which sought to take erotica seriously as a genre. Writers such as Aaron

Travis, Phil Andros, and Lars Eighner published some of the most influential early pornographic works with these and other independent houses.

Apart from these books, for the last twenty years, the publication of explicit erotica was limited primarily to appearances in the pages of skin magazines. For those of us who wrote porn, the thrill of seeing our words in print was dampened by the knowledge that after thirty days on the newsstand, our glory days would be over. Add to that the fact that our stories were competing with the magazines' real selling point—the photographs—and writing porn became a labor of love. It certainly wasn't one of profit.

That changed dramatically in 1992 with the publication of the debut title in John Preston's *Flesh and the Word* series. Preston had already caused a minor sensation in the gay literary world with the serialized publication in *Drummer* magazine of his now-classic porn novel *Mr. Benson,* which even spawned a fashion statement in the form of T-shirts emblazoned with the phrase *Looking for Mr. Benson,* with or without a question mark appended. A self-proclaimed pornographer, and more than proud of it, Preston argued for the respectability of porn as a genre with a strong and reasoned voice. Whether or not he always proved his point, he certainly broadened the horizons of many a reader. Equally important, he also opened doors at mainstream publishing houses, doors that had been firmly closed to erotica and those who wrote it.

The first anthology of gay male erotica published by a major publisher, *Flesh and the Word* signaled a change in attitude toward writing about gay men's sex lives, and toward writing about sex in general. It can certainly be argued that this shift owed as much to the financial rewards to be gained by treating porn with greater respect as to any actual shift in thinking about erotica as a viable art form, but the fact remains that bringing it out into the open and putting it on shelves at Barnes & Noble gave the material a measure of respect it had not previously enjoyed. While the books published by small presses had certainly been popular with a select readership, *Flesh and the Word,* with the help of the advertising dollars available to a mainstream house and the added benefit of being published as part of a serious literary list, was able to reach a far broader audience than ever before. Wrapped in a handsome cover and presented as worthy reading material, the book could safely be taken to checkout counters by readers who would never dream of buying pornography in its earlier, rougher forms.

Suddenly, it seemed that porn (always referred to as the tamer, less-threatening "erotica" by publishing-house marketing directors) was hot in more ways than one. *Flesh and the Word* topped bestseller lists for gay men's books across the country. Collections such as Susie Bright's *Best American Erotica* and *Herotica* garnered respectable sales and equally respectable reviews, even breaking into the lucrative book club market. The highly-successful BadBoy line, still the only ongoing imprint devoted exclusively to gay male porn, even found its way into the chain bookstores at suburban malls, many of which now carried some of the titles that came out following the success of Preston's ground-breaking book. Erotic anthologies of various stripes and predilections appeared in a flurry of publishing excitement, as editors eager to feed a hungry audience sought out material that previously had been taboo.

While many porn writers found this sudden public legitimization of what had heretofore been a forbidden subject a long-deserved welcome into the literary fold, others labeled it nothing more than a trend, and accused greedy publishers of once again co-opting gay male culture and using it to turn a profit. Unused to finding their work noticed by anyone but faithful readers, writers such as Lars Eighner, Phil Andros, and Preston, who had written porn for years in relative obscurity, found themselves labeled cultural historians and saw their works deconstructed as portraits of times gone by. Other writers, including many who previously wouldn't have thought of writing erotica, or at least admit to writing it, suddenly jumped on the bandwagon, declaring writing about sex a worthy pastime. While it's too early to tell whether the publishing of erotic writing is in fact a trend or a genre that's here to stay, the fact remains that interest in sex writing is at an all-time high.

The literary standards and breadth of subject matter in gay male erotic writing have reached an unprecedented level of excellence. Moving far beyond the-mailman-delivered-more-than-mail storylines of the past, porn being produced today offers commentaries on everything from the effects of AIDS on the sex lives of gay men to the role desire plays in our adolescent lives. While the *Flesh and the Word* series is still going strong, now on its fourth volume and under the editorship of Michael Lowenthal since Preston's death, it has never really been a "best of" anthology focusing on material written or published during a particular time period, which can in itself provide a fascinating snapshot of the concerns, interests, and fears writers are experiencing at that moment. And while Susie Bright's wonderful *Best American Erotica* series always contains excellent examples of gay erotic fiction, and should be required reading for *anyone* interested in the craft of writing porn, gay readers and writers deserve their own collection.

I would argue that precisely because of the increased interest in erotica there is a need to collect the best examples of this type of work into one volume. As inevitably happens when anything becomes popular, the quality of what is being published varies from book to book, and many current anthologies are produced with little thought to substance and perhaps too much attention to marketing strategy. While some erotic anthologies that focus on particular aspects of our sexual lives, or are directed at particular segments of the gay community, are excellent, there are far too many mediocre sex at work/outdoors/school anthologies, too many repetitive and just plain boring books. While these books certainly provide opportunities for publication that didn't exist before, and while they are often entertaining, they don't challenge readers' expectations, don't encourage them to look beyond stock plots and ideas. They treat erotica with an outdated "candy for the cock" mentality that effectively pushes porn back into the literary closet instead of really seeking out the varied voices that are out there waiting to be discovered.

What I find missing from much of the gay male porn coming out in recent years is a willingness to go beyond standard suck-and-fuck notions of sex or to discuss desire as it applies to anyone other than perfectly-developed, All-American young men with big cocks. I once asked a room filled with men who had come to hear me speak about erotica if any of them ever read the erotic writing of women such as Pat Califia, Carol Queen, or Wickie Stamps, all writers whose work pushes boundaries in new and exciting ways. None had. A few weeks later, I got a call from one of the men. He had recently read a lesbian daddy genderfuck piece by Pat Califia, and found himself incredibly aroused. He was both surprised and angry. Did jerking off to a story about two women mean he was straight? Did it mean he was bisexual? He wanted answers. Similarly, I have had people write to me saying that they were ashamed to have found themselves getting off on stories I'd written about things they found taboo or disturbing.

It is important for us to stretch the boundaries of our erotic lives, or at least to know what other people are up to. Unfortunately, most of us are conditioned to think that we are limited by what we are "supposed" to like. Ironically, for all of our openness about sex, gay men can be especially rigid in our ideas about what is acceptable turn-on material. The man who finds himself suddenly getting aroused by photographs of soldiers in Nazi uniforms may feel shame at the same time that he's shooting his load over his belly. The man who finds his cock swelling while reading a description of less-than-physically perfect men fucking is more likely to feel confusion than be moved to see if maybe he hasn't fully explored the extent of his ability to be attracted to different types of men. And the gay man suddenly finding himself wondering what it would be like to make love with a woman is conditioned to respond with disgust rather than interest.

The purpose of excellent erotic writing is to explore what makes us feel sexual stirrings. A good story takes readers into a sexual world. This world may be familiar, or it may at first seem totally alien. Expanding this world, and introducing readers to corners of it they might not ordinarily visit, is one of the joys of writing erotica. Yes, gay men can be aroused by a story about a man and a woman, or about two women. And lesbians can get off on stories about gay men. And even if you've never experienced a particular kind of attraction, you can still be moved by the ability to have that attraction, or by someone's description of what makes desire bloom.

When I first thought of putting together an annual collection of best gay erotica, I wanted to present readers with a sampling of some of the many excellent stories in which writers of all types explore the nature of passion, need, and desire from various viewpoints. I was both surprised and overjoyed at the number of writers who submitted stories for the collection, and regret that we can feature only a handful. Interestingly, none of the stories in this collection were first published in porn magazines, the traditional arena for such material. Many are unpublished or taken from works-in-progress; a few came from other anthologies. Clearly, the world of erotica, and of those who write it, is expanding.

Some of the stories here will be expected; others I hope will be surprising, perhaps even unsettling. None, I think, are ordinary. My hope is that, by reading these stories, others will be encouraged to do some exploring of their own.

Michael Ford
New York
December 1995

INTRODUCTION

Scott Heim

Oh god, oh yessss.... Or so moaned the dialogue from the first porn paperback I ever laid my astonished pale blue eyes upon. I was nine, maybe ten. The book was called *The Passion of...* um, some woman's calendrical first name finished out the title; either April or June. My father hadn't hidden the book in any of the usual crannies. Not beneath his mattress, not behind the folding seat of his Ford pickup. Instead, he stashed it in an unused breadbox atop our kitchen's fridge—presumedly a lair beyond my reach. (The refrigerator? My father should have known that me, chubby-cheeked pre-teen porker, would have discovered the book at some point, what with all my openings and closings of that fingerprint-smudged door.)

I was spurred to read *The Passion of April/June* by the photographs on the front and back cover. The female stood in see-through gown, lips parted seductively. But behind her: *voila!* a man. He lounged in a hot tub, waiting for What's-er-name to come tiptoeing back to sluicing jets of hot water. He sported a goldilocks mane of hair, its shiny blond matched by a mustache (instant turn-on for pre-teen me) that curled over his sneering lip. He held a half-empty glass of champagne. A candle flickered beyond his shoulder.

Over the following months, years, I devoured that book umpteen times. Peppering its flimsy narrative were sentences, whole paragraphs, of clichéd dialogue and wild synonyms for both male and female genitalia. I giggled at words like "sleeping snake" and "coral cavern." Later, I passed the book to my friend, Traci, whose favorite phrase was "quivering quim," the meaning of which to this day I'm still uncertain. Nights, with my family harmonizing their steady bedroom zzz's, I snuck to the kitchen, smuggled the book from its hiding place, and sprinted back to my blankets.

Fast-forward. College, grad school, MFA in writing. I only read "classic literature," "serious literary fiction." The language and characters and settings from books like *The Passion* were worlds away from my new canon. I graduated, published my first novel, blah, blah, blah. What I'm leading to is this: how, one summer evening, my pal Mike Ford—in between bites of fish teriyaki—asked me to make the final selections for the anthology you're gripping in your little fists.

Why not? I thought. I enjoyed reading and writing sex scenes, provided they were sandwiched safely between pages of what I'd been taught to recognize as "serious fiction." I wolfed more sesame noodles and accepted, expecting to read slightly varied versions of the same male/male, top/bottom dirty talk. Gay takes on that book I'd read as a kid. *Oh god, oh yessss...* and then some.

One of my immediate assumptions concerned the writers themselves. I reckoned the *Best Gay Erotica* submissions to be from unfamiliar names, pseudonyms for hacks who churned out a story a day, then mailed them off to this or that porn magazine. Not so. Included were writers such as Alex Jeffers, author of the recent highly-praised novel *Safe As Houses;* Michael Lassell, whose book of poems, *Decade Dance,* won a Lambda Literary Award. Also included were names I knew as more familiar to readers of erotic fiction—Michael Rowe, Scott O'Hara, others who continue to remain at the genre's forefront. There were poets, magazine editors, MFA students. There was even—and here, the first hint that my assumptions were poised to be not only disproved, but shattered—a gay erotic story written by a woman.

Surprising me even more than the writers' names were the actual stories. I made the stipulation that each piece had to stray from my preconceptions and admittedly ingenuous expectations. A piece of erotic fiction, I decided, should transcend both the banalities of "porn" language and the predictable setting and/or scenario. After all, most people remember the clichés of certain dog-eared porn paperbacks they warily passed around high school hallways. Who wants to read rehashings of those nasty pages? There are only so many synonyms for *cock* and *cunt.* Only so many retellings of the well-hung TV repairman; the mustachioed traffic cop willing to accept a good, imaginatively perverse bribe; the pair of naughty nursemaids caught sixty-nining in the storage room.

While most of the stories here stray far from the orthodox ideas of what porn writing "should" be, some treat familiar subjects or settings in entirely new ways. For instance, an extended take on the glory hole fantasy, Owen Keehnen's sexy "A Traveller's Relief" swerves from convention in its tone, using an economical and nervy slam-bang style to mirror the quirky urgency of the story's twenty-one-year-old Cody. Despite the bar-cruising scene of Mark David Fennell's "Prime Real Estate," descriptions of the hunky bartender are juxtaposed with the nervy and lonely thought-speech of the paranoiac narrator. In Rick Jackson's "Whiskey Dicks," a Marine story that makes William Higgins' early-eighties porn films seem tame, the boys-on-leave take stereotypical porn-story speech to the nth power, making poetry from its monosyllabic grunts. Jimmy any sentence from "Whiskey Dicks," and you're certain to find something to mutter during your next Marine fantasy.

These stories, perhaps, were easy to like. But what else makes erotica work? I tried to consider my favorite novels' sex scenes. Instead, I kept conjuring moments from favorite movies. In cinema, the erotic moments that explode from the screen do so because they employ certain images or settings to further delineate and set them apart from the average under-the-covers, lights-out tedium. I'll always remember Dennis Hopper and his oxygen mask in *Blue Velvet;* the boy masturbating over the man's iron lung in *In a Glass Cage.* Even something like the wacko husband in *Female Trouble,* using a tool kit to bring Divine to climax. Or *The Entity,* in which a horny but invisible poltergeist fucks the heroine. Why can't more porn writing explore these bizarre, risky, outlandish, sometimes surreal situations? Thank the lucky stars that many of the writers in this anthology do just that. Need proof? Check out the entries by Carol Queen ("Ganged") and D. Travers Scott ("Aegis"). Other stories needled their way into my brain with a single image (e.g., the hair tonic-as-lube, a sort of fictive fetish object, in Simon Sheppard's strangely bittersweet "Hotter Than Hell"); some with unconventional locales (M. Christian's "Stroke the Fire"); some even with intoxicant language (Miodrag Kojadinović's "Loveth Thou Me, Boy?" or Alex Jeffers' beautifully lyrical "The Voice of the Capon").

Conversely, a piece of erotica often succeeds because it positions us within a setting or an experience that we as readers can effortlessly relate to or imagine ourselves in. Scott O'Hara's "Good in Tension," for instance, immediately appealed to me because I'm so accustomed to that alone-on-a-long-train-ride feeling of, well, horniness. And two of the most powerful stories in this collection are about a time many of us remember well: gay adolescence. "The Adored One" by Michael Rowe and "Playing Solitaire" by Mitch Cullin are both well-controlled and nostalgic paeans to sadder, happier, clumsier, often sexier times. As full as some novels, these stories also show how subtle writing about sex can be.

Through reading these stories, I've realized that one of erotic writing's most important characteristics is its ability to get immediately to the heart of the matter, as the saying goes. For proof, read Scott ("Aegis"), Christian ("Stroke the Fire"), Jackson ("Whiskey Dicks"). Read the opening paragraphs of Jameson Currier's "First Shave": what fiction editor of *Story* or *Iowa Review* would pull this from the slushpile, skim page one, and include it in those snooty literary pages? My guess is that Currier doesn't care; he knows what his audience wants, and he delivers. The story's cunning lies in the writer's ability to first snag the reader's, er, attention, then to casually jab necessary splinters of character detail. In "First Shave," the reader learns poignant details of Barry's, Eric's, and the narrator's lives, yet never leaves the hold of arousal.

A similar brand of economy appears in the story by Thomas Roche. "What He Did" works especially well as erotica because of the way it gives us the necessities. Instead of spending needless pages blabbing and hem-hawing about this or that unimportant detail, Roche situates his three protagonists in one no-bullshit sentence:

> "That chick has a crush on you, Paul," John told me as we walked home up Haight Street, through the mid-November chill.

There. We have three main characters. We're deposited in a specific time and place. Okay, I'm starting to sound like a creative writing professor here. But my point is this: In a lot of fiction, and especially good erotic fiction with its primary sex concerns, it's important to stab right into the heart of the matter. In porn, that heart is the sexual situation being addressed, and getting to it is the goal. Sure, there's time for a little foreplay to get things started. In fact, a little bit of teasing can go a long way toward drawing a reader in, especially if he's heading into foreign territory and a little bit nervous. But the heart of a great erotic story is still the sex, that which gets the characters (and if the author does his or her job well, the reader) off. Allowing the reader to touch that heart, to feel it beating with lust, rage, desire, love, or whatever emotion the author is trying to capture, is the purpose of writing.

"Pleasingly," by Matthew Rettenmund, gets to the heart, too, but there's a bit of flesh to dig through first. This story provides a rather startling (for porn, at least) pair of sex partners to spy on. It works because, in its own little way, it breaks a taboo of not only gay erotic writing, but gay aesthetic to boot. The guys in Rettenmund's piece are "chubby in a skinny fag's world"—to borrow a line one character huffs in Bill Sherwood's film *Parting Glances,* they've committed the "gay cardinal sin" of being overweight. But Rettenmund's narrator (who uses the term "Rubenesque" to describe himself) doesn't sit at home and brood. He takes charge. A story about fatties might make the typical body fascist uncomfortable in principle, but in the actual story, it's a turn-on. In this case, erotic writing is vital because it makes the reader realize he can get a hard-on from someone other than his firm-bodied pals at the Chelsea Gym or the West Hollywood coffee shop.

Besides the story of the two chubbies, herein also are tales zeroing in on men over fifty (M. Christian's "Stroke the Fire," a kind of Zane Grey meets John Preston, the literary equivalent of one of Joe Gage's early-eighties porn flicks); boys barely in their teens (Cullin's stunner, "Playing Solitaire"); fetishist raver bike messenger boys ("Aegis," by D. Travers Scott, who skillfully leaves as much to the imagination as he revels in explicitness); family members (Simon Sheppard's "Hotter Than Hell"); and close bisexual pals who indulge in three-ways (Roche's "What He Did"). Carol Queen's gloriously debauched "Ganged" is even narrated by a female, "a bisexual cross-dressing femme switch with a taste for leather daddies." Boy, was I ever wrong in my assumptions about *who* the people in these stories would be.

While the characters in some stories twist porn preconceptions like silly putty, other pieces are unique even in form. "The Yellow," by Michael Lassell, is less a piece of erotic fiction than an example of, say, an erotic essay. It also resembles a graceful, multi-layered poem, incorporating hustling, porn, and promiscuity with world concerns like homophobia and the Gulf War. It subverts the whole genre of porn by blurring the distinction between what stirs our dicks and what stirs our brains—in one paragraph, Lassell is getting us hard with his detailed descriptions of dancers at the Gaiety; in the next, he's telling us what for, compelling us to go kick some oppressor's butt. "The Yellow" is exemplary, maybe, of one direction erotica is taking—past the simpler concerns of fuck paperbacks and jerk-off stories, toward a narrative that makes us think while our hands are busy.

In "The Last Blowjob," Stephen Greco makes us think, too. He paints a careful portrait of the narrator and his lover Henry, a PWA spending his last days in the hospital. But while the story resonates on many levels, it's no Hollywood-style tearjerker. Greco shows us Henry's "head thrown back in ecstasy," not in sorrow or the throes of death. For once, we're viewing a PWA not as a "victim," but as a stud. And that's important. It's erotic writing that whisks us somewhere we haven't been before. Perhaps that's what all of the writers of these stories wanted to achieve—and also, I guess, what Mike Ford and I wanted to accomplish with this anthology. To lift the sex story somewhere far away from tedium, from throwaway porn of the past, from that dimwit "quivering quim" and "sleeping snake" from the hot tub cover of *The Passion of* What's-er-Name.

In *Best Gay Erotica 1996,* nasty talk melts into poetry and politics implodes into porn. Sex waits patiently on the sleeping car of a train, behind the crowded bar, or out in the snowy frontier night. And chubby boys, Marines, tops wielding razors, sufferers in hospital beds, best friends, and girls in drag are all proven sex objects. *Oh god. Oh yessss.*

BEST GAY EROTICA 1996

FIRST SHAVE

JAMESON CURRIER

Barry lies on the bed diagonally and I pull his body closer toward me so that his legs dangle over the edge of the bed. His erection stretches up toward his navel and I grasp his cock and give it a few pumps with my fist. The water is in a large pot on the nightstand beside the bed, and I lean back from where I am standing and dip the tips of my fingers in the pot to wet them, then dip my hand all the way inside, clutching a grip of the warm water in my palm. I lean back toward Barry and drip the water over his waiting balls and cock, his skin soaking in the water as I next run my hand over them, the liquid a slick lubricant as I reach up and play with the shaft of his cock. Barry's eyes are closed, but he smiles as I run my fist back and forth along the head of his dick. I cup his balls with the palm of my other hand, feeling the warmth and wetness of them now, then move my own dick, stiff and needy, to the side of me so that it falls against his balls.

I reach over from where I stand and get the shaving cream from the nightstand, squirt a handful of it into my palm, and rub it on Barry's balls. I let the skin soak this up, and while waiting I use the cream as a lubricant to play some more with his cock. Barry smiles again, wider, 'til his lips stretch almost to his ears, and then he opens his eyes and looks down at my hand, the shank of his neck flushed red from where my movements have excited him. I take my free hand and lightly squeeze his left nipple, and he shoves his head back against the bed, lifting his ass up slightly so that his dick slips in and out of my enclosed fist from the rocking motion he makes himself.

When he relaxes again, I reach for the razor from the nightstand, do a fast check of the shaving cream on his balls, and decide to squirt some

21

more on them. I use one hand to pin his dick against his stomach, then point the razor right beneath the shaft of his cock. I bring the razor down slowly against his skin, feeling the hair on his sack pull a little as I work on him, shaving him in short, firm strokes. Overcome slightly by the reality of my own shyness, I lean back and rinse the razor in the pot of water, even though I could have shaved some more of him. This is my first time shaving Barry, and I feel the tension in the arch of my back. After eight months of irregularly dating one another, Barry finally trusts me enough with a razor at his balls.

Not that he should, of course. We're not lovers, we're not roommates—nor friends, either, really. Merely two men who date one another, something a little more complex than fuck-buddies, however. Barry already *has* a lover. *Isn't that always the story? The way it goes? The good one's always taken? Or at least the sexy one?* Barry's been with Eric for almost twenty years now, and Barry tells me every time I see him that he and Eric haven't had sex in years. Every time he mentions Eric, however, I feel both jealous and envious; Eric has a daily intimacy with Barry I know I will never possess.

Now, using my thumb and fourth finger, I stretch some of the skin of Barry's balls, and with the razor, shave the skin I have pulled taut. Then I push one of the sides of his balls tight against the other, shaving the side of it and slightly underneath. I do the same with the other side of his sack, dip the razor clean, and then play with his cock to make sure he is enjoying all this attention.

Barry first shaved his balls when he started dating a guy who had shaved *his* balls and ass. Not Eric, of course; Barry has been seeing other guys since his relationship with Eric began, when they were college roommates. They never started out monogamous, Barry told me the night he first slept over at my apartment, but they made a rule, right up front, of never discussing their other lovers, dates, or tricks with one another. How Barry explains his clean shaven balls to Eric now, I have no idea, though I think it might have something to do with the absence of sex between them. But if I try to understand the complexity of *their* relationship, I only become frustrated with the inadequacy of *ours*.

I want more than this, of course; or rather, I want more than what Barry is willing to give me. He likes our arrangement the way it is—once or twice a week for a movie, dinner, and, inevitably, sex. When Eric is out of town, one of us sleeps over at the other's apartment.

At first, all Barry wanted us to be was fuck-buddies, an arrangement I was perfectly capable of accepting, though not happily. But Barry wouldn't stop calling me—first for sex, then later, to complain about

Eric. He called from the office, from the car, from the lobby of the theater, 'til sometimes, we spoke to one another four or five times a day. Then he would disappear for a long stretch of time, only to call repeatedly again. I always expected that Barry would have used me up by now, but instead he arrives with little gifts—toys which we will use later, together, in bed—handcuffs, rings, clamps, dildos, flavored lube. That's how the shaving came about. Barry arrived tonight with a disposable razor and shaving cream.

I continue to talk to Barry's body with my hands. His dick is rock solid hard, thick and pumped like his morning erections always are, and I sneak a look at the whole package of him, the hefty, well-fed physique of a well-groomed, middle-aged theatrical producer. What is this thing I have for older men, anyway? Barry is effortlessly a man, however, natural and unrattled as a father, with a chest and stomach full of flat, brown hair, the ends of which are tipped in gray, and full round biceps and an ass you would believe belonged to a much younger body. There is a good twenty years difference between us; Barry says, more often than not, that I look like Eric did when they first met. In spite of his comparisons, in spite of knowing I'm being compared, I also find Barry inherently sexy. I play with myself for a moment, stroking my cock as I look him over, then tell him first to turn over on his stomach, then to push himself up, supporting himself on his knees and elbows.

His ass now—the white, creamy complexion of it—is pitched heavenward into the air, and I cup his cheeks with my wet hands, kneading them first and then giving them light slaps. His skin is baby soft but firm beneath the flesh, and I slap and knead, slap and knead, as Barry shifts himself beneath me to accommodate my grips, his ass pushing itself even higher into the air above him, as if trying to drink in the air through his asshole.

Not long after I met Barry, he told me that he liked the slick feel of his cleanly-shaved balls, and that he would go wild when someone just touched him there, cupping them completely into the warm palms of his hands. Now Barry shaves the evening before he sees me, in case he nicks himself, he tells me, in order to give the skin time to heal. I worry a moment about nicking him now, imagine how I would handle the blood if that should happen. But I shake off the thought, mentally chant it out of the room. *That will not happen,* I tell myself over and over, *because he trusts me. No blood. No blood. No blood.*

I run a finger from the base of Barry's spine, down through the crack of his ass, back down to his balls. I cup them with one hand, then take my other hand and rub my fingers against his asshole. The hole is red and almost angry-looking, and I study the hairs along the puckered surface. I reach over to the still-warm water, wet my fingertips, then run them into the crack of his ass, digging a damp finger slightly into his asshole. I play with the water some more against his ass, then squirt shaving cream into my hand and rub it along the crack.

I tell him to spread his knees even further, widening my view of his asshole. I slap the skin some more, then take the razor in one hand and with my other hand spread the skin of his other cheek—first for support, and then, when I am sure of the flesh, to stretch the skin even further apart.

I shave the base of his spine first, then, in short, quick strokes, work my way down the crack to his asshole, watching the warm, creamy liquid drip down onto the sack of his balls. When I reach the more furrowed surface of his asshole, I slow down, almost tapping the razor against his skin. I can tell he is even more aroused now, imagine my quick, light movements must feel as if he is being tickled there, and I smile at the thought of it and continue shaving him.

When I first started dating Barry, I wanted desperately to fall in love with someone, having just emerged from a string of very bad blind and fruitless dates. The moment Barry told me about Eric, I was ready to end it all. Who wants to be the other woman, after all? Had the sex not been so good, so comfortable, so hot and inventive between us, he could never have convinced me to continue.

I rinse the razor and continue shaving his asshole, using the razor a little harder now to get a closer shave. I run a finger along the clean, finished surface of the skin, testing the smoothness. I decide I want it to feel even smoother, and repeat my strokes along his ass. I stop midway, however, reach underneath him, and pump his cock. He groans and shifts his body. I knead his cheeks, then finish with the remainder of his ass.

The shave is done now, but I touch up the underside of his balls to get a closer shave from this new angle. The cream, water, and shave take only a moment, and I use the excess liquid to lube his dick, feeling as I do the damp sensation of his precome wetting his cock. I place the razor back on the nightstand, wet my hand again in the pot, and then begin to finger his asshole. One finger slips easily in, and I wiggle it around inside him, feeling for his prostate. I find it—a hard little nodule beneath the tip of my finger—and massage it. He groans again, and I wedge a second finger into his ass, move it in and out, in and out, listening to his moans to make sure that they emanate more from pleasure than from pain.

Barry said that Eric hadn't fucked him since Eric tested positive, almost five years ago. Barry is negative, and the difference in their serostatuses, Barry said, not only pushed them further apart sexually, but bound them closer together emotionally. How could he walk out on Eric now, Barry once told me, not knowing what the future could mean for either of them? Of course it upset me when I heard it; it still does when I think about it. Eric is asymptomatic, and Barry, I know, does not *want* to leave him. *This is what I have,* I remind myself, and continue fingering Barry's ass. *This is what I get.* If I want more or something else, I know I have to get out and look elsewhere.

From the nightstand, I remove a condom and slip it over my cock. I lean over Barry's ass and push my dick slowly in. Barry takes a deep breath, and I wrap my arms around his waist as I fuck him from behind, my movements slow and thoughtful, in and out, in and out, so that he feels every inch of my dick and balls against his now-hairless ass.

He groans louder as I go in deeper and faster, and my thoughts change from erotic to frustrated. Barry's sexual appetite is insatiable— I'm not his only companion-slash-fuck-buddy. My friend Martin's seen Barry at the bar picking up tricks; my neighbor, Jon, saw him and a date at a premiere at the Ziegfeld. Barry's even taken me to the bar with him a couple of times when he's been in search of fresh meat. Now, instead of pushing myself harder into Barry, I take deep breaths, rapidly and loudly, wanting to believe, as I do, that Barry is not just another jerk fucking me over, using me as a sex toy. Beneath me, beneath Barry's ass, I reach down and pump his cock as I fuck him. Barry suddenly comes into my fist, and I rub his hot cream back up against the shaft of his cock, around the base and onto his slippery balls.

I pull out of him and watch myself come into the tip of the condom, my dick suspended somewhere above Barry's milky-white ass. Barry twists his body beneath me, twirls around so that his ass rests again on the bed. His eyes look up at me, searching for my own. I meet his gaze and watch his lips purse together as if to speak. For a moment, I think he will say something romantic, caring, but I lean down into him, wanting to cut him off, not wanting to hear some sort of half-hearted remark about how nice he thinks I am. Instead, he stops my face right above his own by shoving his hands against the side of my skull. For a moment, the power between us shifts. Barry is twice as big as I am, and he could easily crush my skull in his hands. Instead, he turns my head so that my ear is right above his lips. "Show me you care," he says lightly into my ear. "Come on. I want you to do it again."

HOTTER THAN HELL

SIMON SHEPPARD

It's back when Buicks had those little chrome-trimmed portholes. The turquoise-and-white Special DeLuxe is sudsy-wet, steam rising in ripples from its bulbous curves. "Shit, it's hot," mutters the lanky eighteen-year-old. He's got on nothing but Keds and cut-off dungarees. His face and forearms are golden tan, but this early in the summer, his torso and legs still are pale. He draws a hand across his sweaty belly, where a line of blond fur leads down into his shorts.

It's the first time this year he's gone out without underwear, and he's acutely aware of the feeling of his tender dick rubbing up against rough denim. His fingers slip down his hairy belly, down to the base of his peter. "Shit, it's hot." His dickhead's sliding free of foreskin as his dick starts to snake down the leg of his cutoffs.

He opens up the nozzle of the green plastic hose. Cool water pours over his head, down his chest, soaks his denim shorts. His dick is still hard, if anything even harder now, the heft of it clearly outlined by the wet shorts.

He leans up against a soapy fender, presses his crotch against the warm, wet metal. He starts humping the two-tone Buick. The cheeks of his trim butt clench and unclench as he jams his dick hard against the car. When he shuts his eyes, bright sun filters through his lashes.

The legs of his old jeans are cut off pretty high, close to his crotch, and his wet dick has slipped out past the frayed fabric. He reaches down and gives his swollen dickhead a firm squeeze, rearranges the shorts till most of his dick is lying naked up against the fender. He reaches for the sponge, squeezes a big handful of warm suds down his crotch. Muscles ripple beneath the white flesh of his back as he fucks the fender, head thrown back. In a minute or two, his hot cum jets out, splattering all the way down to a shiny chrome hubcap.

He looks up. His little brother is looking at him, eating a Moon Pie. No telling how long he's been standing there.

"Mama says to come on in," Little Brother says. "Yer lunch is ready."

"My Jesus, what happened to you?" says Mama, careworn as usual. "Go dry off and change before your lunch gets old and wrinkled."

Over peanut butter, banana, and mayonnaise sandwiches, Mama tells them the big news: Cousin Earl is coming to stay with them for a while. The last time they saw Cousin Earl was years ago, before he went off to fight in Korea. Back then, Little Brother had been very small indeed. Big Brother, though, can clearly recall his cousin. Cousin Earl, nine years his senior, had been every inch a man, muscled and deep-voiced, while he was just a gangly boy. He still remembers the way his cousin's good-bye hug felt, firm yet somehow infinitely soft and tender.

But something happened in Korea, Big Brother knows, something that had landed Cousin Earl in a hospital, not for the body, but for the mind. The details, though, remain a mystery.

"...you boys won't mind," Mama is saying. "There's plenty of room on the sofa-bed for you, Little Brother, while Cousin Earl shares the bed-room with Big Brother."

And the notion of sharing his room with a man, a man who's traveled and fought and worn a uniform, the thought of sharing a room with Cousin Earl instead of his pesky little sibling, that thought does not bother Big Brother at all.

When the day arrives, Big Brother walks to the Greyhound stop, down by the filling station. He gets there early, way before the bus is due in.

Toothless Tom is sitting on a crate in front of the filling station, sip-ping an RC. Toothless Tom is the man who helps out around the filling station. He's old, thirty-five or so, but he's not quite right in the head and he doesn't act much more mature than Little Brother.

"Hey, Big Brother," says Toothless Tom.

"Hey, Tom. Hot enough for you?"

Tom gives a low chuckle. "How hot are you, boy?"

"Oh, hot enough." Big Brother knows what comes next.

Toothless Tom gets up off the crate, unfolds his big husky frame, and shambles into the storage shed behind the filling station. Big Brother follows him. The shed smells of metal and grease.

Tom bolts the door and sits himself on a rickety stool near the workbench in the corner. He takes out his teeth and sets them down on a piece of newspaper on the bench. Big Brother's fly is already open. Toothless Tom takes one last swig of the RC and his mouth, when he puts it around Big Brother's soft prick, feels cool and wet. His tongue, licking and stroking Big Brother's young, sensitive flesh, makes the dick swell up and fill his mouth. The half-wit's greedy, insistent sucking sends shivers of pleasure through the teenager's body. Big Brother shuts his eyes and tries hard to think about Cassie Renfrew and her enormous titties, but instead his mind homes in on his cousin's imminent arrival.

"Just a second," says Big Brother, backing away so he can unbutton his pants and let them fall to his ankles. Looking down, he sees Toothless Tom stroke his tiny, angry-red dick, which sticks out through the fly of his greasy, dark-green uniform pants. The distant roar of an approaching bus cuts through the humid air. Big Brother plunges his hard-on back into the wet mouth, back between the silky-smooth gums, and pumps until the cocksucker starts to gag, until hot jizz squirts down Toothless Tom's open throat. Without a word, Big Brother wipes off his dick and pulls his pants back up. Toothless Tom's dick is still in his hand, dribbling a rope of cum into a little puddle between his shabby boots.

"Ma's made smothered pork chops. She says that always was a favorite of yours."

Cousin Earl nods in assent. Big Brother expected him to show up in uniform, but when he stepped off the idling Greyhound, he was wearing a tan polo shirt and poplin windbreaker. He's older than Big Brother's memory of him, of course, and a little heavier, but handsome in an unpretentious, masculine way.

When they walk up to the front door, dinner's already on the table. Mama seems bubblingly happy to see Earl again, though for his part, he's a little more reserved. He remains distant over dinner. The conversation moves in fits and starts; the boys have been instructed not to bring up Korea, where, apparently, Something Terrible happened to Cousin Earl.

It's still pretty early when Cousin Earl says, "I'm beat. I think I'll head off to bed."

Big Brother heads up to the bedroom with him, sits cross-legged on the bed while the older man strips down to his underwear. Cousin Earl is hairier than he is, has thick, nicely muscled legs covered with reddish fur. The deep U-neck of his undershirt reveals a tangled patch of chest hair. The bulky outline of his dick is clearly visible through his briefs. Cousin Earl wraps himself in a terry robe and heads off to shower. Big Brother goes over to Little Brother's bed and picks up the tan polo shirt. The dark stains in the underarms are still moist. He buries his face in his cousin's sweat. For a reason he can't quite admit to himself, he inhales the musky-sour odor and holds in the breath. It's almost too hot to sleep.

"Nice car."

"It's the best thing Daddy left us." He thinks, *It's damn near the only thing Daddy left us.*

They're driving to the river over by McCullers' Landing. In the three days since his arrival, Cousin Earl's started to open up a little bit. About how glad he is to be back in the States. About the girlfriend he left behind in Mobile. Playing football in college. About growing up an orphan, being bounced from one foster home to another. But nothing about Korea. And Big Brother hasn't dared to ask.

"Shit, it's hot."

"Sure enough."

In the awkward silences, you can hear the radio talking about Senator McCarthy ferreting out Commies in the State Department. Then an ad for furniture sold to returning vets on easy time payments. Then Eisenhower starts to talk.

Part of the awkwardness, Big Brother knows but can never ever say, comes from knowing how he's lain awake just a few feet away from his sleeping cousin, listening to his steady breaths, watching his moonlit body shift beneath a thin percale sheet. *I ain't a fairy,* Big Brother thinks, *but if I ain't a fairy, then what the hell is going on?*

They park by the roadhouse on the edge of town and walk through the woods to the river. Big Brother, walking behind, can't keep his eyes off his cousin's hairy, freckled legs, shorts revealing the play of muscles, solid calves and thighs. When they get to the river, Cousin Earl right off strips buck naked, T-shirt first, then khaki shorts. It's the first time Big Brother has seen his naked ass, the thick red fur running down the crack, and when Cousin Earl bends over to pick up his shorts, his big hairy balls hang low between his pale upper thighs.

"Well, c'mon then. Git yer clothes off."

Now he's turned around. His dick. His big man-dick.

"Shorts, too. What's the matter, you shy?"

"I'll take 'em off when I'm darn good and ready."

"Only teasin' you. So is it deep enough here to dive in?"

"Plenty deep."

Cousin Earl runs to the riverbank, big dick flopping, and jumps in. Big Brother joins him seconds later, relieved to find that the shock of the cold water shrinks his swelling prick back down.

"Hey, Earl, let's go. Mmff..." Big Brother holds his breath as his head is forced beneath the water. Struggling his way back up, he brushes his arms against his cousin's dick. It's the first time he's ever felt another guy's peter and it's all he can do not to reach for it. He tries to wrestle back, but after a short tussle the older man easily overpowers him, grabs his arms, and pins him against his heaving torso. He can feel Earl's muscular chest and belly up against his back.

"I give, I give."

By and by they get out of the river, return to the grassy bank. Cousin flops himself down on the ground, lies on his back with his arms crossed behind his head and his legs spread wide. As the blazing sun warms and dries him, Big Brother's hefty dick stirs lazily between his legs. He's glad he's kept his own shorts on.

"Hey, Earl," he says at last, "don't you think it's time to be getting back?"

Big Brother is short on sleep. The night before, the thought of Cousin Earl's dick rubbing against his arm kept him awake long after the lights were out. When he was finally sure that Earl was asleep, he humped the mattress till he shot his wad, wiping up the sticky mess with a crusted-up old sock he kept beneath the bed.

Things are tense at the breakfast table. Cousin Earl has just told everybody he won't be going to church with them. He's stopped just short of admitting he's an outright atheist.

Mama is chattering as she serves Little Brother his grits and eggs. "So Earl, I told Freddie Wooten down at the American Legion that of course you'll march with them in tomorrow's parade." Tomorrow is Memorial Day. Cousin Earl says nothing.

Bleary-eyed, Big Brother takes a swallow of coffee and says, "Mama, he don't have to march if he don't want to."

Awkward silence.

"Of course I'll march," says Cousin Earl flatly.

"Of course he'll march," says Little Brother.

All the fat ladies in big hats are fanning themselves incessantly, futilely trying to chase away the heat. Sitting in the stifling closeness of the church he's attended since he was a child, sitting there praying next to his mother, who's taking in washing to keep the little family together, Big Brother is thrown into confusion. He does not *want* to feel this way about his cousin, he does not *want* to be a homo. Waves of sexual guilt overwhelm him. After services, Big Brother waits till his family has left the church and goes up to the Reverend.

"Reverend," he says, real low so the Reverend's wife won't hear, "I got something I got to talk to you about."

"Why surely, son," says the Reverend, with a gracious smile. "What is it?"

"It's important, sir, and it's private."

"Well, perhaps you can meet me at the rectory this afternoon at one." Another gracious smile.

At one o'clock sharp Big Brother is at the door to the rectory. Mama's taken Little Brother to O'Connorsburg to see the new Dean Martin and Jerry Lewis movie, a special treat. Cousin Earl is out somewhere.

The Reverend ushers the boy into his sweltering office and shuts and bolts the door.

"So, son, is something troubling you?"

Big Brother, stumbling over the words, explains about Cousin Earl, about feelings that he hasn't asked for, can't handle. By the time he gets to the part about swimming in the river, there's been a noticeable change in the Reverend's demeanor. His fixed smile has disappeared, and he's moved so close that Big Brother can feel his peppermint-scented breath. A glittering drop of sweat hangs from the tip of his nose.

"So you touched his penis, son?"

"Yes, sir."

"Say it."

"Say what?"

"Say 'I touched his penis.' "

"I touched his penis, sir."

"How did you touch it? Like this?"

Big Brother is frozen. The Reverend's hand has clamped onto his crotch. Sweat pours down the Reverend's face. Big Brother wishes he would take his hand away, wants it with all his heart, but the awful truth is that the Reverend's hand feels pretty good there. When the Reverend unzips his fly and reaches in, he offers no resistance. Big Brother closes his eyes in pleasure.

There's a knock at the door.

"Would you fellas like some nice, cool lemonade?" It's the Reverend's wife.

"No thank you, dear," the Reverend says in a kind of strangled voice.

The Reverend's wife clacks off down the hall. The Reverend has an awful funny look on his face. He hangs on to Big Brother's hard dick a few seconds more, then jerks away like he was hit by an electric shock. "Just go, son," he says, standing up with his back toward Big Brother, "and don't tell anyone about this ever. Not if you want your own feelings to remain a secret. Not if you want your mama not to know. You understand, son?"

"Yes, sir," says Big Brother.

The walk from the rectory takes him through the center of town, past the Chat 'N' Chew and the Will O' the Wisp General Store. Past the road that leads to the colored folks' shacks that stand, like an open secret, out on the edge of town. He knows now that there's no one he can trust with his awful secret, with the ugly, sinful mess his life's become. By the time he reaches the white stucco house, he knows what he has to do.

> *Dear Mama,*
> *I have decided to go away for a while. I do not know where so please do not try to find me or nothing. Do not worry, Mama, I can take care of myself. Tell Cousin Earl good-bye and tell Little Brother that I will see him soon. Please do not be angry. I love you, Mama.*
> > *Signed,*
> > *Your son*

When he finishes the letter, he gets up from the kitchen table and goes to his room. Letter in hand, he opens the door. The shades are down. Cousin Earl is asleep, lying sprawled on his back, a sheet barely covering the lower part of his naked body. Even in the dim light, it's easy to see that Cousin Earl's dick is hard.

Big Brother can scarcely breathe. He stands for a good long time, staring at where Earl's coppery belly hair trails off under the sheet.

Gently, he moves his fingertips down to his cousin's armpit, where a flurry of red hair rises from skin shiny with sweat. He strokes the hair, then brings his fingers to his nose, inhaling the deep male musk. Touching the sleeping man's chest, he runs his fingers over a hard pink nipple, down to Earl's belly, to the edge of the sheet. Earl stirs, but remains asleep; his quiet breathing fills the humid room. Slowly, Big Brother moves his hand over the sheet until his palm hovers over the hard dick. He can feel the body heat radiating from the stiff rod. He slowly lowers his hand till it lightly rests upon his cousin's hard-on. Reflexively, Earl arches upward, pushing his meat against Big Brother's hand. The sheet shifts, revealing Earl's swollen dickhead.

With painstaking care, Big Brother lowers the sheet till he can see all of Earl's cock; the large piss-slit, the retracted foreskin, the big pinkish shaft bulging with veins, the luxuriant, bright red bush. Big Brother bends until his face is just inches from the hard penis, till he can inhale the smells of his cousin's sweaty crotch.

Earl's hand descends gently but firmly on the back of Big Brother's head, pushing face against cock. Big Brother's nose is buried in pubic hair. The hand relaxes, allowing him to run his lips up the underside of the shaft, up to the softly throbbing head.

"Why don't you take your clothes off, boy? It's awful hot. It's hot as shit."

Big Brother, naked, positions his head between Earl's thighs, resumes his exploration of the big, meaty cock. When he sticks the tip of his tongue in the glistening piss-slit, Earl bucks his hips and raises his knees. The eighteen-year-old moves his mouth down the dick, down to the hairy, wrinkled ballsac. He tongues his cousin's balls, then licks the sweat-soaked ridge between Earl's legs, moving his tongue until it's up against his cousin's hole. He can feel Cousin Earl open up for him. He swirls his tongue around the earthy-tasting hole, then stiffens his tongue and pushes as far in as he can go and Earl can't stop moaning. Jacking his dick now, Earl screams, "Aww, FUCK!" and comes all over his belly. Big Brother pulls his head from between Earl's thighs, throws himself full length on Cousin Earl's body. His tongue pries apart his cousin's lips. And he humps Earl's hairy belly, slippery with cum and sweat, till with a shudder he shoots, pumping a load of hot cum between their bodies. Kneeling, he rubs his face in the salty stew of their sweat and cum, lapping it hungrily. Then, with a final deep kiss, he curls up in the older man's arms, his face buried in Earl's warm armpit.

He's almost asleep when he hears a noise out in the hallway. Mama and Little Brother are back; he must not have heard the Buick drive up. He's just managed to wipe up and slip into dungarees when his mama calls from downstairs, "How you boys doing? Y'all hungry for supper?"

Big Brother picks up the letter to his mama from where it's fallen to the floor and rips it up into a million pieces.

At the dinner table, Little Brother seems real quiet, real distant. Earl, though, is more animated than Big Brother's ever seen him, which is lucky since he himself, caught up in a muddy swirl of emotions, barely says a word.

"So I figured," says Earl between bites of fried chicken, "I'd head back down to Mobile and ask Muriel if she'll marry me. Golly, you'd like her. She's a real pretty girl."

Little Brother pulls a face.

That evening Big Brother and Cousin Earl go for a ride in the Buick. Sitting there beside his cousin, watching the headlights slice through the night, Big Brother tries to feel guilt, tries to ease it out like his tongue toys with a loose tooth. But all he can feel is happy. "Do you reckon," he says finally, "that what we did was wrong?"

"Big Brother," says Earl, his voice strangely gentle, "after all the things I've seen, I've clean given up on trying to figure out sin."

Cousin Earl has been driving down the dirt road to the river. He pulls off to the side of the road, kills the lights. "You don't have to do nothing more with me. Not ever," he says.

"But I want to," says Big Brother real quietly, laying his hand on his cousin's muscular thigh. Both their dicks are already hard. Earl reaches over to unbutton Big Brother's fly, bends to take his cousin's dick in his mouth.

"Damn, that feels good," says Big Brother, and it's true; he never felt anything so good in his entire life. Earl takes his dick deep down in his throat, backs off, using his tongue to caress dickflesh, then plunges all the way back down, swallowing the shaft.

"Let's get out of the car." The scent of night-blooming jasmine hangs heavy in the air. Big Brother leans against the car door, dungarees down around his ankles, while the older man takes him in his mouth again. Big Brother feels Earl's hands on his butt, spreading his asscheeks apart. When he feels fingers on his hole, he freezes up for a minute before he decides that it's all right and relaxes into the heat of his feelings. Earl takes a second to spit in his hand and then eases a finger up inside his cousin. Big Brother is surprised by how good it feels, how much he wants Earl inside him.

"I got some hair tonic in the glove compartment," he says. He reaches in the open window, gets out the bottle of Wildroot Cream Oil and hands it to his cousin, who's buck naked now, hairy body gleaming in the watery moonlight.

Earl gets his big dick all slicked up with hair tonic and gives it a few hard squeezes till it's standing straight up against his belly. "Turn around and bend over," he says, and Big Brother leans on over, onto the still-warm hood of the car. He feels Earl's oily thumb massaging the tight ring of his asshole. "I'm just gonna open you up real gentle," Earl says, pushing in a couple fingers, rotating them until the muscles give way. Big Brother moans. He wants to be fucked. He wants to be fucked real bad.

When Earl slips the head of his dick inside, it hardly hurts Big Brother at all. And when Earl sinks the length of his shaft all the way in, waves of pleasure wash over Big Brother. Crickets cry loud through the sultry night.

"You all the way inside me?"

"Sure am, boy."

Big Brother reaches back to check that it's true. Cousin Earl's big, furry bush is smack up against his butt. He pulls his hand back to his face, sniffing in the mix of hair tonic and his own ass juices.

Earl is banging away now, and every time he slams into Big Brother's ass, the teenager's sweat-soaked torso slides across the Buick's well-waxed hood. Earl grabs hold of Big Brother's hips and pumps harder.

Just when Big Brother is wondering whether he can take much more of this, Cousin Earl starts bucking real fast, yells "Aww, JESUS!" and shoots his hot load deep into his young cousin's ass.

When he gets up off the car hood, Big Brother feels weak in the knees. He leans up against the car door and Earl is immediately down on his knees, taking Big Brother's half-hard cock in his mouth, sucking it expertly till it expands down his throat, till it explodes with a rush of cum down his throat, cum as sweet as pecan pie.

When they walk in the front door, Mama is waiting there, still wearing the flowered apron she wears to do the dishes, grief and anger on her face. She's been crying. "Little Brother has told me what you two have been up to," Mama says. "How could you, Earl? How could you do that to my boy?"

Big Brother drags himself awake after a night of fitful sleep. He's been dreaming of someone—a senator, a preacher—yelling at him and grabbing at him. He slugs the man, but just before the man disappears, he turns into Cousin Earl, who smiles and takes him up in his big, strong arms.

Big Brother looks around the familiar room. Suddenly he jerks himself fully awake. The bed next to him is empty. All Cousin Earl's things are gone.

It's only when he makes his bed that he discovers a letter slipped under his pillow.

> *Dear Big Brother,*
>
> *Your mama don't know that I'm writing you this. I am real sorry that I got you in trouble. Do not blame your brother for spying on us yesterday afternoon, nor for telling your mama. Whatever happened is all my fault, and I know that going away for a while is the best thing I can do. Maybe your mama is right and you should go talk to the Reverend about changing your ways. I do not know.*
>
> *I do know that being this way is not easy. I want to tell you about what happened in Korea, but you must not tell nobody else. When I was there, I fell in love with another soldier. We loved each other very much. For months, we'd sneak around so we could spend time together. We planned to get through the war and then spend the rest of our lives together when we got back home. That's how much we loved each other. I don't expect you to understand.*
>
> *Then one day he was killed in battle. I watched him die. I never felt so helpless in my life. I could not tell anyone what I was going through for fear of getting kicked out of the service. I had to go through losing him alone by myself, and it made me go a little crazy. That is what happened and why I was shipped back to a hospital in the States.*
>
> *Big Brother, you are a wonderful guy and I hate to leave you at a time like this but your mama and I talked and I think for now my going away will be better for all concerned. Do not worry about your mama, she loves you very much. And do not worry about me. I will be okay.*
>
> *I truly believe that someday soon I will see you again. Until then, take good care of yourself.*
>
> *Love,*
> *Earl*

At the bottom of the letter, *Love* has been crossed out and then written in again, this time in big, defiant letters.

That afternoon, the family goes to the Memorial Day parade at McCullers' Landing. Down Main Street they go, the aged veterans of the Great War, the maimed middle-aged men who fought in World War II, the young vets just back from Korea. All the men whom the world has left damaged. Big Brother doesn't feel much like cheering.

He wanders off, down to the riverbank. Thinking of his cousin, he strips down and lies on the grassy bank. He grabs his balls in one hand and peels back his foreskin with the other. Spitting in his palm, he gets the shaft wet and slippery, uses his other hand to play with his warm hole. "Earl," he says out loud, "Earl, Earl, Earl." And spurts hot cum high up in the air, up toward the heat of an unminding sky.

Big Brother spends the rest of the humid afternoon down by the river, till sunset, till darkness falls on Memorial Day. As he heads off toward home, a few raindrops fall, then many more, until the darkness is split by sheets of lightning and howls of thunder. Big Brother, soaked through and through, can see his way back home in sudden flashes of an unnatural clarity. The heat is broken, if only for a while.

GANGED

CAROL QUEEN

A Tribute to John Preston

We join our protagonist Miranda, a bisexual cross-dressing femme switch with a taste for leather daddies, not long after her meeting with Jack Prosper—the only gay man she's ever picked up who didn't throw her out when he figured out she was really a woman—even after she changed into femme drag.

Jack and I had been running together for several weeks. He knew which bar I hung out in; a couple of times he had sauntered in and found me there. He didn't stay to meet my friends; he'd haul me out and back to his place. We usually only got as far as the alley before his dick was out.

He had been to my apartment only once. It was more comfortable at his place; he didn't have any housemates, whereas I could never predict when mine, Ariel, would come home, half the time dragging a john. So mostly our relationship developed within the charmed and secret space of his rooms.

The one time he was at my place, though, I found him nosing around my room when I came in from the kitchen where I'd gone to get us something to drink. At the bedside table, he picked up a book—a very battered copy of *Mr. Benson.* He grinned, and slung himself on my bed as though he habitually lounged there to read. He held the book in his left hand and of course it fell right open—to the part where Mr. Benson takes his new boy to meet all his friends.

"Stroke book, eh?" Jack was, I could tell, amused.

I just said, "You've read it, I suppose."

"Read it? Honey, I'm sure you were still in junior high. For a while there, this character was everybody's role model—or dream daddy." Jack was fingering the teeth marks where one time I had bitten the book during an especially big come.

I blushed. "Well, that historical moment may be over for you, but the dykes have gotten hold of him now."

"I'm not even sure I can picture that," Jack said. He stroked his mustache absently. "You know, I have a few buddies of my own. But god knows, Randy, you'd embarrass me. You look like *baby* chicken when you're in drag."

I'd all but forgotten about that when I got a call from Jack on my voice-mail. "Okay, Randy, I want you over here tonight at eight o'clock. Punctually. Butched up as much as your fey little ass can get. You won't need your girl drag, but bring your make-up."

I showed up at five minutes 'til eight and sat on the steps 'til it was time to ring the bell. I had on my engineer's boots and Levi's, and in a jockstrap, I was packing a small one. My breasts were bound down and I had a worn black T-shirt under my leather jacket.

Jack answered the door. "Randy, for christ's sake, you look like a dyke."

"Jack, there's hardly any difference in this town!"

"Oh yes there is. Get in here, kid. You need a little more work."

Jack put me into a black leather bar vest that just fit me. He didn't tell me where it came from, but it was much too small for him. He asked me for my make-up. With the dark pencils and mascara brushes he found in the kit he darkened my eyebrows a little and stroked the fuzz on my upper lip with color until I had a mustache. "This stuff better be waterproof," he muttered. Finally he stood back and looked at me. "Where in god's name do you get boots that tiny? If only you were a few inches shorter. I could just tell them you're a dwarf."

"Jack, you're a total bitch. Who's 'them'?"

"Never mind, son. You'll see soon enough. Now drop to your knees, boy."

Happy to be back on familiar ground, I knelt with my cheek resting on Jack's thigh, filling with whatever the emotion was that his Daddyness brought up in me. An instant later, I felt a chill coil of chain wrapping my throat and I started; Jack had never collared me before. At the click of the lock, my cunt spasmed as if he'd flicked his tongue over my clit.

"You're *my* boy tonight, got it? You're going to keep your mouth shut and your jockstrap on. I'm upping the ante on our little social experiment, boy, and you're in it 'til it's over. No safe words, no femme drag, nothing but what I tell you. I'm taking you to a little party. You *might* just be the guest of honor." His eyes narrowed—I could see he was dead serious. "But if you don't keep up your end, you'll never be invited back—and I probably won't either. Don't fuck it up."

I stared up at him, welling up with the weirdest mixture of pride and stricken fear. I had only about a shred of an idea where we were going, but it was pretty clear Jack wanted me to pass on whomever we met. I had no idea how I was going to pull that off. I don't think I'd ever passed on anyone for more than about a half an hour in my life.

He put a blindfold on me before he handed me a helmet and straddled his Harley. I was left to grope my way on, and I held him tightly as the bike's acceleration threatened to knock me off balance. I tried, blind as I was, to follow the turns he took, but I was lost within a couple of blocks, and all I knew was that soon we were speeding up even more, crossing a bridge—I guessed the Bay Bridge, for in the middle the sound changed as we whipped through a tunnel. I clasped him, feeling the dildo I wore nudge his butt-cheeks while his big bike throbbed under us like a very butch sex toy.

He didn't take the blindfold off until we'd entered a house, which might have been in the Berkeley Hills, or Oakland, or who knows where. It was a large house, obviously, and Jack had let himself in without ringing. We left our helmets on a shelf in the foyer. We weren't the only ones here, I noted: some helmets were there already, a briefcase or two, and a profusion of coats. Most, but not all, were leather. Jack instructed me to hang my own jacket on a hook—he always said it was too fucking ratty to be seen in—and kept his on. He led me down a long hall.

The room we entered at the end made me gasp. It was clearly a dungeon, though it was not the low-end made-over-basement I was used to from the city. Somebody well-to-do lived here, and he had obviously put all the care into constructing his playroom that some other gay man might spend collecting art or learning to be a four-star chef just to impress his friends.

At one end, it didn't look like a dungeon, but a really classy den, a library without the bookshelves. It had several wing-back chairs arranged around a low table and facing a fireplace, where a small blaze flickered and cast shadows. A sideboard held a silver coffee service—a nice antique one, I noted—and several plates with sandwiches and other easy-to-eat food. A bottle of champagne lay icing in a silver bucket, but the cork hadn't been popped—no one seemed to be drinking. Three of the chairs were occupied by men in leathers, men who would look just as sexy and appropriate wearing very fine suits as they did in this Gentleman's Club atmosphere.

The other end of the room was, like the part that looked like a den, wood-paneled. It might have been in a restored Victorian, except the rest of the house looked newer. Setting off the dark wood was wrought iron fashioned into cages and suspension bars. A wooden St. Andrew's cross, leather-upholstered horses, and other dungeon implements furnished the place. I had been inside a few dungeons before, but they'd all looked tacked together compared to this.

As Jack stepped into the room, one of the seated men got up and extended his hand. Jack clasped it. "Sir Sebastian," he said, with affection as well as great respect in his voice, "how good to see you again. Thank you, as always, for your hospitality." Sir Sebastian, like Jack, had an impeccably trimmed beard, but it was mostly white, and he had white at his temples, too. I put him at fifty, perhaps. He was distinguished, calm, had seen everything. His grey eyes shone with warmth at the moment, but I could imagine them glittering menacingly; power was all over him. If Jack was my daddy, Sir Sebastian could be his.

"Jack, my darling man. You're welcome here at any time." He had looked me over once, the moment we entered the room, and now he continued, "And what have you brought for us tonight? It's fortunate this isn't a public place, my dear. No wonder I haven't seen you in the bars with this lad."

Jack only smiled. "Sir Sebastian, his name is Randy. In my experience, the name suits him very well, and he is not entirely new to all this. Tonight, of course, will be a test for him." As Jack said my name, I sank to my knees and bowed my head. He hadn't told me what the rules were, except "don't fuck up"; I figured at the minimum I ought to put on good dungeon manners and hope I didn't miss any cues.

"Randy is forbidden to speak tonight," Jack said, "and I do hope none of you gentlemen will take offense when he does not verbally answer you. Also, his cock belongs to me, and neither he nor anyone else may touch it." I had a wild image of popping the little Realistic out of my jockstrap and handing it over to Jack for safe-keeping. "He is bandaged from a cutting, a rather extensive one, so I'd like you to leave his shirt on. Beyond that, however, he will be at your disposal."

At that, my heart jumped wildly. Somehow I'd expected Jack to test my passing skills in a dark leather bar, not in a playroom full of masters. Why couldn't he have just snuck me into Blow Buddies? More was at stake tonight than whether I could keep the dildo on straight. I'm not a heavy sensation bottom, and while this place was beautiful, it could've hosted meetings of the Inquisition. I prayed I wouldn't break.

Jack ruffled my hair for the tiniest instant, then left me kneeling and turned to the other men. I stole glances up at them as best I could. One man was enormous and muscular, his head shaved, his tits pierced. I couldn't tell his age—somewhere around Jack's, perhaps. Jack called him Stone when he greeted him. He addressed another man, a lithe young blonde with icy blue eyes, as Marc. Marc seemed a good deal younger than the others, maybe even younger than me. But he wore authority like so many men in the bars wore leathers with the squeak and smell of Mr. S still on them.

Two more men came in. One was substantially older than the others, his hair quite white, and when he spoke I heard the tones of well-bred Oxford English. He, unlike the other men, did not wear leather; he was dressed in a suit that doubtless came from Savile Row. Jesus, Jack ran with some power daddies! "Ah, St. James, sir," Jack said when he saw the man, reaching to grasp his hand and, I noticed, inclining his head respectfully.

St. James' companion stepped forward to greet Jack, and at the sight of him, I almost forgot to keep my head bowed. Tall, black, with sculptured muscles, he was one of the most beautiful men I'd ever seen. He had a similarly galvanizing effect on Jack. "Demetrius! How long have *you* been back?" he cried, and to my surprise threw his arms around the man. Demetrius laughed and hugged Jack, and even when the embrace was over they stood close, with their hands on each others' arms. I realized I was looking at someone who meant a lot to Jack—a lover, probably—and from my post on the floor, I studied him as carefully as I could. He wore a white silk shirt which draped over his muscular arms and tucked into black leather pants almost as tight as his own skin. His boots were fine leather, unadorned, and polished to a high black gloss. His voice was deep and smooth.

Sir Sebastian had stepped to the sideboard and rung a small bell. A very pretty young man entered the room. He was dressed like a formal waiter, except he didn't have on any pants—only a leather jockstrap. His sandy hair curled around his face—he'd do flawless drag, I thought, then reminded myself that I probably wouldn't be let loose to play Barbie with Sir Sebastian's staff. Maybe Jack could get the loan of him sometime and we could play lesbians. He couldn't possibly have his obvious need to cross-dress indulged hanging around with these leathermen.

The waiter-boy bore a tray with several champagne glasses. He set it on the sideboard and opened the champagne, not getting at all ostentatious with the cork, I noticed approvingly. It exited the bottle silently. He filled the glasses, presented one first to Sir Sebastian, then to St. James, and then to everyone else. He looked at me kneeling, poured a glass for me, and left it on the sideboard. "Anything further, Sir Sebastian?" he asked, and left silently when the man shook his head.

"Well, this is quite a lot to celebrate," Sir Sebastian said smoothly. "Jack has brought his new boy to meet us. And Demetrius has come back from his wanderings. Shall we toast?"

Jack picked up the glass from the sideboard and sat it on the floor in front of me, returning to lift his own glass. "New acquaintances and old friends," said St. James, and as the men all toasted, I bent down and lapped from my glass like a rich old lady's over-indulged puppy. So far, this party was a piece of cake, but that couldn't last. I repeated Sir Sebastian's statement "Jack has brought *his* new boy"—in my head. Well, that was worth several hours of conversation about commitment and relationship status, eh? Jack's collar lay heavy on my neck, comforting as the touch of his palm on my nape. I stole another glance up through my lashes—he had his hand on Demetrius' strong, silk-clad shoulder, but I noted that he was reiterating to him and St. James the rules regarding my conduct. No speech—thank goodness; no removing my shirt, no touching my dick. Jack had done everything he could to set it up so I could pass.

Minutes later, Jack was at my side, giving a lift to my collar. I scrambled to my feet, and at his gestured instruction, placed my hands behind my back at waist level. He beckoned and I followed—to the cage.

Inside the cage, a set of leather cuffs dangled from chains. Jack adjusted them to my height, then held one open. Meekly, I lay my wrist onto the fleece padding, and he buckled first that wrist in and then the other. The cage was tall enough for a full-sized man, but fairly narrow. Even with my wrists restrained, I could move right up to the bars on all four sides.

Jack took my chin, lifted my face up so I could gaze into his eyes. He was not quite expressionless—I thought I saw a hint of a smile. I figured that if we really pulled this off, Jack would feel like the cat that got the canary, and I—well, let's just say like the cat that ate the cream.

Then he released my chin and unbuckled my Levi's—the jeans fell down around my ankles. Jack slapped my ass once and grinned, then the cage door clanged shut; the lock snapped into place. He crossed the room and rejoined his friends.

"The devil never does get enough cock," Jack was saying. "He's a little pig, really. I think I've satiated the little bastard and ten minutes later, he's pulling on my balls again. He's tiresome! I finally decided the only thing to do was bring him here." The assembled daddies murmured sympathetically.

"I'm sure we can help," Demetrius said.

"Oh, I know *you* can," Jack rejoined. "A cock like yours is really the only possible answer."

I listened to Jack with amazement. He was going to get me ganged! I rubbed my dick against the cage bars, felt my cunt simmer.

Sure enough, he returned accompanied by Marc. Each was unzipping his leather pants.

"Now, boy, I know I don't need to tell you to be good to my friends. You're here for our use. Take this."

Jack thrust his cock near enough to the cage bars that I could just get to the pisshole with my tongue. I looked at him imploringly, the look that would have been accompanied by a "Please, Daddy!" if I'd been able to speak. Jack laughed and stepped closer, grasped the bars so he could press his pelvis right up against the cage, and his big cock came in for me to work on. I couldn't get hold of it with my hands—the restraints gave me some movement, but not enough—and so the only part of me that touched him was my mouth. I tongued him all over, the taste of him getting my saliva running, 'til his cock was wet and I could slurp him in. Marc stood just to one side of Jack, stroking his own cock—it had a downward curve, it would slide right down my throat.

"Look at this fucking cocksucker, Jack—where'd you find him? Look at this fucking kid." I knew how Jack liked it by now—he made a low little noise each time his cockhead slipped past my throat muscles, and when he pulled it out, I laved my tongue all around the corona. Once in a while I let it slip out of my mouth so I could scramble for his balls—this part was harder with no hands, but Jack stayed close, his cock bobbing up to slap his belly with a soft thwack whenever its head escaped my lips. I could only get one of his nuts in my mouth at a time, here without the use of my hands—when my hands were free, I knew, if I opened really wide I could just get both of them in, and then I could suckle them. Now, though, I returned to his cock after a little attention to his balls, sucked him rhythmically, my tongue alert as it stroked along his shaft for the first pulsing signs of his load coming.

He didn't give it to me this time, though—gasping and swearing, he pulled out before I could finish him. Marc was in his place almost before I knew there was no cock in my mouth. His dick was a little longer than Jack's, maybe not quite as thick, but substantial, and with that downturn. "Little sucker," Marc growled, "you can have my load, punk, if you can work it out of me," and I went for him.

Demetrius and Stone stood a few feet back now, watching too. As I breathed deeply, opened my throat, and started wiggling Marc's long curved one down as far as I could get it, Demetrius moved behind Jack and grasped his still-high cock in his big hand. Jack moaned, thrust into the fist like it was my cunt, started working it. When Marc's cock was all the way down my throat, I started a fast gulping kind of suck. It flirted with my gag reflex, but I didn't care—that cock fit so perfectly in my throat, I didn't want to pull off it at all.

I was just about to drool from the saliva I wasn't bothering to stop and swallow when Marc started thrusting faster. This added movement pulled the long cock up and out, slid it back down and in, fast, hard, repeatedly, as the blond man built up quickly towards his come. Jack was right on the edge of it too, but he wasn't missing a thing. "C'mon," he growled, "use that pig! Fill him up! Spray it right down his throat, man, that's what he's for!"

Marc bucked, knuckles white on the bars of my cage, and the next thrust, I felt the first hot pulse of his jizz hit the back of my throat. Jack's dirty talk had the same effect on me it always did—added to the sensation of come spurting into me, filling my mouth up with bitter, creamy spunk, waves of come took *me* over, too. I could just reach the bars and I held on so I could keep on Marc's cock even as my come threatened to tumble me off my feet.

Stone had inched closer to the cage. Now the huge man snapped the codpiece off his chaps as he stepped up to take the place Marc vacated. Not only his head was smooth—Stone's cock and balls were shaved too, and a sizeable Prince Albert matched the rings that stretched out his nipples.

"Lick it up, little boy. Get it hard." Sucking in Stone's soft cock with the metal ring felt wild, and I suckled on it the way I liked to suckle Jack's balls. As it started to fill up, he took it out of my mouth and, holding it, nuzzled it around my face, sometimes past my lips, sometimes under my chin. My whole face got slick from the sliding cock, and I hoped the fucking make-up on my upper lip was *more* than waterproof—I didn't think they behaved anything like this in the Max Factor test labs.

"Jack, I'm gonna fuck your kid, okay?" Stone slapped his almost-fully-engorged cock against my cheek. "Sure, just get a rubber," said Jack.

Not an instant later, the beautiful waiter-boy was at Stone's side, bearing a tray. Now where the fuck had he come from? I remembered that I'd heard Sir Sebastian's bell ringing a few minutes before. The boy must have come in then.

I could see his long pretty-boy meat outlined hard in his leather jock. I wondered if the help got to get laid around here, or what.

Stone picked a rubber off the tray, pulled it out of its wrapper, and worked it over his dick. The ring through his cockhead made the rubber fit a little funny, but I figured it'd probably work. Then he took a second one and repeated the process. While he suited up, Demetrius reached over Jack's shoulder and took a condom too.

I heard the sound of a zipper. Whose was that? Stone and Jack already had their cocks out. Then I heard Demetrius say, "Peaches, my pants, please," and the waiter knelt in front of him to help work the leather pants over his shiny boots. Peaches folded the pants carefully while Demetrius shucked the white silk shirt, then took them away. Over at the other end of the room, disguised by the woodwork, I saw a door swing open, and Demetrius' clothes went inside.

Stone, clad in rubber now, moved to the back of the cage. "Get your ass up here," he rasped. He reached through the bars to position me—there was just enough room for me to press my ass against the back bars and still be able to reach a cock fed to me at the front. Peaches reappeared silently, lube on his tray. Stone slathered up his cock, worked a finger into my ass. I shook with wanting this pierced-dicked giant to shove it in.

He didn't shove it, he worked it, and it felt so fucking good I could have screamed. I just grunted, low as I could pitch, and wiggled up onto him. "Jack, you're right, he's a fucking little pig," said Stone, "and I'm gonna fuck him just like one, ready, you little fuck, ready to get it jammed up your fucking pig butt?"

He had only arched into two or three hard thrusts when I felt my mouth opening again for cock—Jack's. I could have died of happiness. I sucked him down, *You want pig, Daddy, I'll show you what a pig you have*—and it was a minute before I noticed that Jack had shed his pants, too. Peaches stood near, still holding the tray which held the lube.

Then Demetrius, rubber on, started working his cock into Jack's asshole. Jack responded with a long groan, and I remembered that he'd been right up under an orgasm ever since I sucked him the first time. I backed off a little to give him time to get used to all the stimulation.

Pretty soon, all four of us turned into a fucking machine, Stone and Demetrius pumping into Jack's and my butts simultaneously, me swallowing Jack's cock each time they did. We were all growling and all three of them were muttering, "Yeah. *Fuck! Fuck* your fuckin' ass, *fuck!*"

Thank god Jack's cock was too far down my throat when he started shooting to allow me any air to scream with—I was feeling like squealing, like the pig that I was—but his spasming cock kept me quiet. The minute he slid out of my mouth, all cummed out, he bent forward and sucked his jism out of my mouth. The kiss shut me up again when I was about to howl. The minute his mouth left me, there was Demetrius' cock, out of Jack's ass, rubber shed, at my lips.

His dick must have been as big around as my wrist—at least. It had the most prominent head on it I'd ever seen—though of course, I couldn't *see* it right that minute. As it popped past the muscle at the top of my throat, it burned, and I tried to shake my head, afraid I'd choke, afraid I couldn't. Stone, behind me and still riding me hard, saw. "*Take* that cock," he bellowed, giving my ass a stinging slap. "Take it, you fucking little punk!" I took it, seeing stars, stretching wider than I ever thought I could, oh fuck, I thought, I'm playing with the big boys *now*.

Jack was back in commission. He was kneeling next to the cage, his face right next to mine, watching me growl and stretch to accommodate the thick meat. "Good boy," Jack murmured, "you're making me so proud, *little* man. Sucking that big hunk of cock. You can suck him, boy, you can get fucked by him, I know you want that, baby, don't you, can't get enough meat, hot little man."

That was it, wasn't it? I was where I'd always wanted to be, and I turned into a little demon, throwing my ass back on Stone's hard-pounding cock, suddenly finding room in my throat I didn't know I had. My hands clutched the bars for support and I worked both men for all I was worth.

"*Chew on it.*" Jack was still right at my ear. "Chew that dick, boy. Don't worry about biting him, he likes it." I growled like a junkyard dog around Demetrius's substantial cock, chewing it like Jack told me to. Freed from cocksucking's one overriding rule—*don't bite!*—I lost myself completely in the sensation of being filled up as full as I'd ever been. Thank god all the head I'd given already had filled my throat with that thick cocksucking slime—it lubricated even Demetrius's thickness. Stone pounded away behind me, and I had a feeling I knew how he'd earned his name.

But at last even Stone, who had been rhythmically fucking my ass for what seemed like an hour, started fucking even harder and faster. "Take it, you pig!" he grunted, really close to shooting, I could tell by his voice, and I felt Demetrius speed up too, both of them about to hose me, mouth and asshole, full of hot cream. "Comin'!" cried Demetrius. "Comin' right now!" And naturally, I was shooting up the ramp right along with them, I'd be a fine pig if I couldn't come right along with my tops, *right Daddy?* I opened my eyes to look at Jack, wanting to know he was seeing this, pumped full of his friends' jizz. I couldn't suck any more—my mouth was open as far as the muscles would stretch it, in a silent orgasmic yell—but that was okay, because the big black man in front of me was fucking my face now with pounding thrusts.

I remember the first half of the orgasm, but not the second.

I blacked out. I lost it, don't know exactly how it happened but it must have had something to do with my engorgable throat-flesh forming a seal with Demetrius' expanding, coming cock. I couldn't get enough air, I guess.

When I came to, I had no idea where I was.

I felt damp clothes, chill air and motion, saw nothing but darkness, smelled the reek of not-quite-fresh piss. Where the fuck was I? A vehicle—a *trunk*? I felt around me in the utter black and yes, I was lying in a capacious car trunk, not bound, my leather jacket thrown over me, some kind of scratchy car blanket under my head, what felt like trash bags underneath my body. If I hadn't had such an extraordinary night, I'd have been terrified—but I was pretty sure this was part of Jack's buddies' idea of a good time.

The vehicle slowed, turned, turned again, and after a short distance stopped. I heard almost immediately the familiar sound of Jack's bike. Next, a car door slamming, then another. Two people? Then the trunk lid lifted.

It took a second for my eyes to adjust even to the dim alley light. We were outside Jack's place, back in the city. Jack and Demetrius stood there with a man I didn't know. He had on a driver's uniform, so I guessed that Sir Stephen had lent the use of his car to get me out of there. What would a distinguished man like him do with a pissy piece of fucked-out chicken? After all. But had I pissed myself? It wouldn't have surprised me.

Demetrius reached into the trunk and lifted me like I was an unwieldy but not-very-heavy teddy bear. Jack had his keys out. The driver stood silently by. Sir Stephen's help weren't a very talkative lot, were they? But at last, as Jack stepped up to the door, the driver said, "Shall I wait, Sir?"

"Yes, do," said Demetrius, and he had me up the stairs and into the foyer.

"Here, let's clean the pig up," said Jack, gesturing Demetrius through his room and into his bath. He had the water running in the shower by the time we got there. Demetrius supported me while Jack stripped off my jacket, the bar vest, which I noted with chagrin was pissy too, and my boots and pants. He was about to thrust me under the hot spray with my shirt and jockstrap still on when Demetrius spoke up. "Go ahead, strip the girl down."

Jack and I both looked at him, eyes wide. I was stricken. I had been so exultant about passing! What gave me away?

Demetrius started to laugh, a low swell of a laugh that turned into a roar when he looked at me and saw my face. "Randy girl, you did good. I don't know what the fuck that was all about, but you pulled it off. No one else noticed a thing. I'm the one who carried you into the car, darling, and I took the liberty of feeling you up. Yes, I know your Daddy made a rule, but I've broken plenty of his rules before." At this, Jack started laughing too. "Well, it's not like my meat hadn't just been all the way down your little throat. I felt further familiarities wouldn't be inappropriate. And your sweet little dick just seemed to come off in my hand. I tucked it back in, of course."

Jack was howling.

"I trust you have a bigger one than that, since you appear to be keeping Jack interested. I liked ganging Jack with you very much, dear, and I'd be glad to do that again any time you two want to give me a call. Jack, I'm back at my former number. *Do* phone me when you get time. I see we have more catching up to do than I thought. Randy—it's been a pleasure." With that, he gravely extended his hand, and as I took it I started laughing too.

Jack still laughed as Demetrius engulfed him in a bear hug—god, he was larger than Jack by almost as much as Jack outsized me—and I went ahead and shed the damp T-shirt and jockstrap and unwound the binding. As I stepped into the shower, Demetrius took a look at me and said, "Sure enough, she's a girl, all right. Jack, you sick fuck! If St. James ever gets wind of this, he'll have his traditionalist boys come and turn your dick inside out. You and Little Bit here can go down to City Hall and register as domestic partners, and then you can spend your afternoons drinking coffee at the Whiptail Lizard Womyn's Lounge. You fucking wild man!"

Jack kissed Demetrius goodnight as I scrubbed the piss off. He ducked his head in the shower and kissed me too, and then he was gone.

Still grinning, Jack dried me off, capturing me for a minute in the big white fluffy towel. "Want some ice cream?" he said. "Good boys get ice cream."

"God, yes, I'm starving, Jack. I passed out before Peaches could come by with the sandwich tray."

Jack installed me in the flannel-sheeted bed, disappeared down the hall, and came back with two bowls. Before he started on his, he stripped down, took a fast shower, and then joined me in bed. "Kid, you're more fun than a barrel of novices. You were terrific. I'm very proud."

I glowed as much from this as from the still very-memorable fuck I still hadn't come all the way down from. The cold ice cream felt so intense on my throat that I almost squeaked. It was pretty sore from all that action. "Jack, I got piss on your bar vest. I'm so sorry. I don't know how it happened."

"No, *I* got piss on your bar vest. Leathers have to be broken in, child. We all doused you after you went out."

"*What?*"

"Sometimes it wakes people up," he said innocently. "Don't worry about going out, by the way. I think the first time I got down on that man's cock I passed out too. I was younger then, of course."

Then he told me what happened after I blacked out. I'd have fallen over but the men's cocks kept me suspended—Jack saw it as soon as it happened, though he let the guys finish coming. At first, Stone and then Demetrius pulled their softening meat out of me, Jack reached into the cage to hold me up, and before he could even call for him, Peaches was there with the key, unlocking the cage door so Jack could undo my restraints.

"Jack, who were all those guys? Why didn't Sir Sebastian and St. James play? Didn't they like me?"

"Don't worry, honey. St. James loves this group of men, but he almost never plays. He's an old-timer. A traditionalist. He doesn't approve of the free-form way so many of us play now. I think he has a group of men he plays with back in London. He wouldn't be caught dead playing in a room with people who switch. Talk to him if you ever get a chance. Not many like him anymore. Sir Sebastian would have joined us if St. James hadn't been there, but he's too flawless a host to let a guest sit unentertained. As to who they are, I'll tell you the whole story of how I fell in with them, but how about over breakfast?"

Jack snuggled me under his arm, the scent of which almost got me going again—but I was just too exhausted. I started to nod off to the sound of his murmurings, mostly of the "good little cocksucking pig" variety.

Right before I slipped under I whispered, "Thank you, Daddy"—and then, "Daddy, can we borrow Peaches?"

PRIME REAL ESTATE

MARK DAVID M. FENNELL

I can feel it in every part of my body.

A numbing sensation. Something's missing.

Numbness is coursing through my blood, pulsing through my muscles, invading my bones.

My hands are weak. My head is weak. My heart is weak.

My heart is very weak.

I am asleep.

I am dreaming.

I am dreaming of him.

His hair is brown and his eyes are green. He is tall, taller than I would like, taller than me. He has freckles on his arms, and a hairy chest. He is a bartender. This is absurd!

I am awake.

I am staring at him.

He is staring at me. No, he is looking at me and smiling. I imagine he is staring at me, but instead he is leaning over the bar and sticking his hand down my shirt. Two hundred other men are watching and silently groaning with envy. I am also groaning, but not with envy. This is the second time he has reached from behind the bar to examine my chest. The first time he smiled approvingly at my chest hair. This time he licks his lips. I cannot hear anything yet I hear everything.

"Did you see that?"

"Mark David, what are you doing?!? You're a tramp."

"Slut, slut, slut."

"Don't give that man anymore to drink!"

I cannot hear anything. I have a nice buzz. He is smiling at me. I have consumed at least one half bottle of Absolut Citron during the last hour and a half. I am staring at what I can see of the cavity between his pectorals. I am finding it hard to breathe. I want to go home. I grin inanely back at him.

"You want another?" He shouts over the drone of two hundred other men.

"Sure."

He twists around, sideswiping the bartender next to him. He has a great ass. I want to touch the back of his neck. He is holding the bottle two feet above the glass and the clear liquid falls out. He is smiling at me. He glides the twist over the edge of the glass and slides it in front of me. His hands are beautiful: the fingers long and slim, fingernails neatly trimmed. He is leaning on his hands on the edge of the bar.

"Four-fifty."

I place a twenty on the bar. He whisks it away and is asking another man what he wants to drink. A minute later he is placing bills and change in my hand; as my hand closes, his hand lingers.

I am asleep.

He is leaning over me. No, he is laying on top of me. His lips are a hair's breadth away from mine. I am barely breathing. He is naked on top of me. I can feel his skin beneath my fingers. I draw a path from his hairline, down his back, over the shoulder blades, down the spine; my hand disappears between his buttocks. His lips still have not touched mine. I cannot hear anything but my heart. My legs are wrapped around his waist. It is an unusual position; I am not used to it. The trail of hair from his stomach disappears where our two bodies meet.

I am awake.

"He has a lover."

I can see the plain band of gold on the ring finger of his left hand. I am temporarily, momentarily daunted. I turn away. He Has A Lover; it echoes. Everywhere I look there are men. There are no women. No, there are no *females*; there are many women, I think sadly. I am becoming tired of routine, tired of men. I am being cruised. Instantly I am amused, flattered. I send the jury out. The verdict: I am not interested, thank you very much, good night. Someone is talking to me. It's not him.

"Hello! Is there anybody home?"

I want to be witty, but cannot. I nod affirmative, turning back to the bar. He is leaning over another bartender, his lips moving, brushing against the back of the other man's neck, his stomach lightly pressing against the other man's back. The other man is laughing and nodding his head. I turn to the speaker.

I am awake.

I am tired but awake.

I go wandering. My friend Ken, who asked me earlier if anyone was home, is following me. We are in search, going where all men have gone before. I smell six different colognes in three minutes. Two a minute. In the darkness, all men are only dicks. I imagine that everyone I pass is really just a phallus in yuppie clothing. I start to laugh. Ken leans forward from behind me to ask what is so funny. I contemplate telling him; he will not understand. Ken wants to get laid. I shake my head, tell him, "Nothing." He frowns and shrugs. As we walk, I see him, the bartender. He has a cigarette pressed between his lips. I am instantly disappointed, but still undaunted. He pulls the cigarette out and grins at me as he approaches.

"Hey," he says. In some stereotypical way, it is what I would expect him to say. It is what two hundred other men wish he would say to them. He puts his hand on my shoulder and squeezes. He continues to walk in the opposite direction, pulling his hand with him as an afterthought, down my arm to my hand, pausing to interlock with my fingers and tug as he continues to walk in one direction while I continue in the other. He is holding my hand. Then he is gone.

My eyes are closed, but I see him.

I am breathing in the smell of his skin; his hair is brushing against my fore-head. He is moving against me, with me. My heart is pounding and every-thing is black and white. I am unaware of everything but him, his touch. His mouth closes on mine, and I am breathing in his breath. He is examining each and every tooth, stopping at the two fillings in my back teeth. His tongue is there, then gone, tracing my lips, slipping into my ear. He pulls me on top of him. His pubic hair is entangled in mine; he is hard and press-ing against my stomach. I am caught in the crevice between his buttocks. This is the familiar position; I am almost there—

I am back where I was standing earlier, reclaiming the prime real estate at the front of the bar. Prime real estate: so dubbed because of its posi-tion relative to the prime beef on the inside of the bar.

"His name is Jim."

Aren't they all? is my first thought.

"He has a lover."

I am tired of hearing about his lover. I wish he would stop teasing me. I'm not completely stupid. I understand it is in his best interest to be...friendly...with me; when does it go beyond friendly? He is looking at me again, and I wink without thinking. He is still looking at me. He is still looking at me with those green eyes, and I am still looking at him. I look down at his hands, and the see that left one is wrapped in a bar towel. I am glad I cannot see the ring. I am getting incredibly wasted, now work-ing on the second half of the same bottle of Absolut Citron, working on my third or fourth lemon, working on Jim, the bartender, Prime Beef extraordinaire. I look at my watch and realize that it is two o'clock in the morning. There are only one hundred sixty-seven men here now. Pairs have begun forming. I've seen this scene before, exit stage left.

I am being cruised again. A very attractive Irish boy. I assume he is Irish, because I am generally attracted to Irish boys, and this one gaping at my crotch has dark brown hair and eyes that are not brown. I cannot distin-guish their exact color from this distance. I stare at this boy a while, debating. I have a dilemma. Do I wait for Jim, the bartender? More impor-tant, do I want to wait until four-thirty, five o'clock? To go home alone?

His breathing is rapid and he is moaning.

His chest is heaving and I can feel his blood racing in my hand. His legs are wrapped around my waist and he is pulling me more tightly to him. I can feel the muscles in his calves expand and cut into my lower back. The muscles in my thighs are straining to keep up with his rhythm, each of my hands locked onto either side of his waist. I can see the sweat on his chest, trickling down his rib cage, smell the heat. My blood is racing, I am frantic. My eyesight is fading, and my body is threatening to hyperventilate. The whole room is swimming, spinning, and I am falling, falling; I have no control over my body. I have become some sort of mutated freak, joined to him like some bizarre science experiment gone awry. The harder I try to pull away, the stronger he is pulling me back, as if I am determined to get away and he will not let me; I am trapped inside him, and will soon get sucked into the blackness.

"What's your name?"
The Irish boy is standing in front of me. His eyes are blue, and he is shorter. Those are two points in his favor. Also, he appears to be as wasted if not more so than myself, which has potential advantages.
"Mark David. And you?"
I'm awake but tired. The Irish boy has a nice ass. His name is Kevin, and I think, *I'll just bet*, but say nothing. The Citron in the Absolut has soured my disposition. Perhaps I should go back to the regular stuff. I look behind me toward the bar. I am the single remaining partner of the Friday Night Prime Real Estate Cooperative. All the other board members have disappeared. I turn away from the Irish boy whose name is Kevin this evening and look at Jim. He does not see me. He is engrossed in conversation with a side of beef at the other end of the bar. Game, set, and match.
"Are you, by any chance, Irish, Kevin?"
He cocks his head to one side, wondering what strange direction the current line of questioning will lead to. He is silent a moment, and then responds affirmatively.
"I thought so," I say, but do not continue. He asks me if his nationality is a problem.
"Quite the opposite," I tell him, and stare directly into his eyes. I am feeling the power. He grins a charming grin and his eyes fall to the floor. Alas, I believe it's time for the Cooperative to close for the evening. I glance back toward the bar again. I blink, take a deep breath and turn back to the Irish boy.
"You wanna get outta here, Kevin?"
Real estate is not a game I'm good at anyway.

I am asleep, but I can feel it in every part of my body.

The quiet breathing next to me flows in rhythm to the pulsing of the numbness in my brain. Something is still missing.

My hands are weak. My head is weak. My heart is weak.

My heart is very weak.

THE LAST BLOWJOB

STEPHEN GRECO

By May, a month and a half after my lover Henry was admitted to Sacred Heart, it was clear that he wasn't going to come home as quickly as we had been hoping. They eliminated the pneumonia within the first few weeks and knocked out the peskiest of the other "little" infections that had bloomed under its influence. But Dr. Ehrlich said that before we could think of transferring Henry to a "home setting," his mysterious low-grade fever and recurring cough would have to be brought under control. But this didn't happen right away and, by late spring, it didn't seem likely to happen at all. Managing Henry's condition had begun to look as difficult as shoring up a big plate of softening jello.

Still, Henry remained optimistic. Attached to an IV pole, he continued to produce his TV talk show by staying in constant touch with his office by phone. He had a small fax machine installed on the table next to his bed, received and dispatched several messengers a day, and even had prospective guests for the show come by the hospital for the standard interview—something he always took mischievous pleasure in suggesting to them. His universe, like that of all hospital patients, may have shrunk to the size a room, but Henry's room—private, of course; we had the best medical insurance possible—encompassed the world.

There was a steady stream of friends and colleagues who stopped by—visitors whose appointments it was my responsibility, as Chief Care Partner, to coordinate. Henry was, after all, not as strong as he used to be and needed to conserve his energy for crucial things, like breathing and thinking and praying. His attitude about being sick was philosophical. He accepted the death that was clearly impending but tried to embrace life as vigorously as ever, since it was still in progress. Not only

57

did I never hear Henry curse the sex-in-the-fast-lane lifestyle that some mistook as the cause of this whole mess, more than once, both to me and among friends who loved to hear him talk this way, he affirmed his faith in eros. Eros is not what got us into all this, he would say; eros is what can get us beyond it. Not that he expected his disease to be cured by this force, nor did he think his body would be "healed" by it (to use a fashionable term he found annoyingly unscientific). There was simply nothing Henry had discovered in his predicament to put him off the conviction that what Freud described as "binding together" with others, whether for work or pleasure, was the highest expression of the life instinct.

I guess that's why I was so disappointed when, after the pneumonia was over and he began to gain back a few of the fifty pounds he had lost, Henry rebuffed a gentle request I made to bind with me. We were slouched together in his bed one night, watching TV, and I fell into the kind of lovey-dovey nuzzlings that had been typical of late-night re-run-watching behavior in our home over the last ten years. But Henry wasn't interested. He stopped me with a limp squeeze of his hand. I let it go at that, not wanting to tax him with a conference, but the next day, as I was shaving him, I brought up the question of sex.

"Honey, do you ever jerk off after I go home?"

"Uh-uh."

"Have you done it at all since you've been here?"

"No."

"Why not? Not enough privacy?"

"There's enough privacy. I just haven't felt like it."

It struck me as odd that the man who had gone to so much trouble to reconstitute his work life around his newly diminished capacities should not have done the same thing with his sex life, which was just as important to him.

"I tried once," Henry continued, "but I got interrupted by Rachel." Rachel was the head nurse. "I know she's seen everything, but still I felt weird. Another time, I couldn't stay awake long enough to do it. And then once, I thought I was getting turned on by a muscle magazine that somebody brought, just when a patient down the hall decided to go Code Blue. The commotion killed the mood for me."

I put down the electric razor and took his face in my palms.

"I could help you feel like it," I whispered.

He smiled wanly. Shaving now not only made my Henry look neat but, since the structure of his handsome skull was so much more visible than before, it also brought a clarity to his looks that I had never imagined.

"Can I tell you," I purred, "that I'm as totally turned on by you as ever?"

"Baby, you can tell me anything you want," he said, his smile disappearing suddenly into a fit of coughing.

We'd always been creative with sex. When Henry had his wisdom teeth taken out, when I broke my leg, when we were both paralyzed with sunburn, we were still able to figure out some way to do it when both of us felt like doing it. And we were proud of our secret history of making love in romantic places on storybook occasions, like the garden of the Taj Mahal at midnight during a full moon in July, or a cramped compartment aboard the Orient Express in the middle of the Alps on New Year's Eve. I was sure there must be some way for me to be with my lover sexually now—pacifically, of course; only so far as his energy and strength would allow, in a modulated manner, the same way I got him to eat in the hospital by dining with him slowly, or, when the meals put before him looked too enormous or too monolithic, by cutting things up and putting them individually into his mouth.

I knew the problem: Henry needed time to adjust to the fact that if he wanted sex, as with work, he was going to have to do it here, in this sanitary environment, because he might never see our Joe Durso bed or the antique oak kitchen table again. It might take time; it might also never happen. I would have to try and remain understanding.

"Well, I want us to keep talking about this, okay?"

"Us having sex? Maybe someday, honey," he said. "I just...don't know how. I promise I'll work on it."

He reached over to give my pec an appreciative tug, then turned away abruptly as the coughing started again.

Henry was the one who got me going to the gym. He was one of the original converts to the pectoral lifestyle, at the dawn of the Nautilus Age, and was one of the first people I knew to fill out the sleeve of a polo shirt with a properly pumped tricep. Now, installed for weeks in his bed at Sacred Heart—perhaps never to stand up unaided again, as a physical therapist rather insensitively blurted to both of us—Henry continued to take great care in his appearance. He made sure I shaved him three times a week and insisted I speak with a nurse if there was the slightest delay in his sponge bath. He groomed his fingernails daily—much more than they needed it—and somehow managed to contort his semi-wasted self into a position to tend to his toenails, too.

And his body, I thought, still looked great. Was I only seeing him through the eyes of a devoted lover, or was Henry beautiful in a new way? Of course there were detriments galore for us in this damned hospitalization, but there were benefits, too: new strengths, new ways of looking at things. We'd made a pact when he was first admitted to be aware of whatever unexpected good could be found in this new phase of our life together. I thought Henry looked like a statue of the emaciated Buddha we'd seen in Japan, a sexy/saintly figure whose every muscle, vein, and bone was legible beneath a shrink-wrap of skin that seemed a gracious concession to corporeality. Most of the weight that Henry had lost was unsuspected fat, I swear; there was a new tautness that gave his impeccably gymmed physique a refined, essential look—as if he'd been madly training for some bodybuilding contest in which bulk meant nothing and definition everything. His complexion was radiant—probably the side-effect of drugs he was taking, Ehrlich told me—and when Henry sat there in bed, now that it was spring, draped casually with a sheet over his waist, no shirt on, his chest looking like something out of a George Platt Lynes photograph, his feet out of a Michaelangelo drawing, I could hardly deflect the thought that these were nipples I still wanted to lick, toes I still wanted to suck. And I was not ashamed of this thought, because desire was the only way I could think of to keep sanctified this piece of flesh that had been turned by diagnosis into an object to be poked and prodded and palpated by an endless parade of technicians.

Henry often said how glad he was to have suffered only pneumonia so far and no skin mutilations. He detested any kind of physical disfigurement and was horrified when I told him about the guy down the hall who had been so transformed by black-and-purple lesions that he was unrecognizable as the cute boy-next-door in a snapshot his mother had put in a frame near the bed. Henry was intact and proud of the fact.

I, on the other hand, felt like I was disintegrating, physically. Cramming a full day's work into four hours at my own office, then rushing to the hospital to serve as traffic cop, baby sitter, physical therapist, and master of ceremonies; squeezing in quick workouts now and then; getting home late and sleeping fitfully, because I couldn't adjust to going to bed alone for the first time in a decade; I was often so tuckered out that even looking twice at boners bulging invitingly under sweatpants in the street seemed too hard to do, let alone striking up a conversation and going home with someone—which I almost felt I should do, since I hadn't had sex with Henry in months and sex is usually one way for me to refresh myself. Anyway, it was Henry I wanted—those arms, that face. Despite brief escapades that we agreed must remain "only physical," could never take time away from the relationship, and were not to be spoken of, Henry and I had always been true to each other, and now that our relationship was probably in its final months, I felt less like hooking up with a stranger than ever.

I hope I don't have to explain why sex in a hospital is such a thinkable proposition. Hell, sex has got to be the most therapeutic thing in the world. Other longtime companions I was meeting in the corridors of Sacred Heart told me about salutary bouts of lovemaking they'd enjoyed with their sick boyfriends on hospital beds. In fact, to hear some of them tell it, hospitals are hopping with sex. One had a friend who, over the years, had been a faithful client of one of the city's top porn-star-hustlers. Now that the hustler was ill and occasionally installed in hospital rooms, the client made it a point to go on seeing him. It wasn't so much about money being exchanged for services as a special kind of friendship remaining intact, I was told. The client would arrive for a visit with a bouquet; the two of them would chat aimlessly for a while, then swing into a highly verbal bodyworship scene that centered on the hustler's cock; those famous ten fat inches would inflate and be deflated in a manner that was usual for them; and the cash would be found later in a get-well card tucked into the flowers. Gay men are nothing if not adaptable.

Another guy told me that the ritual group of men he belongs to had recently visited one of their members who was hospitalized in coma. After words being spoken and hands being laid on, the group masturbated onto the man's motionless body, exactly as he had asked them to do when he was able. And everyone tells me that there are nights now on the phone sex lines when it simply isn't possible to avoid at least one connection with someone whose conversation testifies to bed confinement. One guy I was talking to recently told me he had to hang up because an orderly had arrived to wheel him away for an x-ray.

I was trimming Henry's hair one day, finishing up with a little peck on the cheek, when he pulled me close to him and inserted his hand under the waistband of my jeans.

"Oh, really?" I said. "Frisky today?"

"I don't know," he said with coyness that outside the room would have seemed inconsequential but here seemed practically monumental. "You're so good to me."

"You're good to me," I said, "letting me take care of you...."

"Hmmm," he said, snuggling into my armpit.

After a moment, he reached over to get his wallet from a drawer in the night table and took out a twenty dollar bill.

"Listen, it's not five-thirty yet, is it? Go out to where they keep the linens and give this to that cute nurse with the crewcut and goatee. His name is Eric. Ask him to watch our door for twenty minutes. He's cool."

When I returned, Henry had kicked down the bedding and was stroking himself through his Brooks Brothers boxer shorts. I perched next to him and slipped a hand over his chest and down around his back. He smelled very old but reassuringly Henry-like.

"He's cute, right?

"Very," I said, kissing Henry's ear. But I was nervous. "Has Rachel stopped by with the afternoon meds yet?"

"She came at four. Ehrlich's due around six. Now, I can't guarantee that someone's not going to come barging past Eric, wanting a cup of my blood or a picture of my brain..."

"Let me check once more."

I hopped down and went to the door. The corridor was quiet. Eric smiled confidently when I peeked out. He reassured me that this was a good time and shooed me back into the room. Inside, it was suddenly the baths. There was this sexy guy spread out on a bed, giving me a look and a half. I bee-lined over to him and applied my skull deftly to his cock.

It was like conversing in your native language again after a year among foreigners. Henry's cock was big, but it was articulate. It spoke to me. And I was very good at listening to it. The language was that subtle, non-verbal kind that occurs between body parts that are lavishly endowed with a zillion times more receptor nerve cells than other parts. With the delicate skin of head of cock nestled into the lining of mouth and throat, both of us were acutely attuned, like human polygraphs, to minute fluctuations in each other's temperature, electrolytic balance, and galvanic response, forget grosser signs like pelvic thrust and breathing rate. The taste of him drove me crazy; the very elements he was made of, in their exact proportion to each other, I have craved since the day I met him. And he simply *looked* hot: Mr. Big TV Producer lying there on his back, his weak little limbs as immobile as if they had been fettered by leather straps. Now, Henry and I had never done much bondage, but I think what really worked for us this time was this expression of his passivity, with an undertone of resignation.

He took no longer to come than he ever did. Maybe fifteen minutes. If Ehrlich had burst in with his chart, or Rachel with a needle, or that perky, surrealistically well-groomed patients' advocate woman with one more questionnaire, what they would have seen was me kneeling over this muscular skinny guy, his head thrown back in ecstasy, the plastic urinal bottle empty on the floor, where it had fallen when knocked from its hook on the bed rail. What they would not have seen, but surmised, was the presence of the thick, warm, veiny shaft plugged up inside my head, emptying itself. Henry gave my hair a little tousle when we'd finished. He was beaming like Howdy Doody. I kissed his navel and covered him with the sheet.

"Cold?" I asked.

"Hot," he said, letting me tuck him in. "I've so much missed being that close to you. Listen, honey, can I say something serious? I want you to make sure you have another lover when I'm gone...."

"What!? Henry, I can't believe you're giving me that speech. It's entirely premature."

"Just remember that I said it. Be sad when I'm gone, but get another lover. Think of my saying that as a little gift to you, like the one you just gave me."

We talked for a minute about my not wanting to talk about the matter, then it was time for Henry's nap. I put the room back in order and took off. Eric said good-bye as I left.

That was the last time Henry and I had sex. The *last* last time, that is. The time before that—which I remember fearing, when it happened, could itself be the last—took place a month before Henry went into the hospital. We were in London for the opening of a new play. He had already begun to lose weight "mysteriously" and sleep through any performance we got tickets to. We'd returned to our hotel room in the afternoon for a nap, and upon waking, fell into each other's arms with a hunger I recall from our college days, which is when we met. Another lover! That was the last thing I wanted to think about.

Henry never came home from Sacred Heart. Less than a month after our little escapade, Rachel found him one morning wailing about being "at the wrong gate" and waving a towel like a flag to someone on the horizon. Dementia had set in and from there everything got worse. We lost him in August. I am glad to think that, during the last days, though he seldom knew who I was, he still favored me with a kind of infantile sexual intimacy, as if through gathering shadows there shined the memory of love. In the midst of throwing food at the walls and ripping off his diapers, he'd grasp me affectionately and grin as if to say, "I know who you are and I think you're wonderful." And I would feel completely wonderful.

I was surprised when Eric showed up at the memorial service I arranged for Henry that fall. It was a giant affair. Friends and relatives flew in from all over the country. Dr. Ehrlich was there. Rachel came. And then there was Eric, who strode in looking incredibly cute in a smart linen blazer over a tight T-shirt that definitely showed "something going on" underneath, as Henry liked to say. After the ceremony he came up to me and told me something amazing.

"He was a great guy," Eric said, gathering me into a warm embrace. No, I hadn't realized how muscular he was. "I'm sorry I didn't get to know him until so late. But I thought you should know...that is, he wanted me to tell you, after he was gone like this...that we fooled around in the hospital. A little bit."

At first, I didn't know what he was talking about.

"Fooled around?"

"Sex. He said you'd approve."

Oh, I thought.

"He loved you so much," Eric went on. "He always said that. He and I used to see each other at the gym all the time, before he got sick. I always thought he was totally hot, and he used to look at me in the shower like, 'Someday, mister.' I'd drop the soap, spend four minutes picking it up, that kind of thing. Well, when he checked into the room on my floor at Sacred Heart, it was natural that we should talk to each other, spend time with each other. You know."

"So how did you fool around?" I asked.

"We felt each other up a few times, jerked off," Eric said brightly, "and once I blew him. Mainly in the room, when I knew there would be no one around. Once, he asked me to put him in a wheelchair and take him to the solarium. We did it right there, next to a visitor guy who was asleep on the sofa. Your lover was a very sexy man. Now, he said that this would be good for you to hear...."

"Yeah, yeah, it's good," I said after a moment. "So the day you watched out for us...."

"He told me later that until then he hadn't been able to feel aroused in the hospital. It was only after that that he and I did anything. He said that you had, quote, restored his body to him and that after he was gone I should buy you a drink and tell you all the details."

So it was not with me that Henry had his last sexual experience. Well. It would take some getting used to, but I realized even then, in my stressed out state, that Eric's story hardly detracted from my memory of Henry. It embellished it, really: Heroes of Eros, welcome Henry into your midst.

I wanted to hear more, but I was being summoned by the rabbi. I asked Eric to call me. We would have a drink, talk more. And I was thinking: I'm as happy to go out with Eric as Henry thought I would be. Any excuse to keep talking about my lover was okay with me.

WHAT HE DID

THOMAS ROCHE

John liked guys; there was no question about that. But in guys, as in everything else, he had perverse, somewhat decadent tastes. And he had always liked to put people in situations that would test their boundaries, destroy their resistance, take away their feigned innocence. He liked to see people, particularly men, lose control.

That's why he did what he did.

Adrienne and I worked the same shift, at the comic shop, five to eleven, four days a week. So she and I were getting to know each other pretty well. Adrienne was a fag hag to begin with, that was for sure. You can always tell by the comics a girl reads. And she knew I was into boys. Maybe she just wanted something safe, a guy who wouldn't want to own her, or maybe just a guy who wouldn't bellyache about wearing a condom. She knew I was bi, not gay, but she also knew John and I were together.

That night John came in, he stayed for the half-hour after closing while Adrienne and I cleaned and locked up and counted out the drawer. The two of them talked like old friends, about Wonder Woman and Captain Marvel, sexual innuendos periodically drifting into the conversation. I could tell he was baiting her. I was sure that he and Adrienne were flirting, which didn't quite add up.

"That chick has a crush on you, Paul," John told me as we walked home up Haight Street, through the mid-November chill.

I responded without responding. "Maybe she has a crush on you."

"Nah. She's a fag hag, but she's not a glutton for punishment or anything."

I considered Adrienne in my mind's-eye. Adrienne had the look I so adored, the waiflike black-clad pose, the deathrocker bob dyed black, the studs in her lower lip and nostril and the eyeliner and tattoo of a bat on the back of her neck, the rings of silver around her ears from top to bottom. Her sexuality was just overt enough to snare my interest, not brazen enough to strike me as that of a *poseur*. Plus, she had great tits.

I like guys fine, and I had been monogamous with John for over a year now. I was totally into him, but of course I still looked. And John knew who got my attention.

"Maybe you should ask her out on a date," I said. "And find out. You could take her to the drive-in and fuck her in the back seat while you watch *I Was a Teenage Fag Hag* or something. I hear it's playing down in Serramonte."

"I don't have a car. Besides—you'd go mad with jealousy," he told me, leaning over and whispering into my ear. "You'd take a meat cleaver to the both of us. It'd be a tragic affair. In all the papers and everything."

I snorted in disgust. We let it drop, and that was that. But the matter didn't leave my mind, and hours later, I was still thinking of her as John fucked me from behind on the futon, the two of us tangled in the black sandalwood-scented sheets, his hands on my waist, groaning his midnight pleasures in a cloud of incense and pot smoke. I thought about her as I came: I imagined her stretched on the bed next to us, my fingers inside her as our tongues intertwined.

And it was afterwards, as John lit up our post-sex joint, that he whispered to me, his breath all fragrant clouds and intoxication, "You were thinking about her."

Adrienne was a hell of a flirt. John had been right; she had a crush on me. She wasn't necessarily interested in doing anything about it, though—not at first. At least, that was my reading. She just liked flirting with me, and of course, I responded in kind. Her body continued to impose itself on my fantasies, especially when John whispered to me about her. After a while, I stopped complaining when he did it, and just let the images flow into my mind: John wanting to watch me fuck her, to taste her cunt on my cock. John had never even fucked a chick, and had never expressed an interest in doing so. But it seemed that my desires fascinated him even more than his own.

I began noticing things about Adrienne, little details you only notice about someone when you have a crush on them. Like what sort of bra she wore, how she stood when she leaned up against the counter, where she bought her shoes. How the rings in her nipples would show through her babydoll dress when she moved her shoulders just right. The way she smelled when she got close enough to me. The feel of her ass brushing slightly against me as she squeezed past—maybe just a trifle closer than she needed to be—in the close quarters behind the counter. The way she would blush afterwards.

"You're fucking her, Paul. You're on top of her, pounding into her pussy. You like that, pussy? I hear it tastes real good to some guys...you got her tits in your hands...." This while John was behind me, fucking his rubber-sheathed prick into my ass. His lips up against my ear, his hand around my cock. Jerking it. After I came in slick streams all over his gloved hand, he told me that one day he was going to bring home a sweet treat and share her with me on this very futon.

"All walk and no talk makes a gayboy dull as fuck," I sighed good-naturedly. But I didn't take him seriously.

Adrienne became more and more of a fascinating creature; the shape of her body seemed more exotic every day: the curves of her hips like those of some elaborate statue, the shape of her ass like harem pillows...she paid more and more attention to me. It had gone beyond a crush. For both of us.

I knew she'd been dumped a couple of months before, and her boyfriend sounded like a real creep. She had had a couple of things going with girls, but that was at least a couple of years back. I knew she was on the rebound, and rebounding hard, and that spelled bad news to me. I didn't want to encourage her. It seemed sort of unfair to do so. Maybe it was just a bit too easy when I got that other job at the art store. The dollar an hour more wasn't so much the draw as the fact that I wouldn't have the perpetual sexual tension of being close to Adrienne. She seemed sad at my leaving, and we promised to keep in touch and have dinner some time.

I was glad to be away from the desire. It wasn't that I felt guilty or anything—it was just a perpetual confusion, a desire I felt easier living without.

Still, I missed her. I missed the flirtation, the attention, the chance to look down her shirt when she leaned just so. I missed her sense of humor, her friendship. But I knew it couldn't work, us just being friends. That's what made Adrienne so hot to me. There was a sense of urgency, of a need that could not be denied.

John was disappointed. He kept talking to me about her, and the fantasy grew more intense because I wasn't seeing Adrienne every day. John would work my cock with his hand while he told me, in excruciating detail, how Adrienne was jerking me off. It always got him totally hot.

Maybe John's suspicions and fetishes were encouraged by the fact that I only read straight porn, and sometimes got off reading hetero sex manuals like *The Sensuous Woman* and *Total Sex.* I don't know—it was weird—the thought of all those married straight people fucking like weasels in their suburban houses always got me going. So I probably knew as much about women's bodies as I did about men's, though I'd only been to bed with two women in my entire life, and those were fleeting romances.

I was quite happy in my relationship with John. But when I read about tits and clits and cunnilingus and hetero anal sex, I found myself invariably thinking of Adrienne.

I missed her, all right. I missed the possibilities, and the knowledge that I just might lose control of myself in the stockroom and tear Adrienne's clothes off and fuck her wildly amid stacks of *Love and Rockets* and *Sandman* and *Hothead Paisan.* And she might do the same to me.

John missed her, too. He missed what Adrienne did to me, how she made me feel. That's why he did what he did, the fucker.

When I arrived at John's place, I smelled the tell-tale scent of sandalwood incense. I knew something was going on. John was well aware that the smell of sandalwood made me desperately aroused. But he was also aware that I associated sandalwood quite intimately with Adrienne, who used to wear sandalwood body oil. Perhaps that's why I wasn't surprised when I found her on the futon, sitting cross-legged and smoking a clove cigarette. John was across from her in the big easy chair, the one he'd found at the thrift store. His legs were crossed and he smiled at me devilishly.

"Paul...we were wondering where you got to. Adrienne came by. Well, actually, I invited her...."

Adrienne smiled at me sheepishly. "Hi, Paul," she said. She looked a little nervous. She was as cute as ever. She had on a pair of black jeans and a tight lace top, outlining her breasts and making the rings in her nipples oh-so-slightly visible. I sat down at the opposite end of the futon, and we hugged awkwardly. The scent of her body made me very nervous. Plus, I knew something was up. John hadn't just "invited" Adrienne.

There was awkward small talk, as I tried to figure out what was going on. Then John decided to dispense with the pleasantries.

He was behind her smoothly, quickly, without missing a beat. Adrienne seemed to melt into his arms as he coaxed her head back, and she presented her lips for him. He kissed her, deeply, parting her lips and teasing out her tongue. Adrienne let out a little moan of abandon as John's arms came around her and one hand rested absently on her belly just below her breast.

John glanced up at me, but only for a second. I noticed a smirk as he went back to kissing Adrienne.

John had never kissed a girl before in his life. But he seemed to be doing okay. I felt a momentary wave of anger as I realized that he was doing this for my benefit. Then, suddenly, there was nothing. I was freed from my responsibility to fight off my desire for Adrienne. John was giving her to me. She was the most succulent of gifts, the willing one.

I moved closer to her as she and John kissed. Tentatively, I leaned forward, feeling the pressure of her body against mine.

John released Adrienne, her lips slick with his spittle. She turned to me, her eyes sparkling and terrified, her face pale and ashen. Her lipstick was smeared. She took my hand in hers and begged me with her eyes to kiss her.

As I did, I tasted her lipstick and felt the stud in the center of her lower lip. The lipstick struck me as much stranger than the piercing. It was the first time I'd tasted lipstick in years. Adrienne's whimper was faint, distant, as I descended upon her. John's hand closed around her breast and his tongue explored her left ear while I kissed her. Her smell overwhelmed me: sandalwood and roses. Her hand trailed invitingly up my throat, then her fingertips cupped my face. John reached out and took my wrist, holding me insistently. He placed my hand underneath Adrienne's shirt, and her eyes opened to me as I felt her nipple harden. I slipped my other hand into her hair, stroking her cheek with my thumb. John leaned over Adrienne's shoulder and began to kiss me, his hot tongue sliding deep into my mouth. Adrienne seemed buried in ecstasy, snuggling deep between the two of us and arching her back to press her breasts more fully into my grasp. I stroked the slick metal rings, fascinated by the way they felt. I had a boyfriend once who had rings in his nipples, but they felt nothing like this. The implied sense of bondage or submission was overwhelming. Then again, maybe it was the way that Adrienne squirmed underneath us. John nipped at my lower lip, biting gently, his breath coming sweet and hot as he nuzzled closer and placed his lips against my ear. "She's yours," he whispered, telling me what I wanted to hear. John could enjoy our tryst, could be part of it. I would even make sure he came, and that, John must have known. But this fuck was for me, his gift to his lover. He had brought her to me for the pleasure of watching me have her.

The sandalwood incense had burned down; the three of us went into the bedroom.

John and I began by undressing Adrienne. First came her lace shirt, very goth, peeled away to reveal a matching bra. She had larger breasts than I had expected. The bra opened in front. The rings in her nipples were thick and stainless-steel. I bent forward and took one in my mouth as John removed Adrienne's shoes and socks. The two of us helped her struggle out of her black jeans. She didn't wear underpants, which I found somehow fascinating. She stretched nude amid the tangled sheets of the futon, her face buried in the sweat-scented fabric. John came up behind her, his shirt gone, his arms finding their way around Adrienne's waist as I played with her breasts. She breathed deep, as if the fragrance of two male lovers was better than anything.

Naked between us, Adrienne watched wide-eyed as John and I began to kiss again. As I ran my hand over John's bare chest, Adrienne's breathing shortened; her face grew bright red. She squirmed, unable to contain herself. But she wasn't asking for attention. She wanted to watch us.

That excited me more, and so I relinquished my hold on John's lips and slipped my tongue into Adrienne's mouth. She put her arms around me and sank into my grasp as I kissed her, deep, toying with her tongue. I was fascinated by the feeling of that piercing against my mouth. Fascinated, too, by the feel of Adrienne's naked body between John's and my clothed bodies, rubbing against us, her bare thigh curving over my waist and pulling me closer, harder against her, her breasts pressed tight to my chest. She slid her hands under my shirt and ran them up my back, one on each side of my spine. Adrienne whimpered and moaned slightly; John had slid his hand between her ass-cheeks and was touching her cunt. I guess she liked that. John looked down at her body, watching in amazement, exploring the ways his touch made her feel.

John looked up at me, then, his eyes sparkling. He could tell I was enjoying myself, and that was enough for him. He bent forward and offered me a tender kiss.

His tongue tasted of Adrienne's lipstick. My hand, resting gently against around Adrienne's hips, slid to meet his wrist. I felt the juices running along his fingers, and joined them. The two of us began to feel her up, toying with her lips, tormenting her clit. As we did, we continued kissing, and I felt Adrienne unfasten my belt.

Her hands circled my prick as John and I shared her sex. The curve of her thigh was so different from John's. Adrienne ran her black-nailed fingers up and down the length of my cock, rubbing her thumb on the underside of the head. John slipped his fingers out of Adrienne and lifted them to my face. He stared into my eyes as I licked his fingertips one by one, then slipped them into my mouth, tasting her sex. Adrienne leaned forward to touch my cock with her lips.

She licked up the shaft, and I moaned softly. John looked at me hungrily, and I knew what he wanted me to do. He wanted to see it, wanted to know the texture and the feel of having it done in his presence, but John wasn't going to do it. I began to struggle out of my pants, easing Adrienne back before she could take my cockhead in her mouth.

Adrienne slid further back onto the futon, relaxing into John's arms. He had quickly gotten his pants off, and now the two of them were naked against each other. His cock pressed up against her ass. Adrienne turned her head and the two of them began to kiss again, John's hand lazing gently over her breasts, playing with her nipple-rings. Now the three of us were naked. I lowered myself to Adrienne's belly, kissing her soft flesh and toying with her navel-ring. Adrienne's body went taut against John's, her ass snuggling against him as I parted her thighs. Memories flooded back to me as I tasted her cunt. I licked slowly into the silky wetness, breathing her fragrance. I flickered my tongue across her lips and made my way to her clit. I closed my lips very gently around it and began to suckle. Adrienne choked, her mouth filled with John's tongue. I began to feed on her cunt, drinking the taste and smell of it, swallowing hungrily. I curved my hand under her ass and began playing with her asshole, almost before I realized what I was doing. Adrienne's body stiffened again, but then she relaxed as she gave herself over to the sensations. So I didn't stop. I wanted to explore the feel of a woman's asshole as opposed to a man's. John must have liked that; he could feel my hand at work, and between deep kisses with Adrienne, he looked down at me and smiled approvingly.

John reached out to the nightstand and handed me a rubber glove. Obediently, I put it on.

John next held out the bottle of lubricant, which he poured into my palm. I worked it over, getting my gloved hand slick with it. Then I slid one finger into Adrienne's cunt.

She whimpered approvingly, reaching behind herself to take John's cock in her hand. John slid out from beneath her, rolled an unlubricated condom over his prick and turned on his side so that Adrienne could take him into her mouth. She lay on her back, head turned to the side and propped up on a pillow, as John eased his hips back and forth, sliding his cock between her parted lips. Her hands tangled in the rumpled sheets. Adrienne's ass lifted off of the futon, pressing her cunt hard against my hand. I gave her two fingers, moving them in and out slowly, and from the rhythmic fucking motions she made with her hips, she wanted more. I got three in, which was the most I'd ever shoved up John's ass. Her cunt felt tight, but somehow secure, inviting, hungry.

Guided by my memories of *The Joy of (Hetero) Sex,* I started pressing against Adrienne's clit with my thumb. Her hips began to rock faster. She was jerking John off while she sucked him, her lips closed tightly around the head of his cock. John was watching me as Adrienne went down on him. He looked like he was about ready to do it in her mouth. I had no idea the sight of me fingerfucking a woman would get him so hot. Adrienne was really into it, her whole body moving with the two of us. I had no way of knowing what I was really doing to her, but I could tell from the spasms and contractions of her cunt that she was coming. But she didn't lose her grip on John's cock for a moment.

When her hips slowed down, I was struck by a sensuous and perverse urge. I eased my hands out of her cunt, reaching awkwardly to get more lube from the nightstand. John knew what I was doing. He grabbed the lube and poured it for me as I held out my rubber-gloved hand.

Adrienne stiffened again as I parted her ass-cheeks and touched her tight hole. I could sort of guess from the way she moved that she'd never really been touched much back there. That was what turned me on. I'd spent so much of my adult life getting fucked in the ass that I couldn't let her go without, though I guessed it wouldn't feel the same for a woman as it did for a man. She continued sucking John's cock, making him sway and moan as he crouched over her. Adrienne once again relaxed into the sensations as I worked the lube into her crack and felt the gentle "give" of her asshole. I slowly pressed one finger in, being as tender as possible, imagining that I was with a virgin guy. Adrienne sucked her breath in sharply as the finger slipped into her. She seemed uncomfortable for a second, and then it was all right.

"Oh, fuck yeah," breathed John, watching me intently.

I went very slowly. By the time I had two fingers inside her ass, Adrienne was moaning and John was ready to come. He did so with a groan and a forward slump against Adrienne's body as I managed to squeeze a third finger into her ass. Adrienne writhed underneath him, her hand thrust up between his legs and playing with his ass, middle finger stroking the outside of his asshole, up and down in quick strokes. I knew from experience what she was feeling. The pulse of John's cock as it spurted his cum into the condom. The warm feeling as the tip of the condom filled. The squeeze of his buns as the spasms went through him. The rush of terror at the warmth in her mouth and the feeling: what if the condom breaks. Then the wave of momentary regret, usually just for a half-second, and then, the delicious sensation as the thought flows through you, "so the fuck what...."

I eased my fingers out of Adrienne's ass, knowing she was ready for something else. I managed to get the glove off and toss it into the garbage without splattering anyone. Adrienne looked spent, but I knew there was at least one indulgence she hadn't yet been granted.

She bent forward as John, panting and flushed, handed her a Trojan red unlubed. John reached out and took my shoulders, guiding me back onto the bed. I stretched out as Adrienne got the condom over the head of my prick and started licking down the shaft. She paused over my balls, licking them hungrily, taking each one into her mouth. John joined her, putting his mouth over the head of my cock and pushing the condom down. Then she and John began to kiss, sharing my prick. For a while they worked bottom to top, John at the balls while Adrienne swallowed me, then vice versa, then back again. Finally, John eased his body up against mine and started kissing me while I moaned and writhed. He stroked my chest and face, nibbling on my lips and sucking at my tongue as he squeezed and kneaded my nipples. All the while, Adrienne had her way with my cock.

She had swallowed me again, her fingers curved around the base of my cock. She then rubbed the latex over her face, smearing her cheeks with her saliva while she looked up at me. She stroked the cock between her tits, something I really didn't expect a chick to do anywhere outside a porn movie. But I had to admit it was pretty hot. Then she went back to sucking my cock. I could feel the ridge of the stud in her lower lip, pressing against the condom, smooth but somehow threatening, exciting.

She slipped her hand between my legs, sliding the fingers under my ass-cheeks. I felt her finger going home, stroking my asshole, bringing on my climax. Adrienne knew how to make me come. I wondered if John had had a talk with her.

When I did come, it was like a lifelong need suddenly overwhelmed in an explosion of brilliance. Adrienne's mouth was hot around my cock as she worked my asshole and milked my prick.

Adrienne kept her lips closed on the softening knob of my cockhead for a long time. Tiny spasms went through me as she suckled on my soft cock. Every movement of her lips and tongue made my body twitch in agony/ecstasy. It was too much stimulation, but somehow I liked it. And Adrienne was enjoying herself pushing my limits.

After a while, she stopped sucking me, slipped the condom off and tossed it into the trash.

John slipped away from me, running his hands through Adrienne's hair as the three of us curled up into a complicated ball. I faded in and out of consciousness, losing myself in the warmth of the two bodies surrounding me.

I slept deep and hard, exhausted. I dreamed hard, too, hot and deep like it was reality, the way you dream when you're horny as fuck. But I found myself awake, in the middle of the night, not sure at what point I'd dreamed of myself fucking Adrienne and at what point I'd actually done it. Not sure if the taste of her cunt and her asshole, the smell of my cum as I smeared it over her body, was real or imagined. Adrienne's body was pressed against mine; every inch of our naked flesh seemed to touch. I was in a dazed stupor, hardly aware of what I was doing. Adrienne's legs were spread around my belly and she was rubbing herself hard against me while she kissed me violently.

I could hardly breathe, the excitement was so overwhelming. I had completely forgotten, for a moment, that Paul existed. I felt no guilt, no danger. Adrienne's body felt so good against mine, it never occurred to me to stop for a moment. Suddenly Adrienne, who must have been more awake than I was, got a condom open and over my cock. Then her thighs were spread around me, and she was sitting up over my body as she rubbed the head of my prick between her cunt-lips. She worked the head into the notch of her cunt and sank down on me, her breath coming short. Her cunt felt tight, as if she hadn't been fucked for a while. Adrienne pressed her hips down, pushing my cock into her as deep as it would go so the head ground against her cervix. She bent down and began to kiss me, moaning softly. She started fucking her hips back and forth. I choked on her tongue and on the smell of her hair and body. My cock seemed alive inside her. She pulled on me hard, rolling me over on top of her—over the edge of the futon. The two of us fell the six inches from the futon to the floor and I came down hard on top of her, pushing my cock inside her, fucking her slow and deep. She dug her teeth into my throat, holding on to my ass. She started playing with my asshole as I fucked her. The sensations joined somewhere deep in my body, and it was almost like being fucked by her. I kept fucking her, holding back my orgasm, feeling Adrienne keep the muscles of her cunt tight around my shaft, milking my prick. I rested one hand on her breast, squeezing gently, teasing her nipple with my thumb.

"I'm going to come," she whispered, nuzzling my ear. "Don't come yet. Please don't come yet. Keep fucking me."

I held back, feeding her long, slow, hard strokes into her cunt, keeping the rhythm. Adrienne's thighs closed tighter around me with each thrust, as she got closer and closer. She whispered again and again, "Please keep fucking me...keep fucking me..." and so on, letting me know that she was getting there slowly. Just knowing that she was about to come while I fucked her was enough to keep me working, pumping my hips up and down on Adrienne's supple, spread body, begging her with my cock to cream all over me.

Then she came, a silent exhalation—no moan, no scream, just a long, low breath and a spasm of her cunt on my prick. I started fucking her faster, trying to bring on my own orgasm. Adrienne, satisfied with her climax but wanting mine, started stroking my crack, feeling for my asshole, working me into a frenzy. I finally was able to let myself go, and I came inside her, kissing her hard.

I reached down, holding the filled condom as I pulled out of her cunt. It had been so different than fucking a guy's ass.

Adrienne and I squirmed back onto the futon. I was still half-asleep. I realized in my stupor that John was lying there, awake, eyes wide. He had been watching us the whole time.

Adrienne got out of bed to go to the bathroom. John leaned over and started kissing me—deep, hard, possessive thrusts of his tongue as his hand drifted over my soft cock. He rubbed me down around the base, where my pubic hair was damp and matted with the juices of Adrienne's cunt. Then John rolled over. With his back to us, Adrienne and I slept entwined like straight people. But as he had turned, I had seen that there was a smirk on his face.

The three of us curled up and slept the rest of the night. I felt totally happy. When the sun broke through the sky, Adrienne was gone. She'd let herself out.

John and I fucked long and hard that Saturday morning, him sucking my cock while he played with my ass. As he did me, I smelled her on the sheets, a feminine scent mixed with ours, but strangely, her memory didn't overwhelm me the way it had. I was content to be with just John.

John spread my ass-cheeks, entering me from behind and fucking me for as long as either of us could stand it before tossing the condom and letting himself go all over my back. He licked his own cum up, smearing it into my smooth skin and whispering to me that he loved it when I played submissive. Which was par for the course.

Adrienne and I talked a few times on the phone over the next week. We were going to have lunch together, and soon. Eventually I asked her if she'd had fun that night.

"Of course," she told me, her voice dropping to a whisper. "Having sex with two guys—two queer guys. It was everything I'd ever wanted in the whole world."

I froze, unable to ask her the question that begged to be asked—whether she'd like to come back.

We sort of lost touch, calling each other every few weeks but never managing to get together. I figured she was afraid. I was, too.

John didn't mention her much, but one night he whispered to me, jokingly, that I didn't give head as well as Adrienne. I didn't pursue it, and I wasn't really hurt. Just a little lost.

That was the way it went for a while. For many weeks.

The other day, Adrienne and I ran into each other on the street. We went and had coffee. She was as gorgeous as ever. She kept leaning toward me, her delicious smell drifting into my mind as I watched her, and a couple of times I really thought she was going to kiss me. But she didn't. We promised each other we would get together sometime soon, and as we parted, we hugged longer than we were supposed to. I had a hard-on on the bus later, thinking about Adrienne. It was good to see her. It was really fucking good to see her.

I felt a strange melancholy later, as I thought about what John and Adrienne and I had done that night. John and I had never really talked about it that much. I knew that John had enjoyed it as much as I had, maybe more. I was sure that blowjob he got from Adrienne wasn't exactly just a fringe benefit. It's taken me months after the actual event to understand it, but I knew that in bringing her home, he'd acknowledged an intense attraction for her as well as an intense attraction for me. But even if what got him hot about Adrienne was what she, and her female body, did to me, by the very nature of the situation, it did something to him. That was why he did what he did, the fucker. And now every once in a while, I catch him slipping. He's not the faggot he's always pretended to be, though he still fucks me better than anyone. His brain and his balls are more complicated than anyone might have suspected. I'm only now starting to figure the fucker out, and he keeps throwing me curve balls. I even walked in on him reading my copy of *The Sensuous Woman* once, when he thought I was asleep in the other room. He had a hard-on.

GOOD IN TENSION

SCOTT O'HARA

I was told, many long years ago, in a manner that may have been intended as a tongue-in-cheek effort to see how gullible I really was, that those chains you see hanging off the bottoms of semi trailer trucks are intended to hit the road constantly, to serve as a conductor between the truck and the ground, to prevent a static electricity build-up in the truck and its contents. Not only does this seem absurd to me (have you ever noticed a static electric charge on your car? I haven't), but the solution seems counter-intuitive: Surely a chain striking the roadway would raise sparks? Which doesn't seem like the best thing to have happening underneath, say, a gasoline tanker. But while I have never been very comfortable with the idea of this explanation, I have also never heard a better one (the idea that those chains are just hanging there kind of accidentally, with no purpose at all, is a little bit creepy too), and I've kept it in my mind without comment for many years.

Recent events have caused me to realize that, at least from a metaphorical standpoint, this explanation makes perfect sense.

Sleeping cars have always intimidated me. When I was a child, I associated train travel with the rich and famous, since, despite my parents having taken me on planes many times, I'd never ridden a train. And the sleepers were obviously where all the truly important people rode. Some of them undoubtedly had their own private cars. Well, maybe all this was true in the pre-Amtrak days. To my surprise, sleepers are surprisingly affordable nowadays, and the people who take them are pretty much ordinary folk. I discovered this on a recent trip, after the latest bolt of static electricity from home had sent me flying eastwards with a mission.

You don't need to worry about maintaining contact with the road when you're on a train. The wheels are steel instead of rubber; they don't insulate you from the earth. You're in constant contact with reality, and you can feel every joint in the track, every spike, every penny placed on the track by some curious boy. You have an intimate connection with life, on a train, that I felt I had lost in real life; and I found my train ride relaxing, strangely comforting.

Like most new experiences, the response was immediate: I want to share this with somebody. But who? Yes, there was the man across the hallway from me. He had changed into shorts and a T-shirt the moment the train set off; obviously he knew what he was doing. He had very attractive, hairy legs, too. I wouldn't have minded sharing my space with him, and though it was late at night, my excitement level was too high to allow immediate sleep. But it wasn't clear to me how one cruised between compartments; after an initial exchange of pleasantries, conversation dried up and the contact blew away with the imaginary smoke from the diesel engine. His door eventually closed, and I presumed he went to sleep. I began roaming the halls of the train, instead, going first forward into the coach cars, where I'd always traveled before, where I still felt a closer connection to the other passengers.

In coach, there is often quite a lot of conversation. You're not as crowded as on an airplane, for instance, but you're stuck there, usually, for even longer, so people break down and talk. Connections are made. It's especially fun to walk the aisles after midnight, when everyone (or nearly everyone) is asleep. They're lying every which way, some of them huddled together, some stretched out on two seats, some curled up. A few insomniacs will open their eyes as you pass by.

I've always had a fondness for watching people sleep. I am a voyeur. And it didn't take long at all for me to find my favorite voyees of the trip. In the first car in front of me, right at the rear—barely twenty yards away from my own compartment—were two darkly beautiful men, asleep, leaning casually against each other. Both of them had gold chains around their necks with crucifixes; both were dressed in sweatsuits, appropriate nightwear for a train. I passed by quickly, without too much looking, figuring I'd have a better look on my way back. But I thought I caught a glimpse of one of them opening his eyes as I passed.

When people use the word *magnetic,* they are usually talking about attraction. That is not, of course, the strict meaning of the word. Magnetic forces include repulsion, too. That's the principle behind the new, high-tech trains that various companies have been pushing for the past couple of decades: High-powered magnets that keep the train from ever touching the steel tracks. Imagine, though, the powerful charge of static electricity that must build up in a rapidly moving object that travels so close to the ground, without ever touching it! Gravity forces it down; magnetic energy forces it up. But what, pray tell, forces it forward? Jet propulsion? It's a mystery to me. I only know that the most intense attractions of my life have been to men with whom I never had actual physical contact, with whom I maintained that distance, that tension, for days, weeks, months, years—forever, in fact, in certain cases. There are few enough men in this category: A high school pal or two, a few intense crushes from my later years. When I'm deep in the throes of an infatuation, the last thing I want is to suggest consummation to the object of my affection. That would indicate an End, a finality that does not lend itself to romanticization, and I am nothing if not romantic. As Oscar Wilde said, "There is nothing romantic about an actual proposal. One might be accepted!" Too right, Oscar. No, it's so much easier on the nerves to keep one's self in a state of steady tension, to keep the current flowing, to keep the magnetic field in flux between "repulse" and "attract."

On my return trip down the train, having not found anyone awake who seemed worth the game, I reached the last coach car—and discovered that one of the beautiful Latin boys was gone. The other, in the window seat, had fallen over (the armrest was raised) so that he was partially stretched out in both seats. Quite soundly asleep, mouth open, snoring gently. (To sleep in the coach compartment of a train, it's necessary to be able to ignore lots of things. The noise of the wheels, the swaying of the car—romantic in a sleeping compartment, it nevertheless keeps jostling you out of position if you're trying to sleep sitting upright—and most notably, the snores of a hundred people around you.) I, of course, kept going—directly to the men's lounge which was at the rear of the car, halfway between their seats and my own compartment.

He was in the lounge, of course (there wasn't anyplace else he could've been), standing at one of the two sinks, drinking a glass of water. The doorway to the men's lounge, unlike the ladies', is only covered by a curtain, which sways wide open as the train lurches. I could see him there, leaning over the sink, his ass thrusting out against his sweatpants. He was looking in the mirror, and his eyes immediately met mine. He finished his water—I was standing there, frozen—and opened the door next to him, into the toilet. He went into the toilet. I came into the lounge and took his former place at the sink. As he stood in front of the toilet, taking his dick out of his pants, he propped the door open with his body, so I could watch his every move. I did. Nervous beyond belief, my entire body humming with tension, I reached in through the door and grabbed his dick. He motioned me inside and closed the door behind me.

"Perfection" is a strange concept. It's tossed around loosely in stories like this: His face was perfect, his dick was perfect, his ass was perfect. And you accept the use of the word, because you know it indicates that you, as the reader, are free to picture whatever it is that is perfect to you, without concern for reality or the writer's preferences. When a fiction writer states that something is "perfect," he is calling upon the readers' imaginations for help.

I will not resort to such trickery. His dick was smooth-skinned, with that particular velvety-softness that is rarely felt except on the dicks of men from Central America. It was not hard yet, but it had considerable substance and heft to it, indicating that it was beginning to get that way. There was a snug-fitting foreskin completely covering the head, which he had retracted just a little bit in preparation to piss (or to pretend to piss, I wasn't sure which). The color was darker than the rest of his skin, a smooth dark amber color that made me think of honey. In size, it wasn't spectacular. As it hardened, it didn't grow a great deal, either, merely stiffened and began to bend slightly downwards.

My knees began trembling, and it didn't take more than a slight lurch from the train to send me crashing to the floor, left knee in a puddle of piss, mouth just inches from that intoxicating, pheromone-wafting crotch. I began stroking it gently, while fumbling my own dick out of my pants. His was almost bone-hard by now, but still retained that amazing smoothness and softness on the outside. My own dick, and those of most white boys I know, get all knobby and veiny when they're really hard. Ridged with cartilage or sinew or blood vessels, they look like those "realistic" dildoes that cost so much money. And when a dick is plunging in and out of an asshole, I'm quite sure that the striations and lumps give an extra fillip of pleasure to the bottom. But when stroked in the hand, or stimulating the uvula, the silky smoothness of Latin-American dick is a true marvel, giving pleasure that I will never know from my WASP peers.

I explored the foreskin first, with tongue: Not much taste there, despite my sense that he'd been on the train for a day or two (their seats looked lived-in). I guess he was careful about such things. Pity. I still attacked with all my fervor and gave his still-hidden cockhead a thorough tongue-washing. He liked that; his dick started jumping around, straining towards my mouth with that urgency that practically pleads aloud, "Suck me!" How could I refuse? Not that I wanted to. I took it all (oh yes, size: It was of a size, thankgod, that taking it all was not an undue strain, and there was little danger of marring its perfection with toothmarks; and yet my uvula was sufficiently stimulated to induce an oral orgasm after the first few thrusts), and he gasped and grasped my head to his crotch.

There's nothing like that feeling of first being down on a dick, that moment when you know he's in absolute ecstasy, nervous system shocked into an overstimulated state that approximates nirvana. The rest of the process, teasing him to orgasm, is merely procedural, bureaucratic, with a delightful payoff at the end, true—but it's that initial moment of golden glow that makes a blowjob all that it is. I would be happy to meet a man who did not require the prolonged tease, a man who came automatically the moment his cockhead hit the back of my throat. To flood my throat with praise for my cocksucking abilities, and that without requiring me even to demonstrate them—yes, that is what a truly "perfect" man would do. This man was not perfect. He thrust a few times, and I went through my repertoire of tricks—tongue-swirling and sword-swallowing, then restraining him while I teased his dickhead for awhile. But after the initial shock of contact, it seemed that being sucked off didn't do a lot for him. I backed off, gave his still-shrouded dickhead another exploratory sweep with my tongue (which did make him shiver, again) and stood up.

He immediately zeroed in on my own dick with an immediacy which told me, *Aha, now I know what he likes.* He liked, I gather, big dicks. He was down on mine in a flash, and while he didn't have a big enough mouth to do justice to my dick, he made a valiant effort. I even managed to stay pretty hard—unusual for me, while being sucked, since most suckers tend to scrape it up pretty badly. (Hey, the human body has certain limitations. Mouths can only open so wide.) After awhile, though, I guess he either caught on to the fact that I wasn't really into it, or he just wanted to get off. He stood up, and we stood face to face, each beating our own meat.

I kissed him, tentatively, since that's one of those uncertain things. Some Latin men love to kiss, some refuse to. He seemed a little ambivalent. He obviously loved it, but wasn't sure he wanted to do it with me. I guess that constituted actual infidelity to his lover, or something. His perfect lips (and I beg your forgiveness, here, for using this word, because it was not the physical aspect of his lips that was perfect, but the vulnerability that escaped from them when they were glossed with spit and precum, the tension that I felt in them when I pressed my own against them, the need I felt coming from them, and nothing in life can be more perfect than these sensations) would open against mine, and then he would turn his head and kiss my cheek instead. And I would feel his body shiver, pressed against my own, as if that kiss were almost enough to force him into an unwillingly intense orgasm.

My left hand traveled down his back, to his ass, previously untouched. Slipping inside his briefs (his sweatpants down around his ankles, getting wet on the floor), my hand caressed his butt-cheeks—slender, hairless, smooth—and felt them pressing out against my hand, felt his body begin to vibrate. Gently, I turned him around so that he was facing into the corner, his ass pressed against me, and I began stroking it with my left hand, while rubbing my cock against his right cheek. When my finger strayed near his asshole, his whole body shuddered. Pulling him against me, I laid my dick into his asscrack and began sawing back and forth, running my hands up and down his stomach and chest, inside his loose sweatshirt—and suddenly there were a series of low grunts, his body shook violently, and I knew it was over. I hugged him to me, closely, waiting until the aftershocks died; then I slid down to my knees and lovingly licked the remnants of stickiness from his fingers and under his foreskin until he pushed me away.

How long had it taken? Less time, I suspect, than it's taken to write. One can't linger forever in a train toilet, even at one A.M. Frankly, I think he was more nervous about his lover becoming suspicious than about the train attendant or another passenger finding us. We peeked out through the keyhole (you gotta love those old-fashioned doors), and there was no one there. After pulling ourselves together, we opened the door and stepped out. He stood at the sink awhile, preening, using paper towels to dry the wet spots on his sweat pants (not really very serious), and I stood next to him, asking questions. Yes, he was from Baja California. Yes, that man next to him was his lover; they'd been together for two years, and somehow I didn't have to ask if it was supposed to be a monogamous relationship. Ah, good old Catholic culture! He asked where I was sitting. I told him I was in the sleeper, behind us—where it says *Sleeping Car Passengers Only*—and he said, "Oh, that's why I didn't see you up front." So he'd been looking too, I guess. Then we parted, reluctantly, after exchanging names. He was Isaiah, he said. Charming name; I'll never think of old-testament prophets the same again.

It's amazing, the amount of intimacy that can develop in a five-minute encounter. There was no expectation of permanence, from either of us. I recognized that he was involved in a relationship that did not allow for external attractions or, especially, affections (and, regardless of my feelings about such exclusive relationships, I'm not a home-wrecker by preference). We both knew that this was a one-off. (Though I did take a look into the sleeper, to see if our Guardian Angel was awake. She was, sitting right by the doorway, to make sure no intruders would interrupt our sleep. Drat. I was going to invite Isaiah back to my compartment for a more leisurely repeat, if he was up for it.) But I think he felt as close to me as I felt to him. Being in a sleeper—like being in a relationship—insulates a person from reality. I think both of us felt that we'd just grounded ourselves, and the shock was truly worthwhile.

After breakfast the next morning (I dined early, and when I came back from the dining car, both Isaiah and his lover were still sound asleep), I checked the schedule: Two more hours before we hit my destination. I read awhile, brushed my teeth a couple of times, then decided to take another walk through the train. As I opened the door of my compartment, the door opposite me opened too, and the hairy-legged man hopped out with his shaving kit. Seemed that he preferred using the men's lounge, too, rather than the sink & mirror in his compartment. I could understand that. I followed him north, and as he ducked into the lounge, I noticed another person standing at one of the sinks. I continued, and as I passed Isaiah, now awake, I saw that his lover was missing. I exchanged nervous smiles with Isaiah, but continued forward.

Nothing exciting; two minutes later, I was back. Window seat next to Isaiah still empty. As I passed the lounge, I looked in. There were two shaving kits sitting next to one of the sinks, a towel hanging on a hook by the mirror...but no one visible. I stuck my head in: Empty. But the door to the toilet was closed and locked.

PLAYING SOLITAIRE

MITCH CULLIN

1

I was almost ten when I began experiencing the occasional hard-on. It popped up during soccer practice, when a teammate might bump against me, or when the coach rested his large hands on my slight shoulders, gripping at the joints as he gave instructions. Most often the stiffening occurred on summer afternoons, when swimming at the municipal pool, as my older brother Rick and I dried off in the changing room—our small bodies slender and hairless, with rolls of baby fat here and there. Shrouded in humidity and steam, my eyes wandered to the young men who moved about naked, slipping in and out of trunks, the patches of dark hair above their penises, a revelation. Those amazing bodies were as mysterious to me as the painful arching I attempted to conceal behind my beach towel.

Until then, I had regarded my body as a nuisance. It served no purpose whatsoever, other than to point out my shortcomings. Stuck in that tiny frame was a boy who never ran as fast as his peers, who was unable to coordinate even the feeblest basketball lay-up. I was a sidelined player, envious of my brother and his agile friends; they always stood taller, casting longer shadows, and carried themselves in a manner that seemed more wholesome than I ever hoped was possible for myself.

The night I became aware of what my body offered, of its hidden workings and darker implications, I'd just finished homework for an art class—a watercolor of sunflowers with a fierce bear looming among the spray. The assignment had asked for each student to create a work based on a famous style of painting. My hand pulled "impressionism" from a paper bag.

As I sat in the school library thumbing through various art books in search of my subject, I came across a black and white picture of Donatello's sculpture of David. I glanced around to make sure no one was nearby, then I immersed myself in the image of the nude boy, with his long hair falling over narrow collarbones, thin arms bending, the delicate fingers of one hand wrapped on the handle of a sword, the fingers on the other grasping a stone. I studied his lean and smooth torso, the sinew of muscles, minuscule penis and testicles. There was something of myself in that strange, effeminate creature. The otherworldliness of the boy, the soft smirk, let me know he understood what I felt. And I was aroused to no end, spending the rest of the day dreaming of my new friend.

In my bedroom, I worked past dinner on the painting, basing it on a work by Monet. The bear came as an afterthought, a personal flourish inspired by a poster of Smokey which hung beside my desk. When the assignment was finished, I got ready for bed. I stood naked before the full-length mirror in the bathroom, a smudge of toothpaste on my upper lip, using a baseball bat as the sword, the baseball for a stone. I found myself aching for David in a way that seemed frightening. My brother banged on the door asking me to hurry it up.

I tossed in bed for at least an hour. I squeezed a pillow between my legs, unsure of what needed to be done. I pretended David sat on the edge of my bed, talking to me about the painting, how much he liked it, then I had him finding me unconscious on the bank of some ancient roadway. I rested in his bed and he tended to me, a boy with an indistinct illness and an erection. I rolled to one side, pulling my pajama bottoms and underwear off, then I flipped over, returning to David. That's when I started rubbing my body on the bedding, thrusting a little faster or slower depending on the intensity. There was no ejaculation, but it was still the real thing, unexpected, coursing through me like an electrical charge. What rocketed from within me was beyond anything I'd ever been taught or told. In my bed, face down, out of breath, I felt separate and unique, and, in the moments before sleep, alone.

I wanted to tell someone about my discovery, but I wasn't certain if anyone would understand, least of all my parents. I worried that I was the only boy on the planet who had done this incredible thing with himself. This concern dissolved during my twelfth year when, with great relief, a couple of stunning facts were revealed: one, I was not alone in my nocturnal fumblings; two, my brother was doing it with the aid of his right hand, which was an amazing alternative to dry humping a mattress.

When I walked in on my brother, he was on the toilet in our adjoining bathroom, legs spread eagle, his underwear cast aside on the tile floor next to an open bottle of baby oil. He jerked himself under a heavy glaze of oil. I was struck, frozen at the sight of him, his feet twisting, his knees bouncing. He was biting his bottom lip with his eyes clinched. I don't know how long I'd been standing there before one of his eyes shot open, but I do remember that he continued to masturbate for a few seconds, uncomprehending, as I uttered, "Sorry, I mean, I—" Then he jumped up and struggled to cover his crotch. "Get the fuck out of here, Ben!" he screamed, and I did.

Minutes later, as I perched on the edge of my bed considering the hand action and lube option, my brother burst into the room wearing a T-shirt and sweats. He pounced on me, pinning my wrists with his hands. "What'd you see?" he demanded.

"Nothing," I insisted. "Really. Just nothing."

His face was stern. "That's right," he said, nodding. He climbed off my chest, thumping my forehead with a finger. "Asshole, knock next time." The baby oil fragrance lingered long after he stormed out.

When I knew my parents had gone to bed, and that my brother was in the middle of his late night routine of Atari combat with space invaders in the living room, I stretched naked on my sheets—one hand below my waist, the other holding a well-worn copy of *Boy's Life*. I climaxed soon enough, thrilled by this new form of stimulation, which was more on the moment and acute than my previous experiences banging the mattress. I went into the bathroom, found the greasy bottle of baby oil in a drawer, then returned to my bed and began again.

Soon I spent my afternoons and late evenings searching for the perfect masturbatory lubricant. There was nothing really wrong with the baby oil, aside from the smell of the stuff which my mother had started noticing in my room; however, my brother and I emptied the bottle in less than a week, and neither of us dared ask for another. What he used on himself from then on is still a mystery to me, though I suspect a disappearing container of Texas Bluebonnet Body Lotion to be the answer. As for me, I was inclined toward extreme experimentation.

For a while, I relied on saliva, which was a real hassle. I'd stop jerking off every minute or so to spit on my hand until my mouth went dry. Soap or shampoo worked great in the shower, but once, in pure desperation, I used Crest mint gel—a major mistake, my penis froze and cauterized at the same time. Lotions and various kinds of mineral oils were nice, so was whipped cream, though it needed to be reapplied often. Shaving cream, depending on the brand, produced an effect much like that of toothpaste. I raided the cupboards and refrigerator. Maple syrup and honey were interesting and treacherously sticky. Crisco was wonderful. As far as dairy products go, butter functioned best. Given the chance, I would have messed with peanut butter, but my mother had a preference for chunky style. In the end, Vaseline, with its warming of the skin, became my lube of choice, a favorite to this day.

2

For a brief period in early adolescence, my best friend was Will Dunn. Will and his parents had come from Boston to my hometown, where they moved into the house next door—a whitewashed, weathered two-story dwelling that had been on the market for months. He was a quiet kid, a year younger than I, who always wore a Red Sox baseball cap crooked over a shock of white-blond hair. His father was an outspoken, gregarious evangelical minister, someone my father despised, and his mother was a remote woman who never ventured from their home, except on Wednesdays and Sundays when his family attended church services. Their house, the few times I was invited inside, sagged under the weight of some unspecific pallor. I didn't like being in there, and neither did Will. He appeared on our doorstep the morning after his family took residence in the neighborhood, asking me if I was interested in tossing his baseball around. Of course, I was happy to have a friend for the summer, and my mother made a great effort to make him feel welcome in our home.

It wasn't long before Will was spending several nights a week with me. After hot days of swimming with my brother and his friends, of evenings playing catch with my father in the backyard, we'd stay up late watching TV or entertaining ourselves with video games, something his parents wouldn't allow. We shared my bed, sleeping side by side, and I got great comfort from his body. Some mornings, I'd wake early, excited to find him snuggled against me, an arm across my chest.

In Will, I found someone in which I could share a kind of intimacy; he was the first person I spoke to about those things I always considered to be shameful. Often we lay awake for hours confessing secrets. He told me that his father had left Boston because of an indiscretion with a choir member, that his mother had twice attempted suicide—once using drain cleaner, another time by swallowing sleeping pills, which she vomited on the way to the hospital. He had stolen baseball cards from Kmart, thrown a rock at a Siamese cat with one eye, sipped beer from his uncle's mug. In turn, I mentioned my infatuation with Donatello's David, and how I longed to see the bodies of those fluoridated Cub Scouts in *Boy's Life*. I told him about the treasured glimpses in the changing room, revealing, yes, I'd even glanced at his body. He thought that was hysterical. I explained to him about masturbation, though I was unaware of the exact word or slang for it. I showed him the motions of my hand, telling him about when I caught my brother in the act.

"Like this." I wrapped a fist around one of his middle fingers, started going back and forth. "You see? Up and down." I tightened the grip, smiling.

He shook his head. "Doesn't it hurt?"

"Not at all." I withdrew my hand.

"I don't know." He shook his head again, a perplexed look on his face.

A thoughtful silence fell over us. Will shifted to an elbow. I noticed that he'd misbuttoned his blue pajama shirt, making one side longer than the other, with an unfastened pearl-colored button remaining without a corresponding hole near the neckline. He was smirking in a way I'd never seen before—half of his mouth curved upward in a grin, the other half stayed as a straight line. "I could show you," I offered.

His lips curled into a full grin. He shrugged. "Sure."

I watched him roll onto his back. He slipped his pajama bottoms and underwear past brown knees. The fading tan line above his thighs gave way to blanched and hairless skin.

"It's got to be hard first," I said, reaching to touch him.

"How come?" He put his arms behind the nape of his neck, propping his head so he could follow what I was doing.

"That's when it's ready," I said, toying with him now, and was struck by the amount of warmth coming off his body. I began giving him full strokes.

"It tickles," he complained.

"It does at first," I replied, reducing the caresses across the tip of his penis. "How's that?"

"Feel like I'm going to pee."

I screwed down tighter, adding pressure. His breathing grew fast and shallow. "Does it feel good?"

"Sorta," he said.

"You try," I said, taking my hand away.

He started masturbating himself, and I observed him while jacking off under my pajamas. "No use," he sighed. "You do it."

By then, I was close to coming, but I didn't want to disappoint him. I took over again, and he felt larger in my hand than before. I resumed jerking him off with quick strokes. "How's that?"

"Great," he said. Soon he was hitting his feet against the sheets. I didn't know if he was doing this from pleasure or some new discomfort.

"Want me to stop?" I said, half hoping he'd say "yes" because my wrist was going numb.

"No," he answered.

I was stunned when his arms dropped to the bedding, grabbing fistfuls of the sheet. Then his back arched and his breathing increased. It got me hot seeing him do those sort of things with his body; his head sank deep into the pillow, his knees twisted outward. "Please, don't stop, please," he begged, as if sensing my wrist's fatigue. When he climaxed, a weird groan, like the sound someone makes when taking a punch in the stomach, rose from his throat. "That's enough," he said. "It tickles bad now. I need to pee."

As he pulled his pajama bottoms on, I yanked mine down. He climbed from the bed, dazed, and ambled toward the bathroom door.

After that night, we masturbated each other from time to time. It was always the same; I'd do him, then he'd do me. We never talked about it afterwards. Once, as we rested on the bed with nothing on but our pajama tops, Will leaned over and kissed me on a cheek. I wanted to cry. I wanted to hold him, to tell him that I loved him, but all I said was, "You're my best friend."

Unfortunately, my relationship with Will was short-lived, lasting a little more than two months, from late May to early August. One evening Will's father, Patrick, walked into an empty house, where a Crockpot of beans simmered on the stove. He found a note, written in his wife's hand, placed at the center of the dining room table. She had left, taking their son, while he attended a church meeting that Tuesday afternoon. Though it has been many years since, I still recall Patrick's rapid-fire knocks on the front door as we were about to sit down for dinner. The sight of my father and Patrick standing on the lawn. The way my father reached out, bringing a hand to Patrick's shoulder. And then afterwards, when Patrick returned to his dark house, Mrs. Estes, a neighbor, came over and told my mother what she had seen: Shortly after Patrick left for his meeting, a well-dressed young man in a Buick Riviera arrived at the Dunn house. Mrs. Estes watched as the man helped Will's mother with two suitcases and a steamer trunk, noting that the stoic woman had stepped into the man's car with a smile.

I can't say I was devastated or inconsolable, my best friend's sudden departure was fathomless, but I was shaken. One day I'm climbing the big oak tree in the backyard, Will already dangling his legs from a branch above, the next day I'm told he's gone and might not return; my father's low voice spinning the words, his thick arms cradling my head. It just didn't make any sense, so I withdrew a little, detaching myself from whatever feelings or emotions I'd acquired for the pensive boy with the Red Sox cap. A week before school started, the Dunn house was deserted. A *For Sale* sign stood crooked near the sidewalk.

My brother was kind to me on those last days of summer. Sometimes he'd wander into my bedroom at night and sleep in the spot that had been Will's. He brought me swimming without the company of his friends, and in the evenings, we'd take long walks along our street to a dead end cul-de-sac, beyond which stretched a field of weeds. We talked about many things on those walks, and I'd ask questions like, "What happens when you die?"

"You go to God, right?" He sounded as unsure, if less curious, than I.

We sat in the cul-de-sac, the shadows spreading and shifting in the dimming afternoon. "You're okay," he said. "This is a good place to be." Then he bumped my shoulder, launching into a joke about three nuns and a bicycle without a seat. But I knew there was no good place in the absence of friendship, only darkness, and I cursed God for taking away the one person who I thought understood me.

Several weeks passed before I felt the desire to masturbate again. When I did, Will's solemn face and wiry body flooded my mind. I wanted to touch him, tried to remember his smell, but was already losing sight of his physical appearance altogether. By the middle of sixth grade, my memories of him had become vague and mysterious, his body as alien to me as the first time I saw him helping his father carry a cardboard box into their new home.

3

On a Sunday night, in the pitch of my bedroom, I tensed on the sheets and came. Warm spurts shot from me, splashing across my belly. I was aghast. An index finger went to the mess, which had cooled and was sticky, and rubbed it around on my stomach. In the blackness where I lay, I thought, Oh god, I'm bleeding. I clamored off the bed, fingers wet with jism, and crossed to the bathroom. With tears welling, I pushed open the door that led to my brother's bedroom, saying, "Help me, I'm dying."

My brother's bedside lamp clicked on. He sat up bleary-eyed and not quite awake. "What?" he mumbled, then spotted me standing naked at the foot of his mattress. "Jesus Christ!" he said, his face recoiling in disgust.

I extended a dewy hand, and noticed that the liquid covering my fingers was not red. I glanced at my stomach, observing the same thing, except that the sperm was cutting a trail downward to my crotch. "Something's wrong," I wept.

There was a long silence, punctuated only by my convulsive crying. My brother's face, a mixture of befuddlement and indignation, softened when he climbed from his bed.

"I broke it," I told him, tears streaking across my cheeks. "I kept doing it and broke it."

He stood before me in his underwear, his breath stale from sleep, his hair wild and uneven. "Playing with yourself, right?" He now seemed concerned. I nodded. He looked me over, shaking his head some, and then started laughing. He put his hands on my shoulders, gazing into my eyes. "It's what happens when you play with yourself, idiot. It's cum."

I studied the drying mess on my palm. "It's never done it before," I said, the sobs decreasing little by little.

"God, are you crazy?" He was smiling. "You're going through puberty. That's why you got all the hair and stuff. That's when it happens. It's what gets girls pregnant. Jesus, hasn't Dad talked to you about it yet?"

I shook my head.

"Don't worry about it," he told me. "Just wash up and go back to bed. It's normal."

"Will it do it again?" I said.

"If it's working like it's supposed to," he sighed, "it'll do it whenever you jack off, nimrod." Then he spun me around, aiming my body toward the bathroom door, and gave me a shove forward. I sailed off into lightlessness, my mind settled, my bare feet tripping from brown shag to cool linoleum.

4

The real David materialized during my freshman year in high school. He was too tall for fifteen, towering above his peers with short black hair and a hooped earring in his left earlobe. He wore ratty T-shirts, which usually sported some rock band's name or logo, and a pair of faded jeans with holes at the knees. He was a constant fixture in the school library, slouching along the aisles, two or three books tucked under an arm, his dark eyes scanning titles on the shelves. Once I caught a glimpse of him at the back of the library, sitting cross-legged on the floor, engrossed in Harper Lee's *To Kill a Mockingbird*, another time he sat across from me at a table reading *Nine Stories* by J.D. Salinger. In a roundabout way, I have him to thank for opening me up to the world of literature, because each book I saw him reading I sought out, hoping to gain a little insight into his character.

His full name was David Fitzgerald. I discovered his freshman picture in one of my brother's annuals. In the small photograph, taken a year previously, he seemed sullen, long hair hanging on lanky shoulders, with no earring evident, the curve of his lips parting enough to show braces. He had on a white Polo shirt which made him look more boyish and less intriguing than he did as a sophomore.

For months, I thought David lacked any conscious knowledge of my presence in the library. I spent most weekday afternoons there, hunkered at a table in a far corner, homework spread before me, pretending to be busy, but waiting for him to appear. He'd go walking right past, a thoughtful expression on his face, and move from view behind a wall of shelves. Sometimes I acted like I was searching for some book and followed at a distance. Often I'd make my way along an aisle to where he sat on the floor, an open novel in his lap. I'd step around his bent legs, careful not to disturb him, wishing he'd cock his head to meet my eyes.

It took almost the entire school year before I mustered enough courage to speak to him, and when I did, all I offered was a startled and meek "Excuse me" as I collided with him while rounding the corner between Anthropology and Biography. He gave me a quick glance, mumbling, "No problem." I was elated for days afterwards, feeling that the connection I'd desired for so long had somehow been made in the bumping of our arms.

I spent my evenings listening to the radio, writing his name again and again on loose-leaf paper, then folding the work neatly and praying. I stared at the street from my window as dusk washed across the asphalt. I messed with my hair in the bathroom mirror, combing it from side to side, all the way back, parting it down the middle. I read my daily horoscope in the morning paper. I returned to my prayer note, stuffing it under my mattress with similar stirrings, and prayed once more. And all the while, I carried on cryptic conversations with David in my head.

In the library, I remained as before, reading or doing homework, watching David when he passed, and at night, I paced my bedroom in utter frustration at my inability to communicate with him. Even at that age, I understood that my romanticized ideal of David might fall short of reality, that if he ever knew my secrets, he might hold me in contempt as a faggot, a queer, a freak.

But it was David who sought me out. He sat down at the library table where I was reading *The Catcher in the Rye*. At first I didn't realize anyone was sharing the table, so when I looked up from the book and saw him, his black eyes focused in my direction, I almost jumped with surprise. He pointed at the book, saying, "You know, he's still alive."

"Who?" I said, half whispering, my palms growing sweaty.

"Salinger," he explained. "He's still alive, still writes."

"Oh, I thought he was—I didn't know."

There was silence as he placed a tattered paperback of *Naked Lunch* on the table. "You read all his books?" he finally said.

"Just *Nine Stories*," I replied. "I'm almost through this one."

"They're the best. I've read them all, but those are the two I like."

I stammered, "Yeah, I—this one's good," studying the book's stark cover, then shot my eyes back to him.

There was another pause. David leaned forward, spreading his thin fingers out on the surface of the table. "I see you here a lot."

I nodded. "You too," I said.

I recollect the two of us sneaking from school on warm afternoons, the heat outside hinting of summer vacation. Sometimes we slipped behind the cafeteria dumpster, where he produced cigarettes and matches. He also began walking with me on my way home, explaining the plot of some book or story he'd just finished reading. He told me that he wanted to be a writer, that he'd already written a few stories, that someday he'd buy a cherry-red Ford Mustang and go on the road like Kerouac and Cassady. At night, with the bedroom windows open, the sounds of the nearby interstate lulling me toward sleep, I imagined riding shotgun with David in his dream—the convertible top back, sand blowing across a desert highway, cruising past mesas where a harvest moon shined over us.

By summer's start, we were the best of friends, spending hours in my bedroom talking about literature and music. David would arrive in the evenings with tapes of bands I'd never heard of before. Soon I was immersed in the songs of The Cramps, XTC, and Elvis Costello. Sometimes my mother stuck her head through the doorway, listened to the music for a bit, then said something like, "What happened to The Fleetwoods?" Besides being perplexed by the new music wafting from my bedroom, she was uneasy with my relationship with this older boy, who always greeted her with a handshake, but who struck her as unusual. "He's very odd," she once said. "Does he do drugs?" Of course, my brother had his own notions of David, which he echoed as often as possible: "Why do you hang out with that faggot?" he'd ask. Or, "Is the fag coming over today?" My father took an immediate liking to David, but his interest in him was based only on their mutual passion for televised baseball.

Once, as I sat on my bed listening to No Action at full volume, David came waltzing into the bedroom with a smirk on his face, a wild glitter in those black eyes. He pointed a shaky finger at me, tipped his head back, then started dancing to the music, swaying his body to the rhythm. His eyes shut, veins stood out on his neck as he mouthed the lyrics, and he stretched his arms in what I assumed to be a weird approximation of Christ on the cross. In the middle of my bedroom he began twirling around faster and faster until, as the song faded, he collapsed to the floor on his back, tremulous laughter rising from his throat, his stomach lifting and falling under a red T-shirt. "Play it again," he cackled, slurring the words. I crossed from my bed to the stereo, stepping over him on the way, and felt his fingertips glide across my ankle. Then he laughed harder. I stared down at him as the music played on, a broad grin on his face. The bedroom reeked with the smell of bourbon.

5

Sometimes David knocked on my window after midnight, and I'd dress and creep outside to join him. We roamed suburban streets, cigarette ends glowing, revelling in nights that seemed to hang forever. "We're the last men on earth," he repeated again and again, and I wished it was so. Aside from an infrequent car or barking dog, it didn't take much for us to imagine a world where people simply disappeared one day, leaving an entire town at our disposal. We walked through abandoned playgrounds, a breeze tapping the swingset chains, and sat among the sheetrock and rolls of fiberglass insulation of homes under construction. We stargazed in parking lots, littering our conversations with the sincerest sort of adolescent ramblings: "The universe might just be a molecule in a giant's fingernail." And in the minutes before dawn, as a gauze of sunlight stretched along the horizon, as our eyes wilted with fatigue, we said goodnight and parted.

On an August night, after I'd settled into bed, David rapped on the window. I heard his muffled voice, louder than usual, urging me to get up. When I found him outside, sitting behind my father's Ford, his knees pulled to his chest, rocking, I understood that he was drunk. "I know where we can go," he spluttered.

"Where?"

"I'll show you," then he extended a hand and I pulled him to his feet.

We walked blocks without saying a word. I stared at the sidewalk, watching our shadows spread thin behind us as we moved under the pale luster of streetlights. David led the way, taking swigs from a pint of scotch, his breath heavy with a mixture of alcohol and cigarettes. I realized where he was taking me when we stepped from the sidewalk and cut through the municipal park.

We scaled the chain link fence surrounding the unlit swimming pool, dropping into the darkness of the other side, where still water stood murky just beyond our feet. Then, David resting a hand on my shoulder for support, we walked the perimeter to the clubhouse deck and settled ourselves down into a pair of adjustable deck chairs. We sat there for what seemed hours, sealed in silence, the bottle of scotch empty now on the ground between us. David stared at the black water and popped his knuckles, one by one, massaging the joints of his fingers afterwards. I tilted my head and spotted the northern constellation Ursa Major. The water gurgled and swirled in drain barrels, yet remained calm in the center of the pool, casting the reflections of a few bright stars. Then David started talking about the future, about how he couldn't wait to buy that Mustang, about all the adventures that were ahead. "And you can go with me," he said, no longer sounding drunk. "Me and you, on the road, just the two of us, eating in the middle of nowhere, sleeping outside on nights like tonight. It'll be great. No adults. No teachers. None of that. How about it?" His voice was animated, excited. He was bending forward in the deck chair, peering at me through the pitch. "How about it?" he said again.

"I'd love to," I said, my tone as steady as possible in an attempt to conceal the shiver that had lifted to my throat. He touched my hand and gripped it like no one ever had before, and if he'd been able to see my face better he'd have noticed my tears.

There was a halo of blue and gray outlining his form while he stripped. I watched from the deck chair as his clothing fell around his feet, but was unable to make out the details of his body, only the curve of his back, the pale skin dancing like an apparition. He receded into darkness, tiptoeing toward the pool. Then I heard the splash, and when he surfaced he let out a gasp of delight: "It's freezing," he said. "It's really cold. Come on."

I undressed and went to the edge of the pool. David swam near my feet, kicking his legs, causing small waves to ripple off in every direction. I tested the water with a toe, then felt myself being tugged at the ankles. "Don't!" I pled, but it was too late. I fell forward, my arms flailing, the water crashing over me. When I came up, my eyes burning from the chlorine, David was swimming beside me. He was laughing, saying, "Sorry. I couldn't help it." But I was angry and turned away. His hands slipped around my rib cage, his body pressed against mine. Everything grew quiet. Somehow, in that moment, I understood that I'd never be the same again, that when I climbed from the water nothing would be to me as it was before, except the slow shifting of light at dusk and the stars above.

STROKE THE FIRE

M. CHRISTIAN

Lew always knew he'd die someday. Gotta go sometime, sure: Kicked in the head by a horse, catch flying lead over some kind of stupid shit. Snakebite. Damned Indians. Maybe tainted water. Maybe way too much booze after a good haul of pelts. Could even be a fall—at fifty-two his balance and grip wasn't what it used to be.

But the one thing he never thought it would be was needing to piss.

All around was white. White, his legs, his coat, his arms, and his gloved hands. White. And all Lew could feel was cold. Damned cold.

Seemed a good idea at the time. It was one of those nights when the west wind came right off the mountain and knocked at his front door, or at least scratched to be let in. He'd been up on old Craggy for more than five years, and the sound of that wind was like a bunkmate. Okay, maybe a bunkmate that snored like a gale, made a horrible mess outside (and never put things back), and would kill you in your sleep if you gave him half a chance. But, still, a regular companion on the mountain.

Going out in the middle of a windstorm, then blizzard, to get wood and stopping in the bracing cold to piss against the side of the cabin seemed like such a safe idea at the time. Christ, he might as well have walked outside naked and shaved.

The steep trail that Lew knew so well, that he could have walked in his sleep, had collapsed just enough to throw him down the hillside.

Now he was surrounded by the white of a snowdrift. His leg felt busted-up, and he was going to freeze to death.

At least, Lew thought, looking down at himself—the only colors in the deathly white of the snow—no one would really know he died taking a piss.

96

Some consolation.

Lew really didn't want to die. He wasn't old enough yet (his grip was getting bad but not that bad, and he could still plug a stag at one hundred feet with his trusty Remington), he had a few good crotchety years left in him. Hell, he'd only been to Kansas City once. Still hadn't seen Lillie Langtry. God, he'd never even been to the other side of the damned mountain (just never got around to it)—and he would never see Jeff again.

That's what hurt. Damn it, he was looking forward to going down to Stinkhole (Clearwater to those in the "city" limits) and seeing if he'd come through again. Maybe even try and coerce the range hand up to his cabin ("The huntin's damn good" he'd rehearsed to himself). Even thinking about the last time, about his last trip down to Stinkhole, got him going. Christ and fucking shit, Lew thought, kicking out with both legs—and biting his lip at the pain in his right—I can live without seeing Miss Lily, Kansas City wasn't all that fancy the first time, and, damn it, one side of a mountain looks pretty much like the other (don't it?), *but he was gonna miss Jeff!*

Lew was gonna freeze to death and never get his hands on that lanky range hand again.

The real bad part was that he'd fallen sometime after midnight, and dawn was some four or five hours away. If he could last that long, he might get out of this: Wait till the sun came up, get his bearings, try and either make it back up the mountain or limp it down to Mad Jack's. Now the world was nothing but bitter cold white. In a few hours, just a few hours—

Lew checked his pockets. For Christ's sake he was gonna take a piss, not climb the fuckin' mountain. The only thing he found was a cheap little knife in the pocket of his buckskin coat. Aside from that, nothing but white and the cold.

Almost nothing. He also found a hard-on. Lew's cock was iron in his pants, maybe from fear (heard that kinda thing: A boner when they bury you), but more than likely it was thinking about Jeff.

The last time he'd been in Stinkhole was about two months back: He'd come down from his cabin with sixteen hands of fine pelts, a few nuggets of gold he'd managed to scrounge, and a mean itch to scratch. After a quick detour by way of the assayer's office (for the gold) and Long's Whiskey Parlor (to sell Sissy Dan the pelts), Lew had bee-lined for Miss Sally's for a full bottle of her finest redeye (not the cheapest stuff, but not the good stuff either). Lew didn't like to drink himself stupid all that much, but it was just those few months back had been ones of a meaner and bitterer than usual cold up on Craggy, and he had some long, and very cold, nights to thaw out of his bones.

He would have preferred some other kind of way to spend his hard-earned furs and gold, but while he had been a paying customer over at Miss Lavonia's (particularly of Virginia May, who was as tall as he was and could beat him at arm wrestling now and again), his itch wasn't something that her girls could really scratch.

It was sometime after dark when he'd come out of Miss Sally's less drunk than he thought he'd be, sometime after the first bottle had started to taste like old turpentine (knew Sal watered it down some—Lew just hoped it was just with water....) and he wasn't forgetting what he'd come down from Craggy to forget. So, slightly wobbling, Lew stood outside Sal's and looked out on the pitch, sprinkled with lanterns and stars up above, the night of Stinkhole, and thought that he had might as well get Stubborn out of the corral and saddled up for the long trip back up Craggy.

On the way there, though, he got sidetracked: A hole in the "road" (that Clearwater townsfolk called it) filled with mud sucked in his right boot. Just as he was about to kiss the dirt, this tall, thin fella stepped out of the shadows around the city corral and caught him—saving Lew and his town duds from the mud and horseshit. Helping him back up on his slightly unsteady feet, boot sucking and slurping out of the hole, the stranger had leaned back against that fence and appraised Lew while sucking a hot glow from a thin black cigar.

"Thanks, pardner," Lew had said stomping the rest of the mud off on a large rock by one of the corral gates. "Almost got trapped in this-here hell hole of refinement."

"Going back then?"

"Yeah. Sure forget how fast 'civilization' can run through a man."

"Movin' on myself. Come in 'bout ever two months er so fer mail and supplies. A day's 'bout all I can stand." The man's voice had this steel-string twang to it, something Kentucky maybe, or something deeper south. It was a kind of voice Lew liked to hear, a musical kind of voice.

"That way myself. Only come in ta take a bit of the mountain smell off me and put on a little drunk. Man can only get too wild, ya know?" Lew said smiling.

"That I do. That I do. My smell's range, though. Can't see how you can stand to high Jesus the cold up there and those winds...."

In the white, in the now of the cold, cold white, Lew smiled a bit to himself—and tried not to set his dimestore choppers rattling too much—at that. Cold, yeah, Jeff, damned killing cold. Wish I was somewhere warm right now, Jeff, somewhere on the plains with a nice fire crackling....

"Man's got a home, then that's where he sleeps. Can't, myself, see how you can stand the god-derned quiet out there in the flats," Lew had said, listening to the music of the man's voice.

The man shrugged, the tip of his cigar bobbing in the soft night. "That it be. Name's Last. Jeff Last."

Lew wiped the grime off his hands (and hopefully the fool's grin off his face) and offered his own. "Lew. Just Lew around here."

The handshake lasted a bit too long, long enough for the two men to size each other up. Lew in his Stinkhole clothes was a burly barrel of a man, all beard and round blue eyes. He looked fat from aways, but if you'd ever seen him haul cornmeal or lumber you'd know that it was iron, fella, strong, strong iron and not just insulation against Craggy's winds.

Last was long and lanky, and while the light was none too good in that narrow little ways between the public corral and Miller's Fine Feeds, you could tell that he was a beanpole: Six feet easy, in buckskin and serape. In the dark beneath his wide brimmed hat, his shaved face was carved and as Craggy as Lew's mountain home. The handshake had lasted way too long. Now, he thought, how to get this fine feller up the mountain....

"Gotta hit the trail if I'm ta make Ridgewood by dawn," Jeff had said, and Lew's heart had sunk down to his Stinkhole boots.

"Knows how it is—" he had said, starting to turn, maybe extend a hand, and an invitation for another time.

"But you is one fine figure of a man. Might temptin'—"

Lew stared, unsure of how exactly to respond.

"You think the same, Lew of the Mountain?" Jeff had said.

Even in the low light cast from the lanterns of Sal's, Lew could see Jeff's fine figure, out in all its glory there in the "street" of Stinkhole. Lew's breath was stolen by Jeff's cock. Sure, the mountain man had seen a few in his time. Many. Some were as nicely shaped. A few were as tasty-looking. But none were as gigantic. The size made Lew wonder where the man hid the thing. "I think the same, sir. That I do."

"A man after my own, Lew of the Mountain. Care ta share the same with a stranger?"

What with the booze and the excitement (well, mostly the booze), Lew couldn't match the style of Jeff whipping out his beanpole. Clumsily, Lew fumbled with his overalls till he got a cold (shit!) hand around his own iron and managed to haul it out without doing that Jewish-thing to himself on a brass button. Even with the rotgut in his gut, his cock was strong and—Lew was known for being a modest man, but an honest man—his mighty cock. Even in the dim lantern light from Sal's, his was long and strong: Head capped by the smooth cone of his foreskin.

Jeff took a moment to size-up Lew. "Mighty fine, Lew. Mighty fine."
"Could say the same about you, Jeff."

Jeff's doe-skin glove was warm on the skin of Lew's cock. So soft. It felt like pure heat—and not much else. It felt like the glow from a potbelly stove against the chill night air.

In the snow, in his predicament, Lew fumbled through his few—too few—layers to grip his cock. Thinking of Jeff, feeling Jeff again in his recall, made him as iron as that night by the corral. All he wanted, well besides living to see the sunrise over Craggy, was to feel Jeff again, and to have Jeff feel him again....

"Ah'll bet might tasty, too," Jeff had said that night, stroking Lew slow and steady with his soft, soft doe-skin glove. "Wouldn't you say, Lew of the Mountain?"

Lew looked right and left but saw nothing but Stinkhole, dead asleep. "Few have said so, Mr. Late: Those few who have had such a taste."

Not another word: Jeff bent down easy, balancing himself from falling in the mud and shit with another gloved hand, and wrapped soft lips around Lew's cock. The night was cold, and before his lips wrapped, Lew could feel the wave of heat from his mouth, his breath steaming out from him fogged around Lew's hidden head.

Jeff's mouth was like a warm bath and your hand. It was like a fire in the stove and a good pot of coffee. It was like a huge old buck, just *there* on a rise—waiting for you to squeeze off a shot. It was like dawn on old Craggy. It was, well, the only thing you could compare Jeff's mouth on your cock to was the best of everything.

Lew couldn't help but moan at this. He could feel his breath breathing and blowing warm air on the front of his overalls. The heat of him spread out from his cock down into his belly.

Jeff took a deep interest in his cock. He explored Lew with his tongue, pushing his foreskin back gently to tickle the tip, then wash the smeg away with the vigor of Lew attacking a plate of flapjacks in the morning. Lew could feel the flat back of his tongue, the roof of his mouth, the sudden hardness of his teeth.

Cold, cold, cold, Lew...moaned. He remembered it all, hanging onto the fence, opening his eyes and seeing the stars up above, and feeling a freeing breeze whistle by them, tugging at his beard. His hand was around his cock, feeling its heat, its strength. He pulled a bit, and it seemed like this was the one part of his body not freezing, the one part of his body getting hot....

"Yessir," Jeff said, straightening up and wiping his mouth with the back of a doe-skin glove, "mighty tasty. Mighty."

All Lew could do was smile at the man and give a faint nod. This would have been enough for a long time, something that would keep Lew happily jerking off for months on old Craggy, but maybe that night one of those stars was smiling down on him. Jeff smiled at him and pulled something from under his serape.

Lew felt Jeff reach down to his cock and balls (shifting a bit more of Lew's overall's aside), again—stroking him once more with the heaven of the soft glove. Lew looked up the dancing eyes of this handsome stranger and saw them smile at him with an excited glee.

"Let's saddle up this bronco," Jeff said, that *hahahaha* strong in his voice, those eyes, "and see how he rides."

In the snow, Lew had his eyes pressed closed, lost in the memories of that night, that man; his cock iron in his fist. Maybe it was the cold, maybe it was the heat of the memory, maybe it was the life that came into him when he realized that this was probably gonna be it, but whatever the reason, Lew felt like his cock and balls were on fire. As he jerked to the thought of Jeff's eyes, hands, those gloves, he bit his lip and blinked away drops of water.

Jeff neatly lassoed Lew's cock and balls with a neat length of rawhide cord. Though Mountain Lew, bear-skinning Lew, would never have admitted it to none but himself (and then only in passing) the feeling of that cord around his most private of privates was pretty fearful: To have something tight just looped nice and neat around him like that, when all it would probably take would be a harder tug to leave his cock and balls in the mud by the city corral, was something new and more than slightly alarming to him. Pushing himself up and slightly away from Jeff and his little lasso, Lew scooted backward and almost up top of the fence.

The lanky man laughed, the sound of water draining fast from a bucket, "Take it ease there, stud. There ain't nothing here that's gonna hurt ya none. Rest on back and let this old trained cowhand take the reins."

Those laughing eyes and smiling face, maybe just the softness of those gloves and the skill in their strokes—something about Jeff Last made Mountain Man Lew relax and drop himself back down till his boots were once again in the mud. "Just somethin' new, Mister; can't fault a man fer bein' cautious."

Jeff just smiled at the mountain man, and did his magic with the rawhide, roping it around Lew's straining cock and balls like he was going after a prize calf. In a heartbeat, Lew's favorite sausage was trussed like a, well, like the *sausage* it was: Around cock and balls so that Lew felt fit to burst. His cock had been strong and tight before, but now it felt like someone had stuffed even more cock into his cock. Iron before, damned *steel* now.

Despite a sudden urge to keep his manly composure, Lew moaned and jerked his hips forward into the cool night air.

"There, now, that little doggie ain't goin' nowhere now—" Now Jeff's doe-skin gloves were like, well, they might have been like Heaven before, but now they were the kind of pleasure that surely only a devil could deliver. To Lew's straining and hard, hard, absolute hardest cock, Jeff's gentle and sweet ministrations were a real good drunk, and a gleaming lump of gold the size of a good morning dump in your pan.

Lew's cock felt fit to burst, but that damnable cord around him kept it bottled till all Lew could feel was the cum swelling in him behind the cord and the aching, pounding pleasure in his cock. Somewhere along the line, he had closed his eyes, and in an effort to push himself over the edge he opened them again (maybe then he'd break that cord and come!) and found himself staring into the happy eyes of the man called Jeff Last.

"Howdy," Jeff said, smiling even more, before dropping his head down to Lew's fiery cock.

Christ! Lew felt the man's mouth slip over his cock like a hot wet jacket. But this was just a taste for Jeff. He took his mouth away ("Oh, Jesus, man—" Lew mumbled to the chill night), and careful like, real gentle like, peeled back Lew's foreskin and promptly got right back to it.

Lew was gonna explode, it felt so good. Great before, Jeff's mouth was the glory of warm sunlight after a long freezing night; it was a hand of almost all aces; it was two huge lumps of gold in your pan; it was a pair of fine new boots; it was—hell—it was the reason Lew had come out West in the first place, it was a man's doin' for other men with the wilds tossed in!

Don't ask him how, but Lew also knew that Jeff was jerking his own, too, and that added a fire to his own flame: That he had one of those doe-skin gloves working away at his own long tool, pleasuring himself as he sucked away at Lew.

Moaning, Lew tried to keep from jerking back, and pulling his cock from Jeff's mouth. When he came—and Christ did he!—when Jeff carefully untied his cock, it was pails of sticky cum down the back of Mr. Last's throat. It wasn't a normal come, not as Lew had known them to be (a few jerks of the body, that hit of pleasure that was the reason for the trip), this was a jerking and a thrashing of the body, a moan that turned groan halfway outta his chest. It was a rush like falling off a horse, but lots more pleasurable—

Jeff moaned, too, then and there by the fence on that cold night, a little moan but a good one nonetheless. Lew was aware of Jeff's cum like it was some ways down a long trail, and had a sudden mean hunger to taste Jeff's cum, to feel his cock like Jeff had felt his (wonder if I can do that mean rope trick?).

But, leaving poor ol' Lew there by the fence, Jeff had wiped his mouth again with the back of that so-soft doe-skin glove and had simply said, with that smile too wide and gleaming on his face, in those eyes: "See you around, pardner," and walked off into the night.

Just as Lew was about to call after the stranger, to ask when he might be comin' back through Stinkhole, a voice came from down the street, soft but carrying: "Be back through in two months or so, then we can really ride up a storm...."

But now, *now* in the freezing drift, Lew was just a few days away from those two months. A few days away from seeing Mr. Last again and knowing the pleasures of the man's body, his mouth, those hands, that cock. That cock, that mouth, those hands—maybe because of the cold and knowing that this was probably gonna be his last, Lew pumped his flaming cock. All he could see was Jeff and what they were to do, fucking like deers in one of Miss Lavonia's pretty brass beds—Jeff's long tool down his throat, that same tool in his hands while he played Mr. Last like a meaty flute—

His cum came with a wild thrash close to that very one that night near the corral. It leapt from Lew like an angel's ascent, a shuddering quiver that closed his eyes against the deathly white and made him bite his lip.

Later, he tasted the blood and opened his eyes. White, again, but this time stars looked down at Lew of the Mountain and tinkled like Jeff's smile. The night was cold, yes, but it had stopped snowing. No longer wrapped in a blanket of pure cold, Lew reached up and grabbed the branch of a pine that had been overhead the whole time—but trapped by the white. Pulling, and groaning from the pleasures he inflicted on himself and his smashed leg, Lew hauled himself out of the snow.

A brisk night. Dawn was maybe three hours away. More than enough time to make himself a bed of pine needles and get off the freezing ground. Maybe even enough time to make himself a crutch and limp back up to his cabin or down to Mad Jack's. He knew, then and there, that he would see another sunrise on Craggy and, more than anything, live long enough to get his hands on Jeff.

It was damned good to be alive.

PLEASINGLY

MATTHEW RETTENMUND

I never let myself go, I just *went*.

Actually, if you ask *me*, I didn't really go very far, just spread out a little. I'm not "obese" or "fat" or anything, just soft around the middle, blurred around the edges. I'm...*Rubenesque*.

You learn a lot when you gain weight. Like how big a turn-off spare pounds are to your gay brethren. One week, you're right in the thick of things, cruising and flirting up a storm; the next, you don't get noticed unless you make a funny sound or ask an untoward question...like, "How's it goin'?"

Being chubby in a skinny fag's world leaves you with lots of time to look around unnoticed, to see things. Important things like what's passing for glamorous these days, what makes all the guys' heads turn. When a musclebound, shaven-headed, earringed, *faux* macho-man struts past, the other guys are so busy craning their necks for a second look that they don't even realize *you're* checking *them* out, puzzling over how something so homogenous could elicit such ravenous interest.

I may be chubby, but I haven't lost interest in sex. I've never been much of a slut, always the big talker and seldom-doer. Until last weekend, I'd only ever slept with three guys: two steady boyfriends I ended up seeing for almost two years apiece, and one one-week stand in-between them, with a snarky undergrad when I was a graduating senior and old enough to know better. The latter left me with genital warts, quite a feat considering we both wore condoms at all times. Did the fucker have them on his *tongue* or something? Sheesh.

Don't listen to anyone when they try to get you to, *"Relax...we're having safer sex."* Safer than what? Not having sex at all? Yeah, but still not safe, not ever one hundred percent safe. Sex is always dangerous. One way or another.

I was probably thinking about sex when I first bumped into Christopher. I *always* think about sex; I'm thinking about it right now, even as I'm trying to describe all the things that led up to the most incredible sex of my life, with Christopher, last weekend.

I had been on my building's elevator for so long I was almost convinced it was stuck. Visions of Keanu Reeves appearing at the vent overhead, pulling me to safety, evaporated when the ancient door slid open: Ground floor. Hooray.

I stepped out and made a beeline for my mailbox, hoping desperately that I'd received my copy of *Entertainment Weekly*. The weekend just isn't the weekend if I haven't devoured everything that just happened the week before. Besides, I'd heard that there was a Barbra Streisand cover story, and though I *hate* that woman (I'm sorry, but where's the *pizazz?*), there was a fifty-fifty chance for a photo of her luscious son by Elliott Gould (go figure).

Standing at my box was this guy, this big, chunky guy, trying in vain to force open my mailbox with his key. The nerve! I couldn't believe it was happening; I started to pipe up just before he glanced over at me and flashed me the pearliest grin I think I've ever seen.

"Hiya," he chirped, as nonchalantly as a person not trying to steal my mail, "How're you?"

"Okay."

He'd straightened and was facing me now, allowing the full effect to sink in. I'm not one for physical attraction; I mean, I get turned on by just about any guy, whether he's classically studly or charmingly nerdy, just so long as he's "cute." But this guy—*whoa!*—this guy was unwittingly pushing every button on my panel without even lifting a finger.

He was my height, five foot nine, give or take, and roughly my build, except maybe even a bit chubbier. That would make him about, what? two twenty? Shut up, already—we've both got broad shoulders and big bones; two twenty isn't the end of the world, even if it *is* nearing the end of the scale. He had short, dirty blond hair, a slight scruff on his round cheeks, and a Kirk Douglas puncture wound (read: dimple) in the middle of his chin. His eyes were sort of hazel, and they were looking at me with keen interest. It was like when you catch the attention of a cat—you get the feeling that no matter how hard you try, they're not gonna stop staring at you until they're good and ready.

"I'm having a hard time with my mailbox," he shrugged, "I'm new."

"You might have an easier time if you stuck the key in the right box," I said playfully, pointing first to the *6-E* on my mailbox, and then to the

6-E printed on my key. He did a double-take, checked his key, then flushed scarlet and stammered an apology.

"It's no problem," I laughed, enjoying his cute discomfort, "Any time."

When he retrieved his mail—success!—it turned out he lived in 7-E, just a few feet above my head.

"I'm dying of embarrassment," he said, squinching up his face like a nine year old might. A great big, cuddly nine year old in a twenty-nine-year-old body.

"Really," I replied, "it could've been worse—you could've been trying to get into my apartment." We both laughed and then I took off to the store with my mail peeking out of my backpack. As I walked away from him, I had that familiar desire to be able to suck it in—not my tummy, but my love handles—for his benefit. I miss the days of feeling like I was doing someone a favor simply by turning around and walking away, gifting them with a pleasant view. But as I left the building, I turned slightly and saw that he was standing in the same place, watching me leave. Not so shabby after all, I guess, or was I just imagining things?

Later that evening, I found out.

I shopped, came home, put stuff away, and dropped. I'd been working thirteen-hour days trying to finish a mailing list at work, and now that it was over, I felt every lost hour of sleep and relaxation coming back with a vengeance. I thought I could sleep for days lying there on my folded-up futon mattress. I didn't even bother spreading it out, or changing into more appropriate clothes, I just...

...woke up with the shock of submersion. I was dripping wet, suddenly awake, and too annoyed to do more than exclaim. It was pitch black outside; I'd been asleep for hours and had only woken up because a light but persistent stream of water was drizzling on my face from the ceiling, where it was condensing in a two-foot patch.

Oh, shit. All I could think of was that the new (cute) neighbor had left his tub running and taken off for the evening. I was going to have to call the super and get him out of bed to come over, get into the apartment, and wade across the upstairs neighbor's living room to incapacitate the tub.

I dashed out of my room, out of my apartment, and up the two small flights of stairs to seven, pounding on the door to 7-E.

"Anyone there? C'mon, open up!"

To my surprise, someone did. It was the new guy, and he was wearing an enormous white robe, just like Madonna in *Truth Or Dare.*

"What's up?" he asked, warming to the intrusion.

"Water. Is. Pouring. Out. Of. My. Ceiling," I seethed, "What's the problem?"

"It is? I mean, I don't know, I have no idea..." He stepped back inside his apartment and I followed him to the bathroom, but there was nothing overflowing anywhere. It could only be a burst pipe, and that would be a major pain in the ass to fix.

"Call Juan," he said, handing me his phone, "He'll have to come right over."

Juan did, and was taking his sweet-assed time digging around in the tub and under the sink while Christopher—we'd finally exchanged names—and I sat around watching *E!* and criticizing Bianca Ferrere and Steve Kmetko. We really hit it off like that, just joking around with each other like old pals, no awkwardness at all. The whole time, Christopher was still in his diva robe, affording me a look at his hairy chest and even hairier legs. He smelled fucking terrific, too, like he'd used some amazing bath gel in the shower, or maybe it was just a killer shampoo. With his hair dripping in his eyes, he looked like young Marlon Brando, except doughier, blonder, and more approachable.

"It's fixed," Juan barked on his way out, "Don't be so rough on the pipes."

"Oh, okay," I called after him, "Next time we take a shower, we'll do it real gentle-like."

Now came the weirdness. Up until that point, Juan's presence made the evening harmless. Now, I was alone in the room with a sexy guy who was wearing only a robe and a sheepish grin. He was sitting on the couch, and I was sitting on the couch's arm, feeling like Tweetie Bird balancing on the swing in his gilded cage.

"I better go, eh?" I chattered, getting up to leave.

"No," Christopher said, taking my arm, "Stay."

I'm not lying when I tell you that this kind of shit *never happens to me,* but the next step was complete facial gridlock. He pulled me over onto his lap, holding my jaw and kissing my face like a lonely dog. When he got me on the lips, he had his tongue in my mouth before I was aware my mouth was even *open.* Just the way he pulled me over onto him made me weak with wanting it—he was so aggressive.

I ground my ass into his crotch, my knees at my chest, his arms around my torso and pulling me closer. He kissed my cheeks, licked my neck, nibbled the skin at my shoulder blades—in no time flat, I became shirtless without a care in the world that my belly would be exposed. When he reached up and manipulated one of my nipples, kissed it and flickered his tongue over the tip, I nearly lost it—not only did it make me instantly unafraid that my fleshy body wouldn't be appealing to him, it just so happens that with me, it's *all* in the nipples.

"Oh, yeah, I *love* that," I muttered, forgetting that dirty talk usually does nothing for me. This time, it wasn't contrived dirty talk; it was stuff I was saying because I couldn't *help* myself.

"Suck my tits, lick my tits." I bounced in his lap, luxuriating in the attention he paid to the most sensitive part of my body.

Christopher swirled his tongue around my nipples, ran it from tit to tit and back again, chewed them until they were so raw every touch felt like ten. He was really hard under me—I could feel his prick beating against the underside of my thigh.

I was reluctant to give up the nipple work, but there was more to be had. I stood up and unbelted my jeans, pulled them down and off. (Mental note: Use more bleach on underwear.)

Christopher sat still, expectant, smiling, and winked at me while I got completely naked. I wouldn't learn until the next day that he secretly loves to leave the underwear on, to work around it.

My next move was to open his robe. I don't know why gay guys are so afraid of a little meat on a man's bones, but if anyone could persuade them to change their ways, it's Christopher. He is a hunky, meaty man with a large gut and rounded pecs and just about the most beautiful cock I've ever seen. It wasn't porno-huge—they never are, are they?—but just perfectly fat and artistically veiny, and it was leaking pre-cum like my ceiling leaks pipewater.

Condoms.

He had some, thank God, because who knows what I'd have done without them. Sandwich bags? Or just asking lots of sexual history questions and taking the gamble? I pulled a tight one on him and another on myself. He was admiring my dick, too, stroking it so firmly I had to ask him to lay off—seeing his sexy body all naked and glistening, not to mention the most loving pec job of all time, had me ready to squint and spritz.

I went down on him in one big gulp, wishing that instead of mint, they made condoms taste like dick, with a hint of pre-cum. But rubbing my lips over the shape of his dick was exciting enough for now, at least until we could make a trip to get tested. And the feeling was mutual: Christopher just lay there in awe, mouth agape, eyes closed.

I got a major rise out of him when I licked and suckled his nuts—the most sensitive part of *his* body—and a loud roar when I nipped my way from the tip of his cock to the underside of his scrotum. When I lifted one of his legs, he almost stopped me, thinking I'd suck his asshole. Now would I do that? In a flash, actually, but under the circumstances, I was going to settle for faking it.

I buried my face in his ass, licking his crack and teasing his perineum with my tongue. He smelled great, very musky despite the scent of Ivory soap everywhere. I love the smell of a man's ass, and under safer circumstances, I love, love, *love* to tongue a big man's asshole, make him cry like a baby with so much nasty pleasure. I rolled my face in the crack of his ass, hoping to absorb that scent on my cheeks to smell later, when the lovemaking inevitably had ended.

He pulled me back up to kiss me, dropping his hands to my ass, which he squeezed mercilessly. He bunched my cheeks up in his fists and worked them back and forth, with and against each other, my asshole burning from the friction. I hadn't been fucked in a year, and hadn't ever wanted to get fucked as badly as I wanted it right then. He worked his forefingers toward one another until they massaged my butthole from opposite angles and slipped into me up to the first knuckles.

"Aw, *fuck*," I gasped, wiggling on his fingertips. "I gotta get fucked, man, I have to have it tonight...."

He shushed me, "I know, I know...I'll do it, I'll do it to you good and hard like this asshole," (rubbing the rim of my hole furiously) "needs to be fucked." I hadn't showered, wasn't clean like Christopher—I could smell my sweaty butt and balls, getting all riled up with his touching.

I rubbed his condomed cock with ForPlay, unable to resist jerking it tightly enough to constitute the beginnings of a handjob. He looked like he would've settled for that quick relief, but I couldn't let that happen so I stopped, applied more lube to my butt, and positioned myself over his erection, squatting over it there on the couch. I was preparing to lower myself onto him, but he beat me to the punch. He'd loosened me enough that when he shoved his fat cock upwards at my asshole, it sank halfway in, no problem at all.

"Oh, mother*fuck!*" I called out, seeing stars and losing control. He started pumping up and into me while I held onto the back of the sofa, just squatted there and let him nail me from below. He held my love handles, pinching them hard enough to burn, while he thrust his hips up, fucking me frantically. Toward the end, he was leaping almost off the cushions to get me as deep as he could, and I felt it, baby, I *felt* it.

"I'm gonna..." I stood up on the couch, his prick slipping out of my ass and into his immediately jerking fist. I shot cum onto the bricks of the wall, working my meat with my left hand until I didn't think I would ever come again. By the time I'd collapsed into his lap, he'd spilled all over the coffee table (here's hoping he'd already read that poor issue of *Out*) and was losing his boner, half asleep and satisfied.

"That was so great," I murmured. He agreed, hugging me gently and whispering things I couldn't make out. I looked him in the eye and he looked back, rubbing my belly with one hand, holding me in place—close to him—with the other. I knew then—and I'll let you know if I'm right when the time comes—that I was gonna be with Christopher for a long time. I think he could tell I was thinking that, because he smacked my butt affectionately and kissed my nose.

"Chubby," he whispered to me sweetly.

And then we split a pizza.

A Traveller's Relief

OWEN KEEHNEN

Cody was walking bow legged when he hopped off the bus in Bayetteville. His legs were stiff from being cramped, his back was stiff from facing the window, and his crotch was just plain stiff. The ride was long, but he was excited to see a big chunk of the country.

At twenty-one, he was ready for life. He was born in Macon and had been out of the county on only four or five occasions. This was the first time his watch ever needed adjusting. He got a kick out of that.

Nothing important was left for him in Georgia. The past would be easy to forget. Cody came from a large family that was neither rich nor close. It would only help matters if he moved away. Besides, he had hopes for doing something different with his life. Cody was determined to start anew once he got to Minneapolis, no matter what he had to do.

His connecting bus was still hours away and the greasy guy behind the ticket counter, with prints on his bifocals and fans of obsidian hair coming from his nostrils, said it was running behind schedule.

Cody surveyed the bright yellow room, sat in an orange plastic chair, and fed a quarter into the television. Reception was lousy, but he'd never done this before. New experiences were what leaving Macon was all about. He watched some cartoons before moving to a more comfortable seat at the end of the third bus bench. They were in rows like pews, only facing a clock and not a cross. Cody opened his Ludlum novel and closed it again after a few pages.

He stretched his legs. Five minutes had passed. The anticipation of arriving in his new hometown was making him extremely restless. Standing, he yawned with his hands stretched high above his head. His T-shirt rode up his stomach, revealing a thick stitch of dark hair that

111

ran from his navel to the lip of his Levi's. He scratched his stomach and walked towards the men's room.

Directly inside the door, a man waited beside a standing ashtray. He was thin, with a gray mustache shaped like a staple. He had acne scars, bloodshot eyes, and fleshy lips. Tugging the pouch of his faded jeans, he stared Cody down, following him with his eyes.

Cody turned to look over his shoulder. The man hooked a thumb in his hip pocket and splayed his fingers web-like towards his crotch. Rounding the corner of the L-shaped room, Cody was hit by the stench of urine, cigarettes, and mildew. Still, any bathroom was an improvement over the bouncing broom closet on board the bus.

Looking around, Cody noticed the white tile was marked by brownish-green blotches. The stall partitions were ravaged by rust and covered with graffiti. Cody eyed the detailed rendering of a spurting cock, magic-markered and gouged into the metal stall. He imagined the carving sound and cringed. Below the drawing was a wide hole with irregular edges. Cody saw movement inside.

Moving his wallet to his front pocket, Cody stepped before the second urinal. He heard a match strike and turned. The man that had been near the door was now leaning against the wall by the towel dispenser. He took a drag and rubbed the legs of his mustache as the smoke bowled from his nostrils. Flipping away the spent match, the man lifted one boot back against the tile. Cody turned back to the dingy tiles before the urinal and then towards the stall. Now a finger was hooked on the bottom rim of the hole.

Despite some apprehension, Cody felt his dick stir when he looped the elastic band of his briefs below his balls. His cramped cock and nuts smelled, and a heady cloud blended quickly with the men's room stench. At eye level, SHOW IT HARD was scrawled in different directions between the tiles like random and repeated hieroglyphics.

"Hey kid, let me suck your cock."

Turning towards the hole, Cody saw two fingers now hooked on the opening. He could faintly discern the movement of lips through the opening. The nasty mouth urged him closer, seducing him from the edges of the visible circle. "Come on, stick it through. Let me suck it. Stick it through and let me suck that piece of meat."

The man at the towel dispenser slid his boot down the wall. The scraping sound broke the chant. His heels made a slight click as he crossed the men's room. He unzipped on the way and pulled out his reddening cock even before reaching the urinal on Cody's right. He stared down at Cody's rising member and slowly reached over to wrap a hand around it. He stroked it firmly from base to tip and ran its length with a series of smooth twisting motions. He felt it harden even more as he thumbed the plum crown.

"Nice nuts, kid," he growled in Cody's ear while holding his balls in a cluster. When he stopped his manipulations, Cody's cock was lurching upward. The man reached down and began milking his own uncircumcised dick.

The voice through the hole resumed its seduction. "Come on, look how the eye of that cock is crying for it. Let me work that thing. Look how it's ready. Stick it through and I'll make it feel better than you ever imagined."

Blood throbbed in Cody's head. His cock arched with urgency. The guy beside him was lightly rolling the thin foreskin over the head of his dick and moaning softly. Cody heard nothing but whispering, heaving breaths, and the beating of meat. All sound was enhanced by the men's room's acoustics.

A timed flush put all activity on hold. It rose and faded with a gurgling whistle.

The man at the urinal nodded towards Cody's cock. "Looks like you could use some relief. He's real good. Stick it through. I'll watch the door. The way this place is set up it's impossible to get caught."

Cody looked towards the hole.

"Let me make you feel fine."

"Go on," urged the man beside him, finally pulling Cody by the cock towards the glory hole.

Slowly, Cody put the head of his dick through the opening and into a moist and magical place. He felt a lip near the base of his dick and then a kissing up and down the length of his shaft. A tongue bath followed. His cock was thick with saliva. The man took the head in his mouth and teasingly popped it in and out several times. Unable to restrain himself any longer, Cody slammed his dick deep into the mouth. His hips hit the metal stall wall with a loud slam. The man watching turned and pantomimed, "Shhh." Cody bit his lip and felt a hand run the length of his rod, bobbing in rhythm with the mouth.

"You're a wild one, huh?" said the man watching as he walked towards Cody. "Feels good, don't it?" Cody felt the man behind him, but was distracted by the wonderful sensations on his dick. Nothing else mattered. The man behind him whispered in his ear, "That's it, boy, feed the hungry, give your seed to the needy." Cody could smell the beer on his breath.

The man's callused fingers reached beneath Cody's T-shirt and began tickling his nipples. Once they hardened, he tugged them repeatedly. Twisting away from the fingers, Cody slammed even harder against the partition as the mouth behind it continued to draw the juice from deep within his balls.

"Shoot that load. I can tell you're getting ready; those nuts are tightening up in their sac. Can you feel that cum getting ready, boy?" said the man, running a hand across Cody's solid ass. It clenched to stone at every thrust.

Cody batted the hand away.

The watcher spit on his fingertips and reached between Cody's hairless thighs. He caught the stud's nuts between his fingers and pulled them gently but insistently. He rubbed them in the smooth caress of his palm.

Cody hooked his hands over the partition and widened his stance. He was beyond all concern. If anyone came in, there would be nothing he could do. He couldn't stop, not now. It was too fucking good, and still the sucking continued. Slurps and pops rose as mouth and hand drew a load. Though only a hole, it felt detached and exact all at once.

Cody felt pinned, one hand holding his balls while another pressed his abdomen, and his body was forced against the partition. A great power was lifting the cum from him. Release through his dick was the only way to escape the feeling of being trapped. The eye of his cock was the point of propulsion. He rose on his toes and clenched his thighs, firmly gripping the wrist between them.

His back arched and his ass quivered. A flush of red ran from his toes to his face. His lips curled back from his teeth and his moans grew louder. His cock expanded. The ridge between the crown and the shaft widened as the insistent tongue lapped its circumference. The pounding hand stroked him, sliding on the excess saliva. The head of Cody's cock was everything—the point of escape, of freedom. Cold metal pressed against his chest and flattened his nipples to the cool scratched steel. A loud moan escaped from deep inside him, echoing in the cavernous men's room as he felt himself exploding, bucking the metal partition in freedom and release.

THE VOICE OF THE CAPON

ALEX JEFFERS

Saturday, 13 March 1993

Dearest heart, life yourself,

I could phone you easily enough—speed-dial button A, one touch—although I'd probably wake you up. Or I could take my life, and my key to your apartment, into my hands and venture out into the blizzard. I timed myself once: it takes twelve minutes to walk from here to there. Even in this storm, it wouldn't be much longer. But then again I'd wake you, and you said you'd had a tough week. And you said—these were your words: "It hasn't snowed properly for three winters—you're out of practice." Just a moment ago, I saw the clouds light up for an instant and heard thunder: never before, in a snowstorm.

So instead, I'll sit in front of the computer. I've set it to remind me to save my documents every ten minutes, because the radio warned to worry about power outages. Somehow I still think of snowfall as quiet, a gentle event: I'm a Californian. Around noon, the printer ran out of paper, so I girded my loins and donned my boots for a visit to the office-supply store around the block. First the wind nearly knocked me down, then the snow in my eyes blinded me and froze most uncomfortably in my mustache and nostrils. The drifts on the sidewalk were over my ankles—over the tops of the boots. I couldn't see across the street. Cars at the curb wore six-inch-thick helmets of snow, sat in drifts to their axles, shouldered up against three-foot berms where a plow had passed, blocking them in. And then, when I got to the store, it was closed. As was the twenty-four-hour convenience store next door—that's when I knew this was serious business. Still, I'm sure I could make it over to your place. But the blizzard will have blown over before I'm ready to print this out.

In Elizabeth Bowen's novels and stories, she takes for granted that a letter mailed in the morning will reach its destination across London in the afternoon delivery. This even during the Blitz. This letter, if I were to take it down to the mailbox on the curb, wouldn't reach you for two, three days, even in clear weather—I suppose it goes first to Worcester or Springfield to be sorted. If you want rapid delivery you use the fax or call a messenger. No wonder no one writes letters. Faster to drop it off myself. But in fact in this instance I count on the delay, and count on our being snowed in tomorrow— is your larder stocked, Ethan?—on your going to work Monday morning.

You see, the printer ran out of paper because it was spitting out the new manuscript, five hundred plus pages; I was at loose ends all morning, listening to the printer's annoying thip-thip *(tedious continuo for the Handel* Orlando *I was listening to with the other ear), watching each sheet squeeze through the aperture into the tray. I drank a great deal of coffee. For some reason I didn't want to call you—or anyone else for that matter—and the cats, insensitive as only they can be, were asleep. I thought of baking bread or making cookies but couldn't find the energy or the ingredients. As usual, on finishing something, I sat on that knife-edge between exhilaration and despair when you can't comprehend that eighteen months' labor and passion are* done, *and you can't imagine what you'll do next. It's at these times and few others I feel I ought to have a proper job. I was no fit company—for myself, for Element or Enkidu, for you. The countertenor taking the castrato-contralto role of Orlando went mad for love, his unrealistically high voice dodging from secco to arioso recitative to cavatina and back. I read Jack's book. You told me not to.*

I shouldn't even remember who he is. How long is it since I last saw him—since he broke my heart? The summer before I moved east: 1984, nine years. I shouldn't even remember who he is. The photo on the jacket flap reveals how he's changed—or I've changed; he could be anyone, any man in his middle thirties, hardly even handsome, let alone the beauty I remember. His forehead, always high, reaches nearly to the crown of his skull. I don't remember his face being so round. New beard and unflattering new glasses make it rounder. I remember his profile, his splendid nose as big as Gibraltar.

I fear I would be less distraught, less unhappy, less disoriented if I were in Jack's novel, however distorted the caricature, if there were some evidence that he hadn't plucked me off his skin, crushed me, as easily as if I were a flea, as easily forgotten. But then, I never wrote about him, except obsessively, for a short period, for him alone—with the sure certainty he would never read it.

This is a lie. You know: I wrote to you. What a ghastly archive must be

*your file of my letters. And still there are tricks of him all over my work:
his height (you're tall, but he was taller); his habitual white leather sneak-
ers and a particular deep blue flannel shirt that I often longed to wear and
his little round tortoiseshell spectacles; his big eloquent hands and elegant big nose. Tricks, traces. I don't remember the color of his eyes. I
cannot recall his voice, low, ostentatiously quiet so that one had to lean in,
as though to hear a confidence. Was it baritone or tenor, chest or head?
I've used his apartment any number of times, though it's usually me living
in that spartan studio, not him; I never (hardly ever) write in the direct historical present about San Francisco because—see here—there is San
Francisco before Jack, anticipating, and after Jack, regretting, but I cannot
get a handle on during Jack. I've written him over so many times, so many
times reinvented him, I wouldn't recognize the man if I met him (I don't recognize the author of this dreadful book which I believe I could admire,
while disliking it, if his name weren't on the cover) and yet I remain convinced—vain fear!—that he will recognize himself, and me.*

*You see how (why) I couldn't phone you. All (almost all) of these dam-
aged, fragmented portraits of Jack are simultaneously faulty pictures of you.*

*There is a particular variety of irrealism derided as operatic. I revile that
variety of opera even as I revel (wallow) in the unreal, the overstated case.
I never loved Jack (there: it's said—are you relieved?): I went mad for love.*
Handel's achievement throughout this scene, as elsewhere in the opera,
is to convey a sense of disorder and chaos in music which by its very
nature has to be highly organized; this he does by juxtaposing ideas often
disparate in tempo and rhythm but held together by an unerring control
of the underlying harmonic progressions. *This, from the booklet accompa-
nying my three-CD box, reads better in Italian*—Il merito di Händel in tutta
questa scena come pure nel resto dell'opera, è quello di communicare un
senso di disordine e caos tramite una musica che per sua stessa natura
deve essere altamente organizzata, *etc—just as the libretto does. Oh, if—if
only!—I could take it for my manifesto. I aspire to the eighteenth century
but only ever hit the nineteenth and then, ashamed, revolted, slather over
it a twentieth-century varnish such that even my editor, I think, even my
agent believe I'm writing, as it were, real life. In English.*

As, no doubt, Jack believes he does.

*And you, when you want legitimate vocal music, prefer the austere
unaccompanied sonorities of medieval Latin, the massed, monophonic
tenor thunder of monks. This I adore about you, dear, did you know? The
choirs and cloisters where Gregorian chant echoes in my mind are not,
dare I say, chaste, Christian spaces though they are, yes, holy, dedicated.
Your thoughtful scowl as you listen, immersed. Your distance, your sweet*

concentration, your slowness to rouse. Baroque counterpoint and orna-
ment, I've heard you say, are all very well instrumentally, but add voice—
single, duple, ensemble, choral—it goes all to hell, you can't keep track.

About Jack I don't know. Nine years ago, he said he liked the same
rock I did—or was it that I liked what he did?—but of what one must call
classical music we never spoke. We spoke about everything, I thought. We
talked, for instance, far more about sex than we ever did it.

You know all this. I talked to him—I wrote to you. You know all this.
You, I imagine, have already read the book you advised me not to read,
and if you found me in it you will either tell me or you won't.

Now, for in fact I never stop working, there's never not something else to
work on, I will open a new window on the screen. That last paragraph
admits of no development. There are other projects. With scarcely any evi-
dence of my competence to fill the brief, an editor in Manhattan has
invited me to contribute a story to an anthology of new erotica. He sug-
gests he would prefer a first-person narrative. Shall I write about you,
Ethan—our deepest, most sordid secrets? (Do we have any?) Or about
Jack? Or make something up completely?

I rumpled the cats' heads where they lay snoozing on the bed—Element
snarled at me, Enkidu purred and drooled and asked if it were dinner-
time...at three-thirty in the AM. He followed me into the kitchen, still begging,
when I went to make another espresso. Outside the window, a blowing,
glowing curtain of snow brushed against the glass, scraped with an arid,
hissy noise against the screen. Out there, it must be quite cold. In here, radi-
ators clank and spit and radiate and I stalk about (or sit at my desk) stark
naked, sweating, sweltering. While the espresso pot built up its little head
of steam, I turned on the radio, listened—aghast—to five or ten minutes of
furious alternative rock. It's Sunday now, I'm not in the mood. It's Sunday: I
don't know the Catholic ecclesiastical calendar, but I believe it's Lent. That
is, not Carnival. Carnival, historically, is the season for opera.

George Frideric Handel (or Georg Friedrich Händel), though German
and presumably Lutheran by birth, living in Protestant London and
patronized by a German Protestant king, wrote opera seria to Italian
libretti for the voices of Italian (presumably Catholic) singers. Germany
interests me scarcely at all, Britain hardly more. Orlando, of course, is
based (very freely) on Ariosto, an enduring passion. In the 1730s,
Handel's greatest rival for the allegiance of opera-going London society

was the Neapolitan Nicola Porpora. I have no proper Italian eighteenth-century opera on CD. (There exist, I understand, several Vivaldi dramme per musica on Ariostovian themes, but I've never encountered one recorded.) When, demitasse in hand, I returned to my desk and purring computer, I put on a selection of Vivaldi concerti. Any day of the week, I'll choose Venice over Naples.

"Zanni!" Domenico bellowed my name across the crowded parterre. In case I had failed to hear, he climbed up on his chair and waved his hands over his head, grinning his lackwit grin. "Over here, Zanni!"

I waved back, for everyone already knew we were friends, and began to work my way toward him. His grin widening—many another of his acquaintances would have ignored him—he remained perched on his chair, in plain sight. Ever ready to play the fool, he pulled three bright oranges from a pocket and started to juggle. They flew magically between his hands, someone laughed for sheer pleasure, and by the time I reached my friend, a circle of admirers surrounded him. In the boxes, I imagined, jaded patricians were placing bets as to when Domenico would fumble, hiding behind their painted fans as they peered down from a gilded height, making petty, hissy remarks out of the corners of their mouths. For a fact, a number of those applauding Domenico wore garments of noble quality, though they were, of course, masked. I shouldered one such handsome specimen aside with an apology he had to accept, it being Carnival. Domenico ended his show by tossing two of the oranges to me—I caught them, one in either hand—and collapsing onto his seat in a move that appeared clumsy but was not.

"I knew you'd come," he said when I sat down beside him. Ignoring jocular pleas for an encore, he busied himself peeling the last orange. Little scraps of golden rind fell to the floor; a breath of sharp fragrance wafted up from his ugly, blunt-fingered, clever hands, from the moist red flesh of the fruit.

"Of course I came. How could I not?"

"He won't be as good as they say, you know." Domenico peered at me sidelong, up from under his eyebrows. He was so ugly people assumed he was insensitive and imbecile as well, ugly of soul. My friend took a kind of bitter satisfaction in confirming their expectations, a tactic I appreciated but which appalled me. In affected, swooning tones, he crooned, "Il evirato divino! Il Peccatino!...The sin will be his subjecting us to his voice."

"He'll squawk like a goose," I agreed.

"And the music," Domenico muttered. "I dread to imagine it. These Neapolitan hacks, their scores aren't fit to wipe Maestro Vivaldi's behind."

"Contrary," I said, "This one's said to have studied under both Scarlatti. Perhaps he was teachable."

"Dreamer." Domenico pressed a sour-sweet segment of orange between my lips. Because he expected it, because he was my only real friend, because I loved him even as, often enough, he disgusted or mortified me, I kissed his sticky fingertips. The second bit of orange was followed by Domenico's index finger, the nail scraping my tongue, tickling it. He laughed in my ear, a breathy *heh-heh*, pressed his knee against mine, with his free hand tugged proprietarily at my pigtail. Then, satisfied he'd made a scandal of us both, he sucked a piece of orange into his own mouth and, chewing, said, "It's a Roman cast."

Only in his own temporal state is the Pope able to enforce the Church's ban against women's appearing on stage. Pronounced with the deepest disdain, Domenico's remark was meant to annoy me. I was spared having to reply by the appearance of the composer, taking his seat at the continuo harpsichord. There were jeers. From a balcony above the orchestra, a patrician lady tossed a gnawed chicken bone, her cicisbeo snickering at the fun. No-one likes a Neapolitan. Least of all a youthful Neapolitan who has scored a triumph in Rome and dares to bring the identical show, a year later, to Venice, mother of the opera. Naturally, the house was full. I had had to pay to enter, as, in respect of my profession, I seldom did. But no-one much was here for the music— Domenico and I, perhaps, excepted.

In their boxes, patricians bickered and railed, played at cards, sipped chocolate and coffee and wine, nibbled at pastries and little roast partridges, planned assignations or, indeed, in shadowed recesses, made love. On the parterre, the commons grumbled and fidgeted. Some of us, if we could read, leafed through the libretto—the poet, too, was a rank upstart, though a Florentine; others, still more accomplished, scanned broadsheet scores of arias that were already notorious, although unheard in Venice—tracing the complex staves and humming, perhaps, under the breath. Urchins selling spiced nuts, confits, greasy lukewarm sausage, wandered through the mob, crying their wares in high, desolate trebles, while others watched for ready purses or promised, for the most minimal of considerations, to run speedy errands. "Two sweet coffees, signori? It is done already!" The boy flashed me a grin of startling beauty as he pocketed my coins, and dashed away. One's ears had to be wide open, inured to the din, to catch the orchestra beginning.

The overture commenced pleasantly enough, what one could hear of it. Certain of the musicians, though, themselves were lackadaisical, careless. No Neapolitan parvenu could expect to have the respect of Venetian players. I thought the score nicely constructed, if too pretty, and it annoyed me how poorly they performed the little required of them. Domenico grumbled voicelessly beside me. At his keyboard, the composer doggedly kept time. I could clearly see the malevolent glares he cast at first violin, who, keeping a shamelessly straight face, continued shamelessly to drop or misread notes, throwing the rest of the strings into turmoil. The composer's cheeks went from flush to pallor to flush. Domenico's grumbles grew louder. At length, as the violinist made hash of a fragile cadenza, my friend uttered a belch of outrage and hauled himself gracelessly up onto the seat of his chair.

"Are you a musician, Stefano Manin, or a clown?" he shouted, his voice cracking with scorn. The violinist's bow scraped across the strings with a spiteful shriek and his cheeks blushed the crimson of the velvet curtains across the stage. The second, behind him, a more conscientious musician, took the opportunity to smack his crown with his bow. "In paradise your sainted mamma is weeping for shame," Domenico continued, his tone at once mournful and hectoring, echoing across the suddenly hushed theatre. One was not to be surprised he knew the violinist's name and family. A single startled guffaw rang out from a high box, and the composer, white as bleached linen, covered his eyes with both hands. Glancing up at my friend, his ugly face contorted in fury, I felt as mortified as the composer. "You will apologize at once to the maestro, Stefano," Domenico ordered, "and then you will play the notes he has written for you to the best of your competence, or you will step down and allow a proper musician your place. You hear?"

I watched the composer's livid features as he accepted the violinist's apology—so servile as to be graceful—and when Domenico, satisfied, clambered down from his pulpit, I murmured, "You've made an enemy there."

"Stefano? He'll be boasting of this night for weeks."

The urchin chose that moment to return with our coffees. Trembling with awe, he offered the cups to Domenico, though I had bought them. When I took mine from the tray, he started, nearly upsetting it. Downing his in one swallow, Domenico scowled at the boy, who smiled with beatific terror and ran away.

"The maestro," I said.

"That one?" Domenico grunted. "That milksop? If he's not a eunuch he might as well be." He patted my hand. "Now, sit back and listen, Zanni. I have braved the risk of his hired stilettos solely for your pleasure."

Played over from the beginning, the overture received more respectful attention than, no doubt, the composer had known since hot-house days in the conservatory. Mostly it wasn't deserved. A pointlessly virtuoso passage in the highest register of the strings, which Stefano led with perfect aplomb, inspired a few cries of "Bravo!" I held my coffee to my lips, tasting its sweet-bitter heat on my tongue, awaiting the voices.

A flourish, a fanfare. The curtains swept wide, revealing an exquisite pasteboard set, the formal gardens of a fine Palladian villa on terraferma, though it was meant to represent the palace of King Minos in Crete. A mossy grotto to the side did for the entrance of the labyrinth, and in its shadowy mouth stood a figure meant to be terrifying: a stocky person, in rags, wearing the mask of a bull's head that left jaw and mouth exposed for him to sing, and with tall, gilded horns. From the wings entered the Teseo, a tall, elegant, martial figure, and he, a fine contralto, and baritone Minotaur exchanged recitative threats.

Then, with such subtlety that one noticed the sudden presence, not the arrival, entered the Arianna. This primo uomo, of whom we had heard so much—his like had not been heard since Farinelli's début, they said—wore a great gown of crimson velvet, gold tissue, white linen and lace. Surmounted by a towering elaboration of powder-white wig, face and neck and breast were painted lead white, glistening. Bruised with caustic black cosmetic, the eyes glowed hugely, dark, liquid—dosed with belladonna, doubtless. Parting scarlet lips, he voiced a brief recitative aside on the manly charms of Teseo, expressing regret that he must be devoured by the cruel monster. He sang, the Arianna, this passage at what must be the bottom of his register—he was said to be a high, brilliant soprano—astonishing in its control, very simple and nearly ugly, and then was silent, still as a figure in German porcelain.

With rare subtlety or insane bravado, the young Neapolitan had composed his first aria not for either of the castrati—given more established singers, he would not have dared slight them so—but the baritone monster. It was competent, unexceptionable; the beast sang adequately, accepted with bovine dignity his lackluster applause, and retreated within his cave.

Over tedious continuo, primo and secondo uomi bantered back and forth for a bit, lame verse unredeemed by the trick of one's rhyming the other's lines, the second exercising his clear, promising contralto, the first maintaining his chilling, constrained attack, as affected as a basso's burlesque falsetto. Growing bored, Domenico began to caress my knee. I kept my eyes on the Arianna, willing him actually to sing, to possess the voice that was promised. The technique he had, clearly, to spare.

I was not for an instant convinced that he was a woman, but the illusion was flawless: he was lovely, inhumanly perfect, lacquered, brilliant, brittle. Myself, who had never—to my friends' amusement and disgust—bedded nor wished to bed a woman, I was entranced. The proportions of his face were odd, overstated—the black eyes set far apart and as large in the pointed face as a cat's, the brows rising strangely high in perfect painted bows. The nose was long, with deep flaring nostrils. Settled in a complacent half smile, crimson lips nevertheless stretched wider across the narrow jaw than seemed possible. A black patch—assassina—lengthened the line of the mouth on the right, giving it an eccentric, lascivious little quirk; another—passionata—was applied at the corner of the left eye, a glittering black gem on the crown of the cheekbone.

They moved about, the Arianna and the Teseo, in a grand slow ballet like the movements of stars in the firmament, singing at while never physically acknowledging each other, pacing slow measures among potted shrubs on the stage, the one a donna nobile in red and gold, the other a cavaliere eroico in blue and silver, neither either woman or man. I stared up at the grand figures on the stage, while the composer struck manfully at the keys of his harpsichord, continuo cellist and bassist sawed at their strings, and Domenico kept up under his breath a hummed accompaniment that never faltered, so predictable was the music, despite the cunning forays his left hand made on my thigh.

Both arrived at the front of the stage, on opposite sides, the actors halted. Viols throbbed a little in the pit, and the Arianna sang a question—a query of the other castrato it was, but the singer gazed into the audience. Giving his superbly controlled voice a little rein, he allowed it to move up into the lower range of what must be his proper tessitura, a long, sustained note without the slightest vibrato, and I thought he was staring directly at me. Slowly, heavy eyelids lowered, brushed black lashes at the tops of his cheeks, then rose.

"Ah, dio!" softly exclaimed Domenico, removing his inquiring hand from my lap, for strings and winds had come swelling up over the tinkling harpsichord, and the Teseo launched into his first aria. "The voice of the capon!" murmured my friend, who felt more for music than any other man of my acquaintance.

It is nothing to say the conservatories of Naples train up the most spectacular voices—everyone knows. Our own four ospedali train little nightingale orphans as rigorously, to similarly brilliant effect—my own dead mother had studied under and sung for Vivaldi in the Pietà—but those pious young women are required never to perform on the public stage. A Neapolitan castrato's voice, the exercise of it, is his life, and that city is mad for eunuchs. Of a Sunday morning, they say, when files of gelded orphans wend from conservatory to cathedral, piping in sweet treble all the way, old ladies hang from windows high overhead, lovesick as young girls, tossing flowers and crying, "Angels! Precious angels!" I, who had scarcely ever set foot on terraferma, citizen of the ancient, enduring, misty and watery and most serene Republic of Venice, felt that I might have been happy had I been born a cast-off orphan of that arid, grandiloquent, chaotic southern kingdom with its tyrannical aristocracy that was Spanish, French, Austrian, never Italian. For all that the Neapolitan conservatories raise up—instrumentalists, composers, and whole male singers as well—the castrato is king.

This Teseo was neither the best nor the worst. His tessitura was low for a contralto; the composer might have exploited it better. He strained for his top notes, going strident in the ornaments, where he was perfectly comfortable in a range not much higher than a natural tenor's. Here and in his middle register, he justified a place as secondo uomo, exhibiting perfect clarity and control, ornamenting the melody with admirable tact. If not great, it was a good voice, in the exercise of which his training was evident but did not insist. This was merely the first of his six arias and the least of them; he did not put himself out unduly, was awarded with warm though not ecstatic applause, which he acknowledged handsomely. There were a few cries of "Bravo!"—including one from the seat beside mine. Domenico said quietly, confidently, "Signor Capon hasn't shown us nearly all he's got." Then—my friend had no manners and precious little subtlety—he began again to feed me bits of orange, touching fingertips to lips and jaw in the manner of a caress.

I had listened with appreciation but never taken my eyes off the primo uomo in his extraordinary gown, who had turned half-away when the contralto stood forward to deliver his aria—had lowered the lids over those magnificent eyes and slightly, judgmentally compressed his smile. Now—Teseo having exited—he turned again; once again, so I thought, gazed into my eyes. To the accompaniment of high oboes, breathy recorders, subdued strings, he essayed a plain, simple, andante cavatina. His voice was allowed to open up slightly, promising if not delivering a potent, intoxicating sweetness.

Singing in this pure, artless, old-fashioned manner, he drifted to center stage. Winds dropped out, archlute in bass doubled harpsichord, massed strings commenced a repetitive up-and-down pattern. There was nothing in the world but the castrato's voice.

"Oh!" I believe I said—I moaned in my own lame, famished voice, "oh, sant' angelo!" There are words to describe beauty, to describe perfection, every one of them halt, imperfect, unbeautiful unless they were to be scored for the castrato's voice. There was his voice, there was nothing more, nothing gross or trivial, and I wept. I wept, and the cords in my own throat vibrated and swelled, my lungs ached to contain the volume of burning air that could not be let free, my eyes stared though I wished to close them, in my breeches my sex, idiot child, grossly sensitive to my passion, stiffened. And all the while he sang, the castrato gazed gravely down into my eyes, his own imperturbable.

There was his singing, and there were times when he did not sing. When he left the stage after the third encore of his first aria, I lost my breath, and then caught it again in a solid jagged block that tore at the tender flesh of my throat. I will die now, I thought, fulfilled, but lived on in dreadful anticipation of his return. Besides the three principals, the cast included a basso-profondo King Minos, bluster and majesty; a foppish Cretan prince, tenor, affianced to Arianna and spurned by her; and a boy Cupid who may have been gelded or simply young—his treble was tremulous and, in itself, lovely. I could not bear to hear them, any of them.

During the first intermezzo, when a troupe of gay dancers pranced on stage to sprightly airs and jigs, Domenico led me outside to the water-stairs above the chilly canal. Moved himself, my friend tried to comfort me, to cajole me out of my exaltation. When sly words failed, and acute critiques of the music, the players, the singers—even Domenico's bitter tongue despaired of anything disparaging to say of the soprano—he fell to other, wordless methods.

I wished to push him off but had not the strength, felt defiled by the slobbery pressure of his lips on mine. Distantly, I was revolted by these attentions I had been happy to allow him at other times; when he opened my shirt and scraped the nails of his fingers through the hair on my chest, it seemed that his cold hands were exhalations, coagulations of the stagnant sewage scent off the canal near our feet. Nevertheless, my sex rose up again when he fondled it through the fabric of my breeches, when he kissed my nipples and kneaded them with his teeth. When he opened the breeches to let the thing out, it wilted in the dank winter air, but then he knelt to the clammy step and took it into his mouth. His beard stubble scraped on my thighs.

I remembered the duet between soprano Arianna and contralto Teseo, more duel than duet though they sang of their passion for each other. They sang, contralto forced to the edge of his ability and beyond into brilliances of pitch and ornament by soprano's sure attack. One heard that the lesser singer would be mediocre, next to nothing, without the greater's goading. One heard him aspire to his very height, straining, reach it, and hang there pinned to the empyrean while the other soared effortlessly above. Nor was it simply the one's having the higher voice, for the contralto's part was written low, well within his range; nor did it require less vocal agility, less virtuoso ornamentation, so it wasn't that he was made to sound petty.

And yet, despite the failings of the Teseo and the overarching ambition and reach of the Arianna, their voices played exquisitely together, cello against violin or bassoon against oboe, alternating, or mingling, doubling, or running in counterpoint. At times, veiling his eyes, soprano held back, scarcely grazing the melody, singing at low volume but with such penetrating sweetness that the hair on my arms stood up and sweat burst forth on my brow, while contralto at full pitch ran a single phrase into extravagant confusions of fioritura, tremolo, appoggiatura, vibrato. Then, raising his pointed chin, opening wide his burning eyes that cut into my soul as knives into flesh, soprano would ride over contralto's continuo line, ascending in flame like the phoenix. His top notes lay inhumanly high, yet he reached for them with ease, grappling them like blazing stars, setting them off like pyrotechnics and grand illuminations.

He was staring at me, the great eyes harsh, the voice teetering on an extended trill at unnatural height that went on and on, gradually swelling in fulness and volume, until I was breathless and my skull pounded with the echo of those two notes, and then without warning, on a little catch of his throat, the voice dropped a full octave, as if it were a sob. It ought to have been gratuitous and clumsy: it was devastating. I seemed to see an explosion of vast white light as all the tension in my body released at once, but what I saw was the glistening liquid collected on the lower lids of his staring eyes, collected, swelling to overflow but not flowing, as his voice began again the terrible, irresistible ascent.

Spent, horrified and exultant, I pushed Domenico gently away. He had his own member in his hand. A vagrant gleam of light from a torch guttering in the breeze showed a dribble of slime on his chin, caused a puddle of slime near my feet to glow spectrally. The canal lapped against the waterstairs and the foundations of the theatre. Moored gondolas, my own among them, scraped their flanks together or struck one against another with hollow thumps. Above us, at the entrance where pitch-soaked torches crackled and flared, a small party of masked patricians conversed in brittle tones. One took a pinch of snuff, sneezed, and proclaimed he had seldom seen a woman as handsome as that castrato. "She'd unman you in an instant," replied another. "Why, she's a foot taller than you, man! Your family jewels would shrivel up to nothing in a hand that size."

"Zanni." Tentative, fumbling at the front of his breeches, Domenico sidled nearer.

"No, Domenico. Not now, carissimo. I cannot." I was still hearing the castrato's voice in my head, seeing his eyes. I spat into the noisome waters of the canal. My breeches were still open, my prick still hard. I took it in my hand and it disgusted me. Stepping closer to the water, I held the thing, its gross turgid heft, and pissed into the canal. Over the sound of my own water, I heard one of the patricians saying in lewd tones that it was well known castrati might play some form of the man to a besotted woman, yet they far preferred to play the woman to a proper man.

I continued to hear the Arianna's voice in my mind, singing arioso to a simple accompaniment in the low strings, and it was something I had not heard him sing, something new, something I had never heard before. He was not singing in my head, a disembodied phantom voice vital and necessary as the air I breathed, echoing in the bones of my skull, in the cavities of my lungs, in the stretched, bruised cords of my throat. He was singing within the hall, the least thread of his voice fraying out through open doors, over the jocular laughter of the drunken patricians, the lapping of the canal against the step, and the hiss of my urine hitting the water. The second act had begun. I hadn't heard it.

All the muscles in my body clenched hard on the devastating realization. My pissing stuttered to a painful halt. Stuffing my dribbling prick into my breeches, fumbling at the fastenings like the burlesque buffoon in a street comedy, I stumbled up the slippery stairs, colliding as I passed with one of the patricians. He shouted, but saw, I suppose, that I was not an aristocrat, was a roughneck gondolier bigger than he, appeared not to be in my full senses—he did not follow. Nor did Domenico, my friend, whom I must have hurt. I couldn't care, for I had passed through the ridotto, pressed through a clot of indistinguishable persons at the inner door.

What I had heard from outside was recitativo stromentato—the second act had begun, but no arias yet sung. But full orchestral accompaniment and lyrical rather than declamatory recitative meant to introduce an especially brilliant aria. Arianna and her father were on stage, he gloating over the fate of Teseo lost in the labyrinth, she decrying it and apostrophizing the reel of thread that was to lead him out of the maze should he manage to slay the Minotaur.

Trembling, wiping my fouled hands on my thighs, I found my seat and sank into it. It seemed to me that the castrato acknowledged my return with a slight narrowing of the eyes that might be approval, might be disdain. I took in a great, silent, sobbing breath, my first, it almost seemed, since catching that thread of his voice by the canal. With a last basso chuckle, the Cretan king left the stage. The orchestra commenced a brittle, fast, violent attack. Arianna looked from side to side, turned about in a circle, the velvet skirts of the gown billowing, and sang. I was lost, again, consumed in glory.

Ethan, I will remind you of your grotesquely early call this morning (only you would have the gall, at six fifteen AM *Sunday!, so of course I answered). "What's up?" you asked.*

"My big cock." The right hand slimy with lube and precome, I held the phone in my left.

"Oh—you're writing porn again."

"The precise term is erotica.*"*

"I was going to say it's a day for coffee and cigarettes and toaster-waffles, watching bad TV in our pajamas, and you should come over here, but I guess you've got your hands full."

My handful had diminished considerately. "Have you looked outside, babe? A drift the size of California nearly got me yesterday—I'm not going out there again till spring."

"You're such a wuss sometimes, Alex." I heard you rooting around in the nightstand by your appallingly big bed. "You want some phone nookie, then, to tide you over? Since you've already started the job."

"There are days when I simply adore you, lover."

You snorted. "That's the way it is, hey?"

"No, what I mean is, I'm sorry I'm such a mess. Been such a mess for such a long time. I hit the big one yesterday, Ethan. It's finished."

A whoop in C-sharp. "Alex! Alessandro mio, and you didn't call me—? Well, fuck you, dearest."

"That's what I'm hoping…when the slush melts."

"The hell you say. Did you print it out? Your sordid passions are just gonna have to wait, babes. I've got some reading to do—I'm on my way. I'll bring the waffles. You have coffee?"

"Ethan," I said deliberately. "What are you wearing?"

…Dinner tonight at your place. (I'm listening to Gregorian chant now. Blessèd relief.) I'll bring the manuscript. Speedy reader that you are, you'll have finished it (before my agent gets his copy or my editor hers) before you receive this one in the mail. And how many more times before that day will I have said this very line to you, face to face: I love you. Repeat it. Repeat it again.

OXOXOX
Alex

WHISKEY DICKS

RICK JACKSON

We'd already been deployed together for five long, sweaty, tedious months before we pulled into our Thai liberty port. In that time, I'd spent as much time around Donny Lee as anyone. We were berthed in the same compartment. We worked out together every day. I knew him as well as I knew myself—maybe that was why I was so confused.

We'd no sooner dropped anchor off Phuket, Thailand, than we escaped in the first liberty boat. Both of us were slamming back Kloster's lagers before our feet were dry. By 1500, we were shit-faced enough to rent some whores and a hotel room to do them in and then tend to business. I'd seen Donny Lee naked every day for the last five months as we showered, lay in our racks, or stroked around the berthing compartment trying to cool down.

So why the fuck couldn't I keep my mind on the pussy wrapped around my dick? Why did my eyes keep straying across the few feet to the next bed to watch Donny's tight Marine butt arching up towards the ceiling as he pulled back and slammed everything he had down hard into the rental bitch below him? Why did my mind keep wandering away from the tight, wet hole wrapped around my own unit to worry about what his hard Marine body was up to? Why did the sight of that muscular butt bobbing up and down blend together with the memory of his bitch playing with the thick dick I'd seen so often set my guts to lurching? That dick didn't look familiar, somehow.

It wasn't just a hunk of meat swinging low; it was mystery and adventure and other emotions beyond my imaginings. I'd been used to ignoring it as it slapped between his thighs when we padded unselfconsciously around berthing. A guy checked peckers to see who had big

129

ones or not, but dicks were just dicks—they weren't anything to get excited about. Why were my guts in a fucking uproar?

Humping the hole below me, I heard his grunts and moans of pleasure—and those of the girls, which were somehow irrelevant—as he slammed away. I heard the slap of his flesh against the body beneath him and caught myself almost wishing it were mine. Across the yard of space separating us, every ripple of his hard young body savagely rutting away was a rush. The way he talked dirty to his bitch and clenched his jaw and curled that Corps-driven cock deeper up into her guts with every stroke all seemed infinitely more interesting than anything my busy jarhead unit was into. When he lifted his face from the pillow and glanced in my direction with that bright-eyed smile of his, my guts exploded out through my dick in a surge of spumy satisfaction unlike anything even in my most salacious dreams.

I felt my body contort and heard my surprised barks of confused desperation echo off the walls as I blew my load, but I might as well have been alone. I suppose the girl did her job well enough, making the appropriate noises and clawing at my back—but she and her discomfort at my size were both immaterial to my pleasure. I heard Donny Lee yell shit about not fucking her into a coma because I'd need her later, but the sound of his voice just tore at my guts. What the fuck was wrong with me?

I kept on humping, matching the cadence in the next bed bang for slam, until Donny Lee raised himself up off the bed, still thrusting away, but talking to me while he was servicing his whore. His hard, hairless chest was dripping sweat; looking deep, I could see the vicious shadow of his thick Marine dick stroking in and out of the girl's sloshy hole. I tried to ignore his lunging muscles and thrusting dick to concentrate on the male-bonding shit he was talking, but the strange, simple sound of his familiar voice was too much. For the second time in ten minutes, my balls caught fire and nearly launched my ass into orbit as they jetted out blast after wicked blast of my jarhead jism.

I picked up speed almost at once to blow a third nut, but my whore needed a break, even if I didn't. She gibbered at me in Thai and wriggled her gushing cunt out from under me as I collapsed onto the sheet, a physical wreck. She limped into the head, still muttering about big-dicked Americans and how thoughtless we are.

When I heard the shower start up, I looked back over to Donny Lee and saw him starting to strain. His body was pounding like some extraterrestrial fucking machine run amok, but the expression on his face looked like nothing but the end of a twenty-five-mile hump. He was still grunting shit about how my dick was still hard and how I was a bigger whore than either of the bitches, but his concentration was between his legs. Then his girl started whining about him taking too long and he let slip the awful truth. I'd been admiring his studly stamina and endurance, but the dumb grunt was just shit-faced. He had the whiskey dick of creation and couldn't bust a nut no matter how hard a charger he was.

Somehow the idea that even his pro couldn't take his load pumped my nads like nothing in my young life. I knew I was going to fucking cripple my bitch when she came back, but meanwhile I'd kill some time by fucking with my buddy. Fucking with your buddy is what Marines are all about—I just didn't know how true that was. But, just then, I didn't know dick about life or love or especially, the warrior lust two comrades in arms can feel.

I swear I wasn't trying any fag shit. I just wanted to mess with his mind until my hole limped back to bed to take care of me and mine. When I knelt beside his bed and grabbed his whore's tit, he just kept humping solidly away, slamming that thick dick up into her wet hole as my peter pounded out its need against my belly and I kept misreading the signals like the clueless bastard I was.

When I gave him a wet willie, it just set him to grudge-fucking his bitch all the harder—and made my mouth water something fierce. I moved down between his feet to scope out the action in my first live fuck-flick. The sight of that dick slamming deep, those huge, hairy balls pounding down, and especially that pink pucker of a butthole pulsing with every clenching stroke sent me round the bend.

Even when I reached up and shoved my thumb against his butthole, I don't think I had a clue. Donny jumped about three feet farther up her cunt and yelled back that I was a fucking faggot, but I was too busy weirding out to believe him. I patted his naked butt like an understanding DI with a retarded recruit and moved back up to watch the expression on his face as he slammed away.

By then of course, the babe was dry and tired and was seriously giving him shit, too. He kept his eyes shut and his attention focused, but the dick was just too pickled to breed. Finally, he was about to give up and let his hole join mine in the shower when inspiration struck. For the first time in my life, I was brilliant. The clouds parted, the light switched on, and I knew what I had to do as I'd never known anything before. He'd go off on me later, but later was later.

As his cadence wound down in disgust, I ragged his ass, telling him what a boot he was, a lame grunt who just plain didn't know how to fuck. When I bragged, I could make him blow the biggest load since the Saturn V inside three minutes, he told me what I was full of. We bitched back and forth, but I knew he was hooked. When he bet me twenty bucks I couldn't, I told him to start humping away again and ignore me.

To be a nice guy, I lubed up as I'd never lubed before. Donny picked up his rhythm again and was dicking harder and faster than ever with a new-found determination and the confidence that out of the jaws of masculine defeat, he was at least about to snatch twenty dollars that would go far towards the next day's beer bill. I started on his sweaty spine, easing my hand hard down his back until it hit his tail-bone. I'd had a tomcat once who'd loved having the base of his tail rubbed; Donny went apeshit: "Oh, Jesus! Yes! Fuck that feels...."

He didn't get any farther, because once I'd gotten up close and personal, I shoved my swollen nine inches of jarhead joint hard up his unsuspecting hole in the worst case of back-stabbing buddy-fucking ever to happen in the Corps—an institution well-known for both. His head whipped backwards in reflex, followed by his torso. His dick drilled new ground inside his sweetie, and every howl and shriek and cry of Hell ripped out of his lungs at once. I slammed my hands around his chest, slipping in the unfamiliar country of another man's sweaty body; but I knew at once I'd been right. Maybe I was queer, but if this was queer, they could call me Nellie.

One delicious new sensation followed another like a cascading house of cards: the tight clutch of his butthole about the base of my dick, the slick welcome his guts gave my swollen shank, the foxy way his reflexes ground his ass against my wiry red pubes to scratch our common itch, the smell of man and sex filling the air, the heat from his body as it slammed from me to his bitch and back again, the soft hairless texture of his muscled flanks, the hard hungry feel of his tits, and a thousand others besides.

I felt his body buck beneath me, desperate to escape my ruthless, ravening attack, yet knowing deep down that sparing the rod would spoil the child in him. After perhaps a minute that seemed an eternity of newly discovered ecstasy, I leaned forward onto his back, grinding my chest fur against him as my lips locked tight around his ear lobe and my hips humped my Marine meat up his tight ass. I sucked and nibbled for a moment as his body went wild with terrible, frenetic, soul-shattering seizures. Then some passing god whispered for me to stick my tongue up his ear and the convulsions started. He couldn't breathe, his coordination collapsed into random flailing about as though I'd shoved a high-voltage wire up his butt instead of my bone.

When he finally found voice again, his ejaculations went on for fucking ever. At least it seemed that way. Trapped up his tight ass, I learned how a bull rider feels while he's waiting for the eight seconds to run out. About four seconds into the ride, the feel and sound and smell and taste of my best buddy's nut being blown deep sent me round the bend again, and I slammed his bronco butt hard enough that his dick should have drilled clean through his sweetie.

I kept on slamming—we kept on slamming—together. His tight butt climbed my cock on the upstroke and I slapped it down again. I guess I must have been screaming, too, but just then I knew nothing except that I'd never feel anything so good again and that I was sure as fuck going to make the most of the experience while I could. By the time I had blasted every drop of Marine cream I could come up with off his tight, secret guts and had been reduced to instinctively dry-humping my buddy's hole, I was one seriously wasted grunt. I collapsed onto the bed and saw the girl in the process of heading for the showers. She'd left carrying enough sap from Donny's woodie to repopulate a planet. I was more than half tempted to run after her, spread those legs wide, and suck that creamy load up into my mouth where it belonged.

I half expected him to try to beat the shit out of me. That morning I'd have waxed anybody who'd fucked me up the ass. If anything, though, he was in sadder shape than I was. As soon as I caught my breath enough to be sure I would live until morning, I reached down to wrap my fist around my stiff dick and wiped the thick layers of man-cream and butt-juices onto Donny Lee's bare, cobbled, sweat-soaked belly. Then, with a grin born of inspiration more than self-confidence, I said, "That'll be twenty dollars, Boot."

He gave me a look that was the dictionary illustration of inscrutable and then a nod so curt it almost wasn't there. Then his eyes narrowed to the squint grunts use when they mean business and he told me that if anyone ever heard about this, I was fucking dead. I gave him a wide grin and his cum-soaked belly a splashy little pat with the promise that he needn't worry: I always took care of my bitches. He answered with a long, slow look—as though trying to decide just how far fucking out I was—and then reached down to wrap his fist around his dick. He spanked his messy, purple head against the mess on his belly to jiggle a long, white strand of Corps-cum loose from his piss-slit before he said in a low voice that we'd see who was the bitch.

We did, too. The girls came out of the shower about ten minutes later to find us belly-fucking each other in a mire of Marine love, all arms and legs and thrashing unlike anything from boot camp. We sent them on their way with orders to keep their mouths shut. Since neither of them spoke as much English as the village dog, we'll never know whether they did or not. Once they were gone, we moved into the shower to field day the damage and then back out to our bed of sin to learn our way in the new world we'd discovered.

We both knew all about "pole-smoking" and "butt-fucking" from the faggot jokes everybody on ships tells. It wasn't until much later that I discovered why they tell them—to cover up for what they do on darkened weatherdecks and in secured gear lockers and in hotel rooms on liberty. That long, slow, perfect afternoon and evening, we were partners in discovery—letting our wants and needs guide us completely for the first time in our lives. We forgot about faking our feelings and depending on the happiness of others.

One touch mirrored another as lust bred satisfaction and we learned the endless ecstasies available to warriors who share themselves: the taste of Donny Lee's sweat as I lapped it off his neck and the firm feel of his masterful hands on my ass; the ineffable agonecstasy of his swollen dick breaking my guts apart and the urgency of his lips pressing against mine as he filled me with himself; the hard, bone-crunching grudge-fuck and the tender hours of recovery, cradled each in the strong arms of the other as we shared our hopes and dreams as we had shared our bodies.

Late in the evening, we were both rubbed raw and halfway starving so we pulled on enough clothes to be decent and slipped out for a break. A quick beer and a take-out pizza seemed in order, but within minutes, we both soon knew food could wait. We belonged in bed, alone—together.

The float is long since over, but our voyage of discovery continues. Every day turns up delicious new sensations and a new world of unexplored possibilities. Not everything is roses and champagne, though. That asshole Donny Lee never did pay off his twenty dollar bet. I'm having to take it out in trade.

THE ADORED ONE

MICHAEL ROWE

Today the ground is warm, grass brown like dry death, waiting for the yellow kiss of full spring. Lucas Sebastian watches from the sidelines, eyes squinting in the flat midwestern sunlight. He leans back against the whitewashed boards of the Williams Academy chapel and watches the others play soccer. His Nikon is loaded, and he takes the odd snapshot on the field. His team keeps him off the field this way, telling the coach that he's more useful to the school if can get some good shots of the action for the yearbook.

The truth is, he can't play soccer. He can't kick straight, he throws like my sister, *play him! play him!* the other team laughs, petitioning the coach to send Sebastian out to his death on the field. His team does their best to keep him out of harm's way. *Their* harm, not his. If he was injured on the field, it would solve a lot of problems.

He was the last picked, because nobody wanted a faggot on their team. Just hadda lissen to him *talk* for chrissake. If he wasn't a fruit, he could play properly, like a regular guy. The final proof was always in the playing. So the young gods have spoken, and he is banished from the field. So he watches. And there is beauty in watching, just watching.

Muscles strain. Exertion makes taut young chests pink, shirts discarded in the unseasonable heat. Eager sweat cleaves strong pectorals. Hardening muscles flex artlessly beneath the smooth, untanned skin of the half-naked soccer players.

Sebastian sighs to himself, and scans the battle-scarred turf, shielding his eyes from the furious sunlight, and the vision of Trask. He feels his heart quicken, feels the color come hot to his cheeks.

Trask had a first name, but he was held in such awe that his last name, simple, monosyllabic, omnipotent, was all that was ever needed. Calling him anything else would be like giving God a nickname. Trask was the captain of the other team, and it gave Sebastian a private pleasure to silently cheer him on, to wish him well, to hope he caught the ball and bounced it off his forehead into Sebastian's own team's goal net, the way regular guys did.

Sebastian rarely had a need to utter Trask's name out loud. They moved in different stratospheres. But he always whispered it before he fell asleep in his dorm at night. He whispered it quietly, his face in the pillow, like a prayer, too low for his roommates to hear. Sebastian lived in terror of talking in his sleep, of revealing his secret love, his secret sin, the most fierce and private part of him. He nurtured it like a sweet cancer. He knew it was wrong. The headmaster, the Reverend Doctor Power, had told the students that God had reserved a special burning seat in hell for homosexuals. The Headmaster always said *homosexual*, never *gay* or *fag* which were the words the other guys used. To him, these words meant nothing. They could wound, and frequently did, but they bore no resemblance to anything he could feel. He loved Trask. But that was another thing altogether. Dr. Power's word sounded worse to Sebastian, like a sentence from God: sonorous, permanent, and utterly damnable.

But the Headmaster was inside, in his office, surrounded by hockey trophies and lithographs of the Risen Christ, not out here on the field in the searing sunlight watching soccer. Sebastian was as alone as he could be under the circumstances, and he watched.

Sebastian adjusted the focus on his camera, panning it across the field, following the action through the comforting detachment of the lens. He sought out Trask, pulling him into sharp relief, blurring the background. Trask effortlessly bounced the soccer ball off his forehead, neatly passing it to his co-captain. Sebastian fired the motor-drive, stopping the action. Good, good. He spun the zoom dial, trapping Trask's face inside the rectangle of the viewfinder. He wondered what it would be like to feel hands, rough from football and farm work, against his chest. Warm lips, chapped and bruising. The unfamiliar scrape of stubble against his soft cheek. Trask was slickered with sweat, and the rivulets that ran down his chest soaked the front of his white Umbro soccer shorts, grass and dirt-stained at the seat. His skin was winter-white, and his hair was the color of pale dandelions. Soaking tufts of the same gold peeked from beneath the heavily-muscled arms.

As though reading Sebastian's mind, Trask paused in mid-turn and looked directly at Sebastian. His eyes were in shadow, and Sebastian could not read their expression. He fired again, the whir of the motor-drive sounding as loud to him as a rifle shot.

Sebastian lowered the camera and stared at the ground. He felt a sudden horrible stirring below the waist as he hardened inside his track pants. He shifted his position, turning on his side, away from Trask. Terrified, Sebastian thought of girls, pretty and fresh, in order to make the hard-on go away before anyone saw him. Before Trask saw him and realized he was just a little fag after all, for real, and beneath all contempt. He rolled over on the grass. The contact between his erection and the hard ground went through him like a flashfire. He shifted again, waiting until the desire to grind his pelvis against the ground passed, praying that he wouldn't be called, made to stand up, with his stiff sex making a tent in his pants.

But he wasn't called to play. He was ignored, as usual. There would be no Sebastian side-show for his peers that afternoon: No missed goals by Sebastian the retard, no soccer balls to the face, no exclusion from the gladiatorial fraternity of the jocks. No abject, ignominious humiliations in front of Trask.

And the soccer game, of course, finally did end. Sebastian had discovered that one way of dealing with these daily rituals of degradation on the sports field was to imagine them as finite blocks of time, with beginnings and ends. Once he adapted to this thought process, he realized that although it seemed like a game would go on for all eternity when he accidentally scored on his own team, or when the ball knocked the glasses off his face, it *would* end. Eventually. Between four and five P.M., he lived his life in four blocks of fifteen minutes each. Half-time was a promise that there were only two blocks left.

At six forty-five P.M. dinner was served in the large dining hall. Sebastian sat with his group of cronies who had also managed, from their very first day at the school, to find themselves with some sort of immutable label which shrouded them like a miasma and kept them just outside the periphery of the group known as the crowd.

The crowd consisted, for the most part, of the most ordinary boys imaginable. Not bright, not stupid, not particularly accomplished athletically, but who knew all the rules to all the games and never found themselves on the soccer field in basketball shoes and brown denim pants, getting their glasses knocked off by a wayward soccer ball they were supposed to be bouncing off their heads, like regular guys.

In short, they fit. They would grow up and graduate into lives and careers of stultifying normalcy, but at least here, at the school, life left them in some sort of bovine peace. If any of them were sensitive, they hid it with stunning alacrity.

At the far end of the dining hall sat the rulers of the school. From Sebastian's perspective, watching them eat their dinner, all he could see was brawny backs, mostly clad in well-worn button down shirts, or Williams Academy athletic T-shirts exposing biceps corded with thick ropes of hard sinew. The students were allowed to wear jeans after classes, and if there was ever an outward manifestation of the school's hierarchy, it was here.

His group, the outsiders, wore jeans that never seemed to lose their dark blue color, no matter how many times they were washed. The second group, the crowd, wore jeans that faded normally, as jeans tended to do.

The third group, Trask's group, were the denizens of the far table. They wore jeans that were faded to the glorious sky-blue of truly ancient denim. The seats and crotches were bleached almost white with constant wear, and they looked like they would remain that way forever. "Mount Olympus North," as the school's fatboy, Olivier, dubbed it one night in his unfortunately shrill voice. No one liked Olivier. He was, if possible, more of an outsider than Sebastian. But Olivier was unrepentant in his criticism of the demigods of the far table. He hated them all. Sebastian, on the other hand, worshipped them, however silently.

When he thought of Trask, sauntering through the hallways with textbooks held against one lean hip, he always thought of his blue jeans, gripping the round, muscular buttocks and full crotch perfectly, not too tightly, loose in all the right places, as though they had been designed by Sebastian himself during one of his fevered dreams, the dreams he was always afraid would cause him to cry out loud in his sleep.

Once, after a soccer game in the first week of school, Sebastian had caught his first glimpse of God. He'd gone into the shower room after he thought everyone was finished. Through the billowing clouds of steam, he'd heard the subterranean polyphony of water exploding on tile. The shower room was lit with two overhead lights and they were both densely shrouded by coronas of soap-scented fog.

Through the gloom, he'd been able to make out a naked giant at the far end of the shower room, powerful arms crossed, eyes closed beneath the pounding spray. Sun-streaked blond hair soaking, hanging to his thick shoulders like a truncated lion's mane, wet skin burnished with a summer's-end lifeguard tan, it had been the first time Sebastian had seen Trask naked.

Sebastian had stood rooted in his spot near the first shower feeling thin and naked and cold. When he accidentally turned on the hot water full blast and scalded himself, jumping away from the jet and yelping, Trask had looked up and gave him a derisive smirk before turning away again and looking down, leaving Sebastian wishing the tiled floor would swallow him whole. When he'd adjusted the shower temperature, Sebastian stood awkwardly beneath the spray. And lovingly, secretly, he began to explore Trask's nude body.

When Trask briefly turned away from him to reach for the shampoo, Sebastian saw the white ghost of racing trunks against Trask's tanned back and rear. His ass was hard-muscled and marble-white, a man's ass, not a boy's, with sharp indentations delineating each cheek. Sebastian had heard one of Trask's soccer team-mates bragging that Trask had spent the summer at a football camp known for its harsh training regimen. *Linebacker,* thought Sebastian crazily, singing the exotic mantra in his mind. *Halfback, fullback, quarterback, gridiron, pigskin, touchdown, hut! hut! hut!* He imagined Trask straining out endless pushups beneath the blazing summer sun: A helmeted, padded, jock-strapped warrior.

So male. So...*other.* The vision made him reel.

Sebastian's eyes adored the soft hollow at the base of Trask's throat. They reverenced the raw strength of his chest muscles, the athlete's flatness and ridges of his abdominal muscles.

Scarcely breathing, Sebastian had dared to look further.

Between the powerful thighs, Trask's heavy cock was half-hard. Feeling the beginning of an answering response in himself, Sebastian looked away. But as he did, he caught Trask's eye.

Trask stared back, a half-smile touching his lips. He reached down with his hand and lightly caressed his half-erect penis. The gesture was at once defiant and curiously intimate. Sebastian had stared, slack jawed. Then, Trask reached up and turned off the shower. He reached for his towel and secured it around his waist as he swaggered out of the shower room without looking back. Sebastian had felt the moist air move against his bare legs as Trask swept past him.

He'd dreamed of the naked giant that night, unformed, submissive dreams of self-abasement and receptive lust, heat and wetness. He'd dreamed of Trask's hardness, his otherness. But there had been nothing further between Trask and Sebastian, which was right and proper given their relative positions in the school's constellation. Trask never looked at Sebastian again, and never spoke to him.

But today, oh today, he'd looked.

After dinner, there were chores at Williams. The Reverend Dr. Power was a firm believer in the leveling power of manual labor. At the beginning of every school year, each boy was assigned to a duty detail which, among several crews of ten boys each, was responsible for the maintenance of the school property, inside and out. Each crew was supervised by a senior. Sebastian was on the clean-up crew, supervised by Halliday. His job was mopping the front hallway.

Lost in his thoughts of Trask, dreamily mopping the floor, Sebastian missed Halliday's approach. He felt a slap to the back of his head sharp enough to bring tears to his eyes.

"Wake up, asshole!" Halliday snarled in passing. "Quit slacking! I don't want to see any streaks on the floor, Sebastian. If there are, you can expect double-duty next week. With me. And we're doing outside crew. You don't wanna do outside crew with me, Sebastian. You'll wish your mother had never had you."

Squeezing his eyes tightly, Sebastian mopped the hallway with renewed vigor, re-mopping when boys, deliberately or not, tracked mud across the wet surface. He passed the hour this way as the pain in his head subsided into a dull throbbing. There would be a bump there tomorrow. Halliday didn't put in another appearance, which Sebastian appreciated too much to find odd.

Towards the end of the hour, he heard the sound of workboots approaching behind him. He sighed, thinking only of mud on the clean floor, and wondered whether or not he was going to pass Halliday's inspection before the bell rang for study hall.

The footsteps stopped. His stomach clenched, his hands gripped the handle of the mop. Turning, he saw that it was Trask, not Halliday, who stood before him, thumbs hooked in the pockets of his jeans. Instead of relief, he felt the supplicant dread of a pilgrim on the holiest soil.

"Sebastian," said Trask warmly and softly, as though jocularity were the usual currency of their relationship. "How's it going?"

"Fine..." Sebastian stammered. The sound of Trask's voice speaking his name as though he knew who Sebastian actually was made him dizzy. He still couldn't bring himself to pronounce Trask's name.

The older boy suddenly grinned at him, and Sebastian's world went white at the edges. Trask reached out his arm and touched Sebastian lightly on the shoulder. The pain of Halliday's slap vanished from memory. He felt the heat on his shoulder even after Trask moved his hand away.

"I've got a problem I think you might be able to help me with," Trask purred.

140 MICHAEL ROWE

Anything! Anything! Aloud, he said, "Okay."

"I saw you on the field this afternoon." Trask's smile widened, and Sebastian felt he might fall into it. "Get some interesting shots?"

"Yeah...I mean, yes I did," Sebastian squealed.

"Get any good ones of me?" Trask smiled languidly.

Sebastian gaped, and said, "Yeah! I mean..."

"I know," Trask said, smiling broadly. "What you meant to say was, 'Yes, Trask, I did. You're my hero.' Right? Am I right?"

This time Trask laughed, full and warm and golden.

Sebastian felt a horrible little giggle welling up in his chest, but before it could erupt and humiliate him one last, terrible time, Trask cut him off.

"I heard you were handy with cameras and photography and stuff," Trask continued. "I'm editing the yearbook this year, and I need someone to help in the darkroom. You up to it, buddy?"

Buddy.

If Trask had mistaken him for someone else, Sebastian was not going to give himself away. At the very least, his doubts about the existence of God had, by now, completely disappeared.

"Yes sir!" squeaked Sebastian. Trask laughed softly.

"*Good man!* And by the way, Sebastian? Call me Trask, not 'Sir'. Better yet," he said with a lazy smile, "call me Joe. But only when we're alone. You know how it is."

Sebastian felt an odd pressure in his chest, not comfortable but not unpleasant. He knew how it was all right, but for the first time, it didn't matter. If this miracle friendship was to be kept a secret to protect Trask's white light from being sullied, he would keep the secret. He would do anything.

"Okay...Joe," Sebastian breathed.

"Darkroom? After study hall tonight? I'll get you a pass from the Duty Master."

Trask smiled again, and turned on his heel. Sebastian watched him walk away down the hall. Trask never looked back.

Sebastian wasn't aware of Olivier coming up behind him until the mop was snatched from his hand.

"Olivier, for Christ's sake," Sebastian snapped. The last thing he wanted was the intruding presence of the school's fatboy. Olivier placed one hand on his hip, and banged the mop handle against the wall with his other hand. He was furious.

"It's my night off!" hissed Olivier, face the color of summer tomatoes. "I've been told to finish your job for you. I have to mop the fucking floor. Your job Sebastian, you fucking slacker!"

"What?"

"Halliday, dickhead," Olivier whined. "I don't know whose butt you've been kissing, but it worked. Way to treat a friend, like I don't have anything to do myself?"

We're not friends, Olivier. We're just two misfits stuck in the same place. If one of us was cool, he wouldn't piss on the other if he was on fire. You know it, I know it. And I don't need any "friends" like you. Not anymore.

But Sebastian didn't say any of this out loud.

Study hall was endless. Each tick of the wall clock was like a drop of water on his forehead. He tried to read his Dickens, but the text kept dissolving, replaced by a pastiche of images: Trask, running. Trask, laughing, his arm flung around Sebastian's shoulders, both of them suntanned and equal. Trask, scoring a goal in soccer, saluting him like a knight to his lady.

Miracles, he thought, and sighed louder than he intended, attracting the disapproving frown of Mr. Gladd, the mathematics teacher, who had pulled study hall duty.

"For God's sake, Sebastian," he shrilled. "Stop daydreaming and get to work. Your grades in my class, for one, are appalling. Study hall is not for sighing like some lovestruck Victorian heroine."

Sebastian reddened and opened his math text. The study hall tittered. Mr. Gladd smiled primly, knowing that he had picked on a favorite school target and had therefore curried temporary favor for himself with the others. There would be no further trouble from anyone tonight. He sipped his weak tea and smoothed a hand over his sparse gray hair, content that discipline reigned.

But for Sebastian, the study hall creaked interminably forward, and when his enemy the clock finally granted him clemency from his sentence, his excitement was fever-pitched.

As the boys gathered up their books, Mr. Gladd pounded his desk with the wooden paddle he kept with him always.

"Boys!" he shrieked. "Silence! I have two announcements." The noise died to whispers.

"Schimkus and Doolan, you are to report to Dr. Power's office immediately after study hall, to deal with incomplete homework assignments and disciplinary action.

"Mr. Sebastian," he continued crisply, turning his haddock's eyes on Sebastian, "is to report to the darkroom." He clapped his hands irritably. "Please pick up your hall passes immediately."

He could barely suppress a smile at Mr. Gladd's prissy, congealed grimace when he handed him the pass, co-signed by J. Trask, Jr. Sebastian thought he saw something glitter in Mr. Gladd's eyes as he took the pass, but he would not realize until later that it had been jealously.

The darkroom was dimly lit, the red lamp in the corner casting the unfamiliar bottles and canisters into a weird twilight of garnet-red and blue shadows. Sebastian inhaled the pungent chemical smell as he surveyed the walls. They were papered with photographs taken by the photo club, some even taken by Sebastian himself, mostly of boys playing sports. Here and there were images of churches, the school's sled dogs, boys studying. Photographs littered the floor, some of them cut off at the neck, faces among the debris, smiling tightly.

Sebastian turned when the door opened slowly behind him. Trask's face was wreathed in shadows, his powerful body backlit by the naked bulb in the hallway. *Gods don't need faces,* Sebastian thought giddily as he steadied himself against a table. He could fill in the face from memory.

The door closed. Sebastian felt a rush of heat rise to his cheeks, and he was grateful for the soothing red darkness. Trask's voice was low, and there was an unfamiliar tightness to it.

"Hey," he muttered. "Sebastian..."

Sebastian's heart began to pound, and he heard the answering blood thunder in his ears. He looked towards the door and realized that Trask had locked it. Trask saw him look, and smiled.

"You can ruin film if someone opens the door when you're developing," Trask said reasonably, advancing a step towards Sebastian. The locked door was like a caress to Sebastian, secure and comforting. He felt his erection growing in his dark blue jeans, pressing against the rough fabric of the denim. Each breath seemed individually negotiated. The pungent, chemical-laced air pressed against his hot face, thick and heavy.

"So," Sebastian stuttered. "What are..."

Trask placed both hands on the boy's shoulders. *Oh yes,* thought Sebastian, *hands rough from football, from farm work.*

"I saw you watching me, Sebastian," whispered Trask. "I know what you are. I know what you want. But you have to say it to me. Say it."

How can I say it? I don't know what to say!

"Say it, Sebastian, right now. Say it, or I'll leave!"

"I don't know what I am!" cried Sebastian. "What do you mean? What do you want me to say?"

"Fuck you, Sebastian," Trask said. He removed his hands from the boy's shoulders, and Sebastian felt cold air rush to the spot where Trask's hands had been. "Go to bed."

"Please," Sebastian whispered, reaching out. "I...want you."

Sebastian saw Trask smile then, saw all of his beautiful teeth at once. Trask reached over with his jock's ease, and flicked the light off, plunging the room into complete darkness except for the red safe-light.

He heard the rustle of cloth on skin. His wrist was grasped tightly and guided below Trask's waist. Trask's cock was hot and hard and smooth. Sebastian felt Trask's fingers wrap themselves tightly in his hair, forcing him to his knees among the snippets of discarded photographs, imprisoned memories of afternoons he could no longer see in the red darkness.

He cried for two hours, tears of shame, anger, and violation. Afterwards, he had lain in bed, unable to sleep. The night's images replayed in his brain like a flickering horror film. The pain had been excruciating, and any pleasure that had been taken had been taken by Trask. More bewildering still were the words Trask whispered hoarsely in his ear: awful, foul words, the words he had heard flung at him since he arrived at Williams. But, confused as they were in his mind with the desire which scalded him with its ferocity, the words took on a cunning new meaning.

"Is that what I am?" he whispered into his pillow. "Is it?"

When Trask had climaxed, he shoved Sebastian away from him and began to sob harshly, muffling the sound with his hands. Sebastian, sprawled on the floor, his pants around his ankles, reached out for Trask.

In spite of the burning pain that seemed, when he moved, to cut him in half, the thought of Trask suffering was more than he could stand.

On his knees, still supplicant, he murmured the only words that came to mind.

"It's okay. It's okay." He spoke the way he would have spoken to a frightened dog, or a child who had lost his mother. Mutely, he held out his hands, reaching.

And then Trask hit him in the face.

"Don't you fucking tell me that it's okay you little faggot!" Trask sobbed furiously. His eyes, swollen and streaming, flickered to the locked door. "Who the fuck do you think you are? *You're* gonna tell *me* that it's okay? You? You're fucking *nothing! Do you know who I am?*"

"Trask..." whispered Sebastian. He felt the fire of each finger across his cheek. He felt the imprint of Trask's heavy football ring above his jawline. Tears stung his in his eyes, and he tasted copper in his mouth.

"Fucking right! *I'm Joe Trask!* Fucking *right!* You made me do this, you little cocksucker! Fucking little asshole. Loser! You're nothing! I hate you! *I hate you for making me do this!*" He grabbed the front of Sebastian's shirt and slammed him against the counter. "Get the fuck out of here you little faggot," Trask rasped. "And if you tell anybody about this, so help me Christ, I'll kill you!"

His fury seemed barely under control, and for the first time ever, Sebastian feared for his life.

Breathing in shallow hitches, he pulled up his dark blue jeans and fled the room, fled the sight of his brilliant golden soccer-god, huddled in a corner, the handsome and perfect tear-streaked face puffy and red, like a baby monster freshly born and covered with slime.

The next day, there was a little more green on the ground, and a warm wind blew white clouds from the west. The students at Williams Academy spent as much time as possible outdoors, and there was a barely-contained euphoria in the classroom. Mr. Gladd lost control of his grade eleven calculus class, paddling Schimkus and Doolan afterwards for what he called disruption. He could have paddled the sunlight instead, or looked for a culprit in the crystal blue of the sky, or the white of the clouds.

After classes, there were the compulsory sports until dinner. Sebastian had gone to the nurse, who was also the Headmaster's wife, and asked for a note to be excused from soccer. He wasn't feeling well, he said. He felt woozy.

She assessed him coldly, her lemon-sucking mouth puckering with distaste.

These nancy-boys were an embarrassment to Williams, always trying to get out of the character-building athletics her husband's school strove so hard to provide. She, for one, saw no reason to make it easier for them to shirk.

"I think you're fine, Sebastian," she snapped. "What you need is a little fresh air and sunlight."

Sebastian changed into his soccer gear and trudged out to Oxford Field. Walking was painful. The blood had stopped, but it still hurt. He didn't tell Mrs. Power. His camera dangled from its vinyl strap, banging painfully against his thigh.

Sebastian heard the pounding of cleats as Trask and Halliday came running up behind him. He flinched as Trask snaked out an arm. But Trask didn't hit him. He slowed to a jog, and clapped his arm around Sebastian's shoulders. Halliday looked, first at Sebastian, then at Trask, horrified.

"Trask! Are you fucking *nuts?* What are you *doing?"*

"Relax, Red," he said, punching Halliday manfully in the arm. "This is my man Sebastian."

"Your *what?"*

They were rounding the quad, and Oxford Field rolled open before them like the battlefields of Troy. Trask smiled down at Sebastian, his eyes shining like sapphires in the rosy bronze of his warrior-prince's face.

Trask tightened his grip on Sebastian, beaming heartily. No one saw the fingers dig brutally into Sebastian's arm, squeeze once, painfully, then release.

Trask jogged onto the field to a raucous cheer from his team. Sebastian rubbed his arm to take the sting away, and went to his accustomed spot by the chapel to wait. He wouldn't be called to play today, he knew it. Things would change for him at Williams. The snickering would stop, at least to his face. The catcalls would be for others now, not for Trask's anointed. No one would risk the divine wrath of the far table, and Sebastian was safe now in its shadow. He felt a flicker of pity for Olivier, the fatboy. And he felt envy.

A bargain had been struck. The protection of Trask in exchange for his silence. It would be honored by both of them, he knew.

Reflexively, he reached for his Nikon, but instead of raising it to his eye, he aimed it at Trask as though it were a gun. The motor-drive sang its sharp report. A few heads turned, but not Trask's. He watched Trask rocket across the field in a blaze of alabaster and dandelion, sweat flying like a sun shower. Dazzle, dazzle.

Sebastian shivered in the dying dirty-gold light of the afternoon and thought about the death of gods. Felt a cold like dark winter. Prayed he would be warm before summer.

AEGIS

D. TRAVERS SCOTT

Soon, Ian thought.

The razor glided across his scalp, leaving a smooth, pink wake in the lather. A chill followed the razor's swath, cold air touching exposed skin. In contrast, a warm razorburn glowed. The hot/cold juxtaposition reminded Ian of raves: flushed Ecstasy-forehead heat against cold menthol jelly on lips and eyelids.

Hot and cold make tornadoes, he thought.

Stevik was steady, careful.

Ian shifted his concentration from top to bottom as the razor made another pass.

Feet flat against the floor-tiles, back braced against the goal posts of Stevik's legs, Ian held himself still as possible. The tattooist's knees jutted out through torn black denim, the cotton fray and kneecap hairs tickled Ian's earlobes. Ian's arms circled back around Stevik's calves, the hard swells from years of bike messengering wedged solid inside Ian's elbows.

Ian focused on the tactile sensations underneath his fingertips and sweaty palms. Stevik had put him on a steady diet of L-arginine, niacin, pantothenic acid and choline to heighten his sense of touch. Boots and jeans flooded his system: Rough canvas cord, cold metal eyelets and supple leather, smooth spots on frayed laces, and rough denim all weave against his armflesh. Stevik's shins ran down his bare back in sharp verticals.

Focusing on these sensations kept Ian motionless. Stevik could work around a nick, but Ian knew he'd prefer perfection from the onset and wanted to give it to him. He opened his eyes. The sun, low on Belmont,

147

shot orange verticals of August evening slicing through the windows of Endless Tattoo. Stevik's boots glowed black-red; the silver ring on Ian's fourth finger gleamed in bright contrast. The oblique light carved deep shadows into the inscription, *BOY*.

Ian fought a shudder. It would take several sessions to do a piece as elaborate as Stevik had promised, as elaborate as the work he'd done on Toad: The outlining, fill, shading, color.

Finally, they were approaching the home stretch.

Once Stevik had marked him, it would happen.

"So," the pierced guy with dreads drawled, "who gave you the ring?"

Ian turned around, surprised.

"No one." Ian's eyes, burning underneath thick, furrowed brows, darted around the club. They lit on the dreaded guy. "Gave it to myself."

The man held his gaze, unblinking. "Self-made *Boy*?"

Ian looked away.

"Someday..." Ian glanced at his half-peeled Calistoga label. His eyes danced briefly onto the pierced guy, gazed past him out into the pit.

"Someday, someone'll give me one to replace it."

The man curled out his lower lip thoughtfully.

Ian scowled into his bottle.

The man with the dreads rose, took one of his two singles from the counter.

"Yeah. Someday," he muttered.

Ian's eyes trailed his dissolution into the crowd.

"There."

Hot/cold prickles ran over Ian's clean scalp, down his neck.

"OK, Ian. I'm done."

Ian stared at the ring, and his pale fingers gripping Stevik's black laces. He didn't want to let go. He'd waited so long for this—and what would follow—he almost feared its arrival.

"Ian, I gotta get you into the chair to do it."

Ian tilted his freshly-shaved head back against Stevik's lap, looking up into his eyes. Stevik's brown dreads circled down around his face like curtains. His face was a series of long shadows and gleaming sparks from the stainless piercings: Labret below the lips, Niebuhr between the eyes, septum, eyebrow. Ian traced them with his eyes, drinking in the details of the man's face. His black goatee curled down in a point; scars striped his eyebrows. Two dark brown eyes terrified Ian, their enormous potential energy, poised to spring deep into him.

Ian smiled.

Stevik's lips curled into a fond snarl.

He spat.

The hot saliva splattered beneath Ian's right nostril. His tongue stretched to gather it up.

"Fuck," Stevik sighed. "I get so hot thinking about marking you."

Ian nodded. He squeezed Stevik's ankle and laid his face against his thigh. He breathed in sweat, dirt, and crotch-funk through the stiff denim, nuzzled the coarse fabric, sighed.

"I know," Stevik murmured. "Won't be much longer, boy. Not too long. And it'll be worth the wait. You'll have earned it."

Ian exited into the gelid night. LaLuna's neon tinted the wet street hyper-cobalt.

Town always looks like a fucking car commercial, he thought.

Assorted young queers drifted past with affected chattering, unlocking station wagons and Buicks, strapping on bike helmets, revving motorcycles, stretching into raggedy sweaters and backpacks.

Ian kicked around the corner, disgusted. Another wasted night. Tweakers, smoked-out groove-rats, slumming twinks. Even at the freak convention, he felt the freak. The kids, his peers, had all been babbling about the Psychotronic Circus coming down from Seattle, trashing a new all-ages called The Garden, comparing notes on which of the street kids arriving for spring were fags and which ones would fuck around anyway, for money or a dose.

And the older guys: Trolling, married, shut-down, falling asleep...fuckfuckfuck.

What I'd give for one fierce guy.

He cut through the alley, staring at his black Docs scuffing the gravel, listening to the regular jangle of his wallet chain. Chink-chink-chink. Another regular beat, some industrial ambient dub thing. Mix in a little Violet Arcana, maybe, and it could've graced the clove cigarette smoke in the chill room.

Chink-chink-chink-

Juh-jangle.

The dissonant beat startled Ian. He stopped, looked up.

The dreadlocked guy, one hand supporting himself against a dumpster, stood across the alley from Ian. Facing the club's rear, his suede jacket glowed a scabby red in the halogen streetlight.

The man looked over his shoulder. "Oh—you. Hey."

He turned, releasing a splattering piss-stream against the mossy bricks.

Ian stood silent, watching the piss steam slightly, frothy trickles pooling around his boots.

The dreaded man looked back over his shoulder.

Ian didn't move.

The man's boot-heels ground into the muddy gravel. He pivoted to face Ian. His piss-stream, spewing a circular arc like a suburban lawn sprinkler, rained across the alley between them.

Ian met his gaze. The man frowned.

Ian dropped to his knees, immersing himself. The bitter piss ran into his eyes, dripping from his forehead, shoulders and chest; gathering and falling from his face in thick, round drops, splattering on the earth.

The man shook off the final drops, tucked, buttoned. Ian's jaw dropped, the dour drops hitting his tongue. His eyes burned; his T-shirt, soaked and cold.

"Come on," the man whispered.

Ian followed him out of the alley.

"We'll just aim for starting the outline tonight. Just see how far we can go."

"I can take it."

Stevik's hand sifted through Ian's hairy chest, callouses stretching out a nipple like fleshy caramel. "I know you can. I know you can."

He jerked out a couple of hairs from around the aureole. Ian stiffened, inhaled briskly.

"I'll give it to you," Stevik said. "All of it and more. You know I will. But not 'til you're mine."

Ian's hard-on thumped against his belly, disconsolate.

Stevik unlocked the door of the metal Quonset hut. Ian followed him deep into the high-arched space, filled with only a few chairs, a couch, some cinder blocks. Eight-foot sheetrock walls set off a room in the far back corner. In the ceiling's dark recesses, rain splattered against the corrugated metal.

A light clicked on beneath the furthest wall. Ian shut the door behind him and twisted the deadbolt. He felt his way toward the light.

He stood in the doorway, blinking in the light. Stevik sat on the edge of a bed which descended from the ceiling on heavy wooden braces.

Stevik looked up, almost surprised.

"What?" Stevik stopped, holding one boot in his hand. "What do you want?"

"I—ah—" Ian struggled for a response. "Well, why'd you bring me here?"

Stevik rolled his eyes and yanked off the other boot.

"Why'd you follow me here?" he shot back, tossing the boot onto the floor.

Ian shrugged. He took a step toward the bed.

"Look!" Stevik barked, "I don't want to touch you, get it? Little fuck; I don't know shit about you, if you're even worth it. I just.... You can stay here, tonight, if you want."

He jerked his thumb toward a pile of dirty clothes in the corner.

"There. Sleep over there if you want."

Ian stared at him. Stevik rolled away, still in his clothes, and jerked a plaid comforter up over himself. He clapped twice and the lights went out.

Ian found the pile of clothes in the dark. He could smell them.

Ian climbed off the floor into the chair. He stared ahead at the screen Stevik had set between the chair and the store's windows.

"Bet you've dreamed about my dick," Stevik said, rolling open his station's drawer.

Stevik pulled out a rustling sheaf of carbon papers. Ian had seen him working on them. It was the design, the tat for his scalp. Stevik hadn't let him see it finished.

"What it feels like, how it smells. You've only seen it pissing. You don't even know what it looks like hard, how it feels in your hand, all hot and heavy."

At the apex of the Broadway Bridge, Stevik told him to stop.

Ian stared at Stevik, a few feet before him, hands across chest. A curtain of vertical lights rose behind Stevik, a skyscraper-light mirage that made Portland look, at night, like the metropolis it wasn't. The verticals of lights were only expensive houses rising up along the West Hills, but it had fooled Ian that night, years ago, when he'd leapt off the freight train beneath this very bridge.

"Take your clothes off, jack off, and don't look at me."

Stevik sauntered over the walkway's railing and leaned back.

Ian pulled off his T-shirt, unbuckled his belt. He was elated to have run into Stevik again, but wondered where things would go this time. He kicked off his Boks, pulled down his jeans.

Just the boxers left. If someone comes along....

"I said don't look at me, dogshit!" Stevik kicked Ian's shirt out over the bridge's lane gratings.

Ian scuffed off his shorts. He leaned back against the cold metal girder, its single-file row of rivet-heads pressing into his back like a formation of soldier-cocks. He licked his palm and rubbed his shriveled dick, trying to coax a hard-on. He kept his eyes moving to avoid Stevik: The tiny scythe-blades of moonlight on the Willamette River, the splintery wood planks of the walkway, the kitschy yellow lily of the suicide-hotline sign.

A dull roar grew. Cold whiteness rose up his bare side; Ian kept a steady rhythm pulling on his soft dick.

A breeze whipped against him as the truck plowed by; the bridge vibrated against his back and ass and feet. Silence. Ian was raging hard.

Relaxed, he stared up at the stars. Orion guarded him above, bow drawn. Ian stared at his jeweled belt, and came.

"Good," Stevik said. He was standing right at Ian's side, holding Ian's shorts.

"Here."

Ian slipped them on, his jeans, socks, shoes.... He looked over at his tire-tracked shirt stretched across the grating.

Stevik set his jacket on the girder and pulled his own T-shirt off. "Here. Yours is trashed."

Ian swallowed and pulled the shirt over his head, Stevik's smell surrounding him.

"You don't always have to wait to just run into me, you know," Stevik said jovially as they descended the bridge. "You can just come by the shop."

Stevik sprayed disinfectant onto Ian's scalp, minty-cool mist dancing across his raw skin as it evaporated dry.

"I bet you dream about it in your mouth, going down your throat, sucking it dry, swallowing all the cum I can shoot out."

A sticky bar ran across his head, leaving residue. Ian smelled of Mennen Speed Stick, a cloying musk of ineffectual father-macho.

Ian waited across the street at Subway, watching Stevik work. He chewed pepperoncini thoughtfully. Watching Stevik from a distance afforded him moments of striking lucidity, quite distinct from the blind heat saturating his mind in the man's close proximity.

This is so weird, he thought. It was one thing when it was so—casual, but now.... Fuck, Ellen's already rented my room out to that sculptor-guy.

He's never hurt me, though. He's never done anything I haven't loved.

"And your ass just itches, don't it? It hurts—don't it hurt so bad, the way you want it? You think of me up there, my arms crushing your chest, my tongue in your ear and my dick, that dick of mine you dream about just ramming away up inside your ass, plowing into your hot gut. Goin' in and out."

Stevik pressed the carbon against his scalp, the design transferring to the adhesive deodorant.

"Put some music on," Stevik muttered as they entered the loft. He wandered into the kitchen for a beer. Ian flicked on the living-room light and rifled through the CDs.

"Wanna Sheaf?"

"Yeah, that's great." Ian hummed happily. Stev had never asked him to pick out the music before. Some old Front Line Assembly would be fun, he thought. Or maybe more mellow—This Mortal Coil or something. Or Coil—yeah, that'd be the perfect combination.

None to be found: Marc Almond, Everything But the Girl, Annie Lennox, Edith Piaf, Billie Holiday—

God, I've gotta unpack my discs soon.

Stevik walked into the room with the two brown bottles of Australian stout.

"God, Stev," Ian quipped, scowling at the track listing on *Billie's Blues,* "you got anything besides all this diva-queen crap?"

Stevik set the bottles down carefully on the floor. His fist plowed squarely into Ian's gut.

Ian collapsed to the floor, gasping.

"Put on the headphones—and listen to that CD," Stevik seethed through grit teeth. "Don't go to bed 'til you get it."

He picked up both bottles and stalked into the bedroom, slamming the door behind him.

Four A.M.

"Stevik."

Stevik rolled over, blinked.

"Can I go to sleep now?"

Ian was crying.

"Yeah."

Ian knelt to spread out his blanket.

"No—"

Stevik pulled off the sheet, stretching out in a black T-shirt and shorts.

"Get in here. You ain't gonna get anything, and don't cling on me all night, but—just go ahead and get up here. You don't have to sleep on the floor anymore."

"You think of me fucking you and you get all weak, doncha? Like your knees giving out."

Stevik peeled off the paper and set it on the counter. Ian stared at the ceiling, feeling the vinyl and chrome of the chair beneath him. Stevik spoke in a steady monotone as he set out his supplies. The ink bottles clinked against the individual glass wells as he dispensed and mixed the colors.

Ian waited on the floor beside the chair.

"So you're Stev's new boy, huh?" The woman looked down at Ian, balancing her water bottle on the shiny black hip of her PVC hot pants.

"He marked you yet?"

Ian smiled, shook his head.

"Oh, so you're still in the—uh, trial run." She laughed. "He let you talk?"

"Yeah."

"But he told you to wait here for him, right?" She smirked. "Been gone a long time, hasn't he? I think he's up on the roof fucking my sister."

Ian bit his lip and tried to sound polite. "He didn't tell me anything," he said, "I just want him to be able to find me whenever he wants. So I'm staying in one spot."

"Not bad," she appraised. She turned around to face the crowd at the far end of the Quonset hut. Stevik broke through, dragging a skinny bald guy under his arm, both howling loudly.

"Well, your wait's over, it looks like. He's bringing over the ex for introductions."

She looked back over her shoulder at Ian, eyebrow arched. "You must rate."

Stevik and the bald guy tossed her happy nods in passing. They planted themselves loudly before Ian.

Stevik slapped the bald guy's chest proudly. His chest, arms, neck and scalp were a myriad of designs. In the dim light, Ian could barely sort out the intertwined images: An octopus sat on his head, tentacles creeping down the neck. Two figures hung down his pecs, crucified at crossed wrists just above each nipple. Geometric spirals rose out from the waistband of his black leather pants.

"This is what real skin looks like, boy, see this? This is real work! This is the kind of work I do when I give a shit about someone."

The bald guy beamed proudly, his blue eyes sparkling brighter than the glinting four-inch steel spike through his septum.

"Don't take all the credit, now!" The bald guy grabbed Stevik's crotch. He crouched down, confidentially, to Ian. "Stevie, now, he didn't do all this, mind you. But, eh, he got it all started."

"Look at this fag's shit!" Stevik yanked Ian's T-shirt, pulling it up over his head.

"See? He's a little lost tribal boy, look at that. My!" He grabbed Ian's arm and stretched it up high. "A chain around his arm! Tough shit! And wait, there's more!"

He reached over and grabbed the back belt loop of Ian's cords.

"Stand up, fuck," he muttered.

He spun Ian around and pulled down the back of his shorts, exposing the dogpatch hair leading down to Ian's ass. Off to the left side, where the hair faded into pale fawn-down, was an ankh.

"Wook! It's a wittle ankhy-wankhy!" Stevik sneered. "Itn't it twoo tweet?"

Stevik howled. His friend belched. Ian stood, patiently waiting.

"Toad," Stevik said to the bald guy, "this little turd wants me to mark him. He wants me to put my art on the same skin with all this other piss-ass shit." He snorted.

Toad smiled. "Now why don't you just, eh, cut out those old ones, eh, Stevie?"

Stevik laughed. "Nah, no scars for him yet. Maybe we get Ben to brand him someday. For now I want his skin clean."

Toad nodded. "Then you'll just have to cover."

They stared up at Ian. He held his head bowed.

"Look at me, fuck."

Ian raised his eyes to the short, dark man.

"You really want to get marked by me? Like Toad here?"

Ian nodded.

"I had to earn this, you see," Toad said with quiet pride.

"I understand."

"It was quite difficult."

Ian nodded.

Stevik and Toad exchanged glances. Stevik shrugged.

"Go let Toad fuck you, asshole. Head's clear."

Stevik jerked his head toward the crowded rear of his space.

"Keep the door open," he called out as they walked away.

Stevik shifted weight in the worn easy chair cushions, his boots propped up on a cinder block. He watched across the space 'til Toad's serpent-entwined arm shoved Ian out through the bathroom door, to the cheers of the crowd. They gathered around Toad, laughing.

Ian pegged his shorts back up. He looked around the floor by the chair for his shirt. It was soaked with beer and cigarette ash, marked in the middle with a bootprint where it'd been used to swab the floor.

Ian wiped the wet cum-muck off his face with the back of his arm. Sticky smears clung to his hairy abdomen.

"Sit down," Stevik muttered.

Ian sat, wrapping his bare arms around his chest.

Ian looked at Stevik's boots. He leaned forward.

"Touch me and I'll beat the living shit out of you, right here."

Ian froze.

"Christ, you stink."

"Like you wanna cry. You think about how bad you want me inside you, how you want my dickhead kissing your heart, my cock's shit-smeared blessing. You want it so bad you can't stand it. You think of it and you think you'll just collapse in a big whimpering, slobbering mess, begging for me to do it. Doncha? Doncha?"

He slapped the boy's naked stomach.

Ian nodded, dislodging tears that dripped onto his chest, trickled down the sides of his neck.

Ian heard Stevik tear open the needle package.

"But you haven't, have you?"

Ian shook his head proudly.

"No, you haven't. You're tough. You never even asked me for it, never went around with your ass in the air like some damn cat in heat."

Stevik ran his gloved hand down the side of Ian's face, wiping away the saltwater, the rubber dragging across Ian's lips. Ian kissed.

Stevik kissed the clean scalp.

"You already got it, man. You already got it. Everything I'm ever gonna give you—you already got it."

Studying the Alliance of Professional Tattooists manual and the Oregon state regs, Ian imagined Stevik marking him. He imagined Stevik fucking him, 'til the two fantasies meshed.

The tat machine and Stevik's all-but unseen, imagined, longed-for dick merged—the machine's rabbit ear screwed into the base of Stevik's pubis, its mechanism sticking out from the pubic hairs. The armature bar shot upward as the base of his shaft; DC coil, spring contact points and base all curled into an electromagnetic nutsack. The rubber bands were black neosporene cockrings. A dark brown foreskin stretched out over the armature bar and sanitary tube—it skinned back to reveal a five-point grouping of liner needles arranged in an X like five dots on a die, like a man spread-eagled. The red cock-needles shot in and out, woodpeckering Ian's scalp through scaly layer, epidermis, into dermis. Stevik pushed his cock needles further, standing above, Ian bowed at his feet. The needles mixed Stevik's precum-ink with Ian's head-blood, sucking the serum up into the foreskin tube through capillary action, Ian's capillaries got some action, filling with Stevik's Number C Hard Black spunk. Stevik marked deeper, aiming for Ian's fontenels, poking through the skull-joints' cart, past the blood/brain barrier. Ian's whole body spasmed, muscles fibrillating with abandon.

Ian's fantasy lost physical specifics at this point. He couldn't visualize or verbalize, only feel a destruction, absorption, union.

Stevik stuffed cotton wads into Ian's ears.

Ian looked over at the tat machine in his hand.

Time slowed down. Ian watched. Current flowed through the coils and the base of the machine. Electromagnetized, it pulled the bar down, pulling down the needles and opening the silver contact points. Opening the points killed the magnet, and the spring assembly brought the bar back, causing the needles to move up and contact the points, conducting current and repeating the cycle. Again. Again. A cycle of opposite motions and polarities, endlessly repeating.

The first of the needles broke his skin, the ink penetrated his dermis, hundreds of times a second.

LOVETH THOU ME, BOY?

MIODRAG KOJADINOVIĆ

By Thursday night, the boy's pale skin has turned the color of meadow honey, pseudo-tanned with a motley assortment of bronzers he gets complimentary at men's cosmetics at The Bay, where he is a shop assistant. The red-tinted light shades it to the nuance of the most famous local food staple: smoked salmon. He is growing a droll goatee.

Years ago, when I had a summer job as a hotel pool attendant in Pontresina, one in the cluster of chic but, to my concept of the world, godforsaken townships around St. Moritz, employees would sometimes get leftovers from the banquet tray as a special treat. Scottish lox was hors d'oeuvre of choice for the guests, most of whom were monstrously obese former Nazis turned Bundesrepublik foreign trade officers, businessmen and such, whose prosperity was built on the bones of my grandfather, killed at the age of twenty-three. But the predominantly South European maintenance crew of the Grand Hotel Kronenhoff thought little of it: They preferred the much bloodier venison cold cuts. I alone cherished the smooth texture, the salty silkiness laid atop the rough edges of coarse rye wafers.

The boy's hips barely gyrate, but the sturdy loaves of his bum rub invitingly against each other at the crack. His lower torso undulates in the void, floats to and fro, desirable, vulnerable, alluring. His glance steals to check my reaction—I was naïve enough to show him I cared—then is quickly averted. He won't admit he wants me too, not just yet. In the operatic world of pretense, once he has made it out of Amherst, a miserable quasi-historic hamlet in Nova Scotia, he won't be a sucker ever again.

Exhibitionist at the core, I lift my arms vaguely towards him, teasingly

158

stretch the rubber strands, wind them around my fingers, raise the whip high in the air and hit the wall hard. *Whoosh!* Oh, yeah, baby, here comes the staff for the insubordinate younger brother. A swishy sapling for the butt of the prodigal son. Father in heaven may pardon you, but I'm gonna sign my name of a Top in crimson welts on the pink pages of your lower cheeks. Brand you with my supple yet commandeering bull-whip. Claw you with the cat-o'nine-tails, the flaccid surrogate for the cock-which-never-was-nine-inches.

The boy snorts, presumably disgruntled, and turns round the nearest corner. I stand in the darkness, excited that I may finally get the chance to tame him, the wild colt. I feed on his fear. I breathe heavily. Blood foams in my nostrils. I hope he'll be back. Soon. Tonight. Now.

I have not been to many concentration camps, and when I have I did not find them sexual in the least. I appreciate Susan Sontag, but think that *Under the Sign on Saturn* is greatly misunderstood by Gentile readers as having a context beyond what it explicitly deals with: Anti-Semitism. The argument that S/M is necessarily and only a will to annihilate I find ludicrously infantile. I am, indeed, aware that the West Coast of North America may be schizoidly obsessed on the one hand with avoidance of pain at any cost and on the other with super-specialization in leather sex. I, myself, however, grew up immersed in the great Mediterranean myth of purification through suffering, that paramount prototype of the Western thought, manifested through a dualism of Mitras the bull slayer, a self-centered whimsicality of Artemis of Ephesus, crying for the blood of boys whipped at her altar, and a dogmatic relativity of all transitory things versus a good old over-the-knee spanking in Kochelet (Ecclesiasticus).

The boy drifts back in, walks past in a semi-circle, vaguely delineated by the reach of the short whip I fiddle with; pretending not to notice me, he sits on a low bunk. Half-licks his palm, half-spits on it and coats his cock with saliva, starts pulling. Then wriggles, purportedly to make himself more comfortable, managing to move closer with every twitch of supple muscles that wobble under the skin as grass on the prairie reels in the wind. On a someone with so softly boyish a freckled face as his is, an eight-incher is always striking. He is twenty-four, but looks hardly a day over twenty.

His stare is glued to the screen; he pretends he is not interested in me. Still, of all places he chooses to jerk off right here where I stand. In the dim light, I can clearly see the slow movement of his hand as it squeezes the shaft and he delves into his own exhibitionist fantasies. *Tough luck, sweetie, I too am immature and self-centered!* By now he is so close that I could reach out and twist his right nipple. I could put a cigarette out in the middle of the crudely made tattoo on his left shoulder. If I smoked, that is. But it's been almost a year since I quit.

I should bend, lean on his shoulders as on a windowsill, and chew on his slightly droopy earlobes that he is so self-conscious about. Or I could bite the ridge of his nose, the back of his neck, hurt him ape-like into obedience. I could, probably, kiss him, drill aggressively into the wetness of the wound. Go. Pierce through the warm darkness of the slit, at first resisting and then opening as a bud forced to flower early in the greenhouse perfection of an artificial universe; the tip of my tongue slides through the canyon between his almond-shaped teeth to touch the palate, then back down to wrestle, subdue, and playfully entangle with his fleshy and bashful speech muscle.

I am an intruder in this mouth, a guest who jumped on the host. I seek the well of youth in the boy, the green freshness of early, not-yet-ripe cherries. I could have been his older brother, his childhood friend. I could marry him, grow old with him.... I suddenly see us, two white-haired old men, sitting on a bench somewhere under the eucalyptus trees, perhaps in Athens. It is late summer, of course, and one of us leafs absent-mindedly through the newspapers, which no longer carry any real news for people our age, while the other feeds the pigeons. And the sun shines so warmly, so gloriously on our parched skin. The supreme mystery of life: Happiness in small things. I hold his hand and the world is a good place where two old men can hold hands, as friends, as lovers, as brothers do.

I pull back up from the deep plunge into his being to fill my lungs with air, look at him from above. And I lay the knots of the whip in the hollow where the low arch of his neck tapers to the yoke-like curve of his shoulders, I let the straps slip over his spine. As the boy shudders, I sneer a vicious smile. And I make a noose-like loop of the cords and put it around his neck, I pull the handle. And he looks me in the eye, inquisitively, to which I barely nod, abiding by the etiquette of the place, which requires that we remain butch throughout. And I see him decide to give in, and he rises slowly and lets me lead him, amidst the fake snubbing of jealous onlookers, as on a leash. And in my room, I slap his butt repeatedly with my palm, but when I hit him with the whip he groans and bites his lip, his chin trembles.

I know it's all way over the head for him, so I order him on his knees. And as his lips glide over the buckle of my patent leather shoe, I want to lift him up and look through his eyes into the depths of his soul, to find the well of innocence to quench my thirst. But I only shove the tulip of my cockhead in his mouth, and at first he just lets it lie there, a tear glittering out of the corner of his left eye, the mirror of feelings.

I then start waving back and forth, as in a prayer, and his mouth envelops me as a soft mitten. His whole world now is this cock; he would drink nectar from Siva's lingam, suction the Milky Way all the way in, partake in the Dionysos frenzy. But I decide to turn him over and squat to offer his now fully ecstatic mouth the axis mundi of my twinkling butthole. And as he laps hungrily at it, I want to hold him in my arms forever; and as he fucks me deeper with the fleshy strawberry of his tongue, I sprinkle my semen over his chest and stomach. And as the bouquets of fireworks fade into a purple cold, the gaping void opens again in the skies, and I know none of my childish dreams of a love eternal will ever materialize, for this is America, and 1995. Therefore I give him two minutes to shoot his load, which he hastily does, and usher him out of the beige veneer cubicle and lock the door behind him.

And as the memory of the faraway stars that loom in icy indifference overhead reawakes in the marrow of my bones, I start weeping. Bitterly.

THE YELLOW

MICHAEL LASSELL

For John Preston,
who said "Write about what you know,"
and meant it...
and then published it.

It begins, of course, with desire—or, rather, *in* desire—this time on a Passover Saturday night in New York City, the night before Easter, too. Where the desire begins is anybody's guess, perhaps in fever. This time it began in the sky, in a cloud cover so low—the way it gets in spring— you feel...immersed, caught in the act, drowning. And the Empire State Building is lit up a kind of yellow that doesn't exist in nature, not in healthy nature, but you can't see the top of the building, anyway, because of the clouds: a translucent mist rendered opaque by mass, volume, density—the whole thing looking like special F/X for hell or some urban apocalypse movie.

You know the sort of film. They were popular in the seventies: It's the year two-thousand-something and the Island of Manhattan is a penal colony, blah-blah-blah...young men encased in tight muscles and leather vests, headbands. Hollywood shit. But not ineffective. The kind of thing that gets under your skin no matter how you resist: hard rival males, little more than school yard Caesars, battling for supremacy and the nubile charms of this year's pouting starlet, a fight to the death that establishes the right of the fittest for supremacy (fitness being measured not only by strength but by cunning and moral rectitude, movies being fiction, after all, and not the glandular dance of the cobra and the mongoose).

162

Yes, it's on nights like these that the city seems most Darwinian, nights that conjure the Tortugas, amphibians crawling out of the ooze, nights of survival, jazz, and ejaculation.

Soaking into the fog like amyl into cotton, the light looks like an incandescent blotch on heaven—God's urine in stained glass on an awesome scale, a hotly contested work of art, perhaps, by a painter/photographer of Latin-American extraction, or a cathedral, say, in Rome, the flaked and scaling plaster mapped by brackish water and mildew, a cathedral where the Polish pope is no doubt droning Easter mass right now, it being later there than here, so probably tomorrow already. And it's spreading, the yellow fog, like sweat on sheets or hatred. That's what the light of Easter through the unseasonably raw Saturday reminds me of. And of London, Jack the Ripper, fish and chips in yesterday's *Evening Standard,* of unheated bathrooms, longing, and brandy hangovers in an Earl's Court bed-sitter.

I'm watching this sky from the bed of a fourth-floor flat on Ninth Avenue where a somewhat overweight but extremely intense young blonde is finger-fucking me while sucking my dick. No condom. It's still sort of safe now, or it isn't, or it sort of is, or some people think it is, or people are so sick of everybody still being dead they figure, *Who gives a shit?* Resurrections, like the Japanese yen, being in greater demand than supply these days, we pilgrims settle for a naked hard-on incubated for an hour or so in mucous tissue at ninety-eight point six degrees Fahrenheit.

The hair's a dye job, of course, and actually *streaked...*or *tipped*—a subtle distinction, to be sure—but it started out reasonably fair and it's long, the way I like it, and smells sweet—like papaya. There's some kind of scented candle thing going on, too, but they all smell like wax to me. But sweet. All burning things smell sweet. The day after the old ghetto burned the whole neighborhood smelled like marshmallows, but that was long ago and far away—well, about sixty miles on I-95. It smelled like roast fowl, too, but that's because the Mesopotamian next door kept a flock of guard ducks that never got out of their pen.

You just dial, you see, seven little easy-to-remember digits. *Punch in* is, of course, more accurate, since you need a Touchtone phone to proceed. Listen to the "menu," then poke the six to listen to the "*actual voices* of New York's *hottest professionals.*" "Hi, I'm Jim. I'm five-foot-ten, weigh one-fifty. I give a hot-oil full-body Swedish massage with a sensual release, and more." *Oooh, baby.*

Take notes. Choose. Call the number. Leave yours on the machine. Wait. Dial again. Leave your number. And again. Wait. Wonder if any of them will call back. It is, after all, a holiday Saturday night. Desperation rises from the smoldering coals of desire: You will agree to see whoever calls first, no matter how much he charges, no matter where in the city he lives, even if it's the Upper East Side. Desire—sprung from the ether like crocus through the unsuspecting snow.

His name is Chip. Right. He's six-two, one-eighty or -ninety, twenty-four, from Massachusetts. Shaved balls for some reason. An angel puppy with a hot mouth—and I've got the bite marks on my unshaved ass to prove it. I did his lover yesterday, who is better looking but less enthusiastic. Neither of them know. It's my little secret (and, by the way, I'd like to have them both together).

A hundred bucks. It doesn't seem like much until after you come. Well, holidays and all...and one from each side of the family tree. Special occasion, that sort of thing. He's Caucasian, not my usual choice. They look better dressed as a rule. Maybe it's the northern light. Too much unrelenting pallor for passion, perhaps, or for honesty, as far as that goes. There's something about white that lies on its face. If you pass white light through a prism it breaks down into its component colors: puritan purple, repression red, entitlement green, conformity yellow.

This white boy is an exception, I think, as I watch the Empire State Building through what looks like the steam that water turns into when hosed onto an inferno. Back in the early eighties, there was a bath-house in San Francisco that had a steam-room maze. I sucked weenie until I practically passed out from dehydration. I learned about chemistry in bathhouses—not from the red tin box of chemicals I got from my parents the birthday I asked for drums, or from the minister of our church, who did little lab experiments on compulsory Wednesday night services during Lent, turning some clear liquid red, which was supposed to remind us of Our Lord and Savior Jesus Christ's first miracle (turning the water to wedding wine at Cana). I don't imagine that indemnity carriers allow toy companies to market chemistry sets anymore. Although it was all pretty benign. Nothing at home ever turned colors. Just into a sludge, like powdered chocolate that stubbornly refused to dissolve in milk.

In bathhouses, in the pitch dark, you can touch a dozen men and feel nothing but flesh—the same feeling you might get rubbing up against an old woman on the uptown local. And then you touch another man, his arm or chest or waist, and your dick leaps to attention like it's on a spring and you are engulfed by him. That's chemistry, when the elements overcome the prejudices the mind has insulated the senses in.

This Empire State Building yellow is the same yellow they lit it that Friday night after St. Patrick's Day, as I recall, the first time the poor oppressed Irish Catholics who run the city of New York refused to let any queers march in their boozy parade (I keep track of holidays by how much pain they cause—ask me about Fourth of July of '76, or Halloween, 1970). There was, of course, the year the Empire State Building was illuminated especially for the troops in the Persian Gulf. Before it was a footnote—Desert Storm? The war in which American G.I.s were poisoned by chemical weapons invented here and supplied to the enemy by us. It's almost as ironic as the fact that Irish faggots march routinely in St. Pat's parades in, for example, Dublin and Belfast. It's only Fifth Avenue that's too narrow for fairies.

Of course, even piss yellow was better than the red, white, and trite fucking blue they were shoving down our throats before the war was over. Patriotism. Sounds lethal. Like botulism. And it is. You'd think they'd go for something less cadaverous, chromatically speaking, for so prominent and phallic a landmark—a nice white-inspired yellow, like wheat or a Yalie's argyles, suburban kitchens of the 1950s, or sunlight on the arm hairs of a Norwegian sailor, a sapling swabbie on leave abroad and not sure where to berth his buoy, not some revolting color that looks like what's been sitting in a stopped-up toilet at the Eros All-Male Cinema on Eighth Avenue for a week or two underneath that scrawny nude kid who'll take anybody or anything into his mouth or up his ass or all over his body. You've never seen hunger until you've said, "I don't think so," and looked into those eyes while you let loose your stream into a nearby urinal while that scabby desperado nearly weeps to see you waste it. It's nice to be so sure of what you want. I envy that. It's the obsession that frightens me, for obvious reasons.

Here's what makes me puke: that washed-out bow-ribbon yellow florists were doling out to tie around trees in working-class Republican neighborhoods in Brooklyn and Queens during the Desert Storm fiasco, the satin ribbon they paste gold paper letters on to spell out *Congratulations* and *Beloved Uncle Guido* and so forth. Of course, even that isn't as bad as the yellow they aim at the Empire State Building, at enormous cost no doubt, a yellow that has some Gaelic emerald in it left over from the No-Pansies Drunken Mick Pig Parade—or else some khaki in it to remind us how cool America is for having the biggest army in the whole wide Western world.

How long has it been? A year or two, and it's so over it's like it never happened. Except for the dismembered orphans and the troops of veterans who are rotting slowly from the inside, thanks to the American army. All those dead people, and nothing to show for it but an oil slick the size of Nebraska. And don't get me started on Vietnam, where a hundred thousand American boys are buried in rice weed. It's a tourist destination now, and I'd go if I could. Just to be near the place where Ralph died—in the days when boys still died one at a time and not in droves like the firstborn of Egypt. The angel of death doesn't pass over very many any more, ram's blood or no. Maybe blood just isn't as repellent as it used to be now that the national immune system is...compromised.

So the roiling midtown sky is blazing like it's National Water Sports Week instead of Easter. And Passover. Like the skyline is an Andres Serrano "Architectural Icon Suspended in Urine" lithograph. And the country's finances, like those of its citizens, are in the toilet. It was Kenny's humiliation that he could no longer get himself onto a toilet seat that finally did him in. The will just cracks, like the Liberty Bell, like Easter eggs boiled too fast on a gas stove, or a vial of poppers. Twenty years ago, when I was young and Ralph was already dead, on the night of a lonely birthday, I got smashed on beers at a bar uptown and this blazer homo named Wayne took me to his luxury doorman tower to piss in his mouth, which, as I remember it through an amber haze of guilt, memory, and a dozen bottles of brew, kept turning him yellower as I let loose—pulling hard on his scab-crusted nipples all the while—yellower than hepatitis eventually turned my eyeballs: mustard-gas yellow, the spewing sulfurous billow above a chemical plant in Baghdad hit by a US scud, the pus color a kid's legs get when they've been blown off at the knees and there aren't any antibiotics left in the country so the kid will die real slow of infections, of peritonitis, just like Bette Davis in merciful black and white, without brain fever and hallucinations in Arabic. Maybe we didn't really kill tens of thousands of Iraqi civilians, as impartial international observers insist. But, knowing us, we probably did, killing being the thing we do best. I'm so proud to be an American I could just shit shamrocks.

So what do you think, it's a coincidence that the same day Irish queers march for the first time in the St. Paddycake Parade (unauthorized, of course, by the Ancient Order of the Ku Klux Hibernians), two undercover vice goons bust a naked dancer at the Gaiety Burlesk for solicitation? So now there are no more private shows because the Greek broads who run the place are paranoid city, and Joey Stefano says, laconic as August in Ecuador, "Pigs are pigs," and eats a cold McDonald's single burger by the pay phone in the Get Acquainted Lounge, which used to smell of grass, cash, and impending sex, but now only smells of ammonia from where a Lebanese kid mops up the room behind the stage so the dancers won't slip on the generic-brand baby oil they use to get their dicks hard before working the runway for their second of two numbers.

I've spent a lot of time on floors in my day. Wooden floors of backroom bars passed out on coats, linoleum floors of peep show arcades working my jaws over any available hunk of sausage, tile floors of bathrooms in places like the Chelsea Hotel (coming to with dead Danny's dick up my ass), cement floors of various...institutions, let's say. And what I remember most is the smell of Pine-Sol, industrial strength. It's an aphrodisiac to me now, like glue, however toxic when inhaled. Behind the screen at the Gaiety Burlesk, it used to smell like semen and the mellow illusion of possibility, now it just smells like sweat. There'd be a lot less hypocrisy in the world, I always say, if human odors were indelible. Of course, there'd be a lot more flies, too.

I've spent a lot of time at the Gaiety Burlesk, too, and a lot of money in that sleazy little temple of priapus where you tend to run into people like the clerk from the mail room at work and David Hockney. It's a microcosm, you know, although too many of the dancers on any given night are likely to be white. Most of the clients are bigoted old queens who get up and leave the auditorium when the black dancers come on, or the brown ones. Well, one thing about fags, we have not got our race shit together. But there were lessons to be learned at the Gaiety Burlesk, and not all the boys were white.

There were Latin boys of such devastating beauty I could get off just touching their flawless skin. Hairy Italians who all wanted you to think they were tops, and, okay, some of them were. Asians who set off every nerve in my body with their fingertips. And a black man once, a model in need of some emergency cash, who didn't want me even for money I was so fat at the time, but who got so turned on backstage when I went to work on his nipples he came when I did.

And there were special cases, too, boys I'd fall in love with just at the moment I shot a load all over the floor behind the screen wishing I had drenched them in that special way I have of spewing a load so big even the professionals gasp (and I'm not just bragging), and I'd visit them time after time.

Luis, or whatever his name was, a Puerto Rican from New Jersey who was working his way through landscape design courses at Rutgers, I'll never forget. I'll never forget the curving angle of his enormous cock-hard dick as he kneeled over my head at the Paramount Hotel (before the chichi renovation), or watching him shower, or his smile, or seeing him again in L.A. and taking him to dinner, and wanting him so bad through my pants I could feel them dampen. If I still had his phone number, I'd call him right now and dump a load anywhere he'd take it.

And there was Vladimir, of course, who got famous on late-night cable TV, Vladimir who was named after the vampire in a Dracula movie his mother saw once, who came home with me one night-before-Gay-Pride-Parade-Day and waved to his fans along Christopher Street (I was so proud), and then stripped in my bedroom and made leisurely, reasonable love with his bulked up body for an hour or more. And Rocky, who got famous for a minute or two, too, when he teamed up with Madonna for a book and a video, but whose real name he told me when he came to clean my apartment—fully dressed—which was his legit day-job way of making money. Told me once in a hotel room he'd never been fucked (like *that* surprised me) or ever even fucked a man, which did take me aback—I mean, what with his muscles and dick and tattoos and dazzling smile and all, not to mention his profession, I'd have thought there'd be men around with enough cash to cajole him into it. And what was the most amazing thing to me was how he just seemed amazed that gay men could like it, not that he thought it was disgusting or anything, just outside his experience (which extended to war).

There was, of course, Brazilian Julio (in Portuguese, you pronounce the *J*, as in Juliet), who was, as I was, born in July, a real dancer, with career potential. "You are so big," he said to me that first night we met, the night of the hotel that overlooked Lincoln Center's Christmas tree, "You are so big you can do anything to me," he said. So I did. I fucked him—again and again. I fucked him in hotel rooms and I fucked him in my apartment when I finally moved to New York and I even fucked him behind the screen at the Gaiety Burlesk, which ran strictly counter to the dancers' code.

"You are crazy," Julio said once while I was fucking him off the floor by the emergency exit, alternating my dick and half a hand so I wouldn't come too soon. "Do you really think so?" I asked, wondering if it was true. "But it's okay," he smiled, "because I'm crazy too—I love it." And he did, this sweet and generous boy/man who was as beautiful as any many I've ever desired, even in Carmen Miranda drag, which he wore to the Gay Parade for years. He was beautiful beside me at the ballet, too.

He was the tiniest man I ever had and I wish I had him again now, to toss in the air and catch on my dick like a game of quoits.

Yes, those were the glory days, when sex was encouraged right smack on the premises, like a cut-rate brothel. But the Gaiety is not the scene it was before the Gulf War (not, strictly speaking, named for the oil company, but obviously fought on its behalf). So...what? You think the bust at the Gaiety was related to the war at all or just a coincidence? Or the parade where you have to be an RC het-breeder to be Irish? Or are the war and the parade somehow linked to this crack-down on grease-smeared ass-cracks just by the general, you know, ethos of the time, the odor of *facismo* on the rise numbing its prey like a giant water beetle?

So, I told myself the first night I turned up at the Gaiety after the "No Sex, Please, We're Busted" message went out, "Well, you might as well tie a yellow ribbon around Rocky's cock since you're not gonna get your lips around it, not tonight." So I stuck my middle finger straight up for those shit-Mick douche bags who booed and spat on the Irish queens in the city's lousy St. Pat-my-ass Parade. I stuck it straight up the fuckhole of a new dancer named Daniel in his room at the Milford Plaza, which cost me a whole lot more than backstage folderol but turned out to be worth it.

Daniel's American-born, but he's one of those border-town Lone Star Latins with hair longer than a girl's and crooked teeth in front. Couldn't be more appealing (as at least one big deal photographer has discovered), though I could do without the safety-pin tattoos. His eyes are swimming in something he uses so his brain won't see things the way his eyes do. He calls me Daddy Bear and has the usual gigantic uncut dick, which is nearly blue it's so dark, but I don't care, even if it does remind me of Roberto, dead and alive. I just want something up his ass. I'd use a shillelagh if I had one. He'll take my dick if I'm willing to re-negotiate, and there is nothing I'd like better than to sink myself up to the ruby pubes in those fleshy buns of his, but I'm not making the bucks I was, so we settle on fingers, which I give him 'til we both come, simultaneously, which I take as an enormous compliment, since even at his age, he can't afford to come with every trick, so most of them don't ever. I've been lucky that way, since I don't find a lot of pleasure in it unless I'm turning on my partner in the process.

"It's a gusher," he drawls in his cutesy way when I geyser all over his too-fleshy middle. He eats a banana, chugs a politically responsible Bud Lite, belches real ladylike, and says, "I don't know, I think everybody's queer." It's a hustler's perspective, sure, but you gotta admit there's some truth in it. In the elevator, there's a Chinese escort hostess in silver rhinestone shoes and fake leopard coat who clocks our number before we drop half a floor, and a little blond girl with brand-new breasts who's here on a school trip from Virginia and who hasn't got a clue and never will, unless, of course, she winds up working this same hotel. It can happen. Even in Newport News. She looks like she's dressed for a junior prom sometime before the Beatles' TV debut. It'd be a fun group to get stuck on an elevator with, but of course we don't get stuck (that waits until I'm trapped with a hysterical sumo wrestler who hasn't bathed since Tito died).

We sashay out of the elevator, across the lobby, through the criss-crossed laser glares of the Jamaican security staff, their scrutiny thick as chemical warfare, but nobody says jack shit. That's what business is all about: that smell of printer's ink, of fine engraving and finesse. Which is why it's so funny not long after when this rich Italian entrepreneur gets busted at the Milford Plaza for bringing a far younger and far more African young woman to his room for immoral congress (US legislature take note). Only it turns out—big oops here—the young lady is not exactly working. She is exactly the Italian's *wife*. Red faces everywhere and banner headlines in the *Post*.

Speaking of which, I don't think it's all that much a coincidence that the *Post* does this giant cover story—right after the mayor of New York—the good one, not the one we have now—marches down Fifth Avenue with a clutch of lilting laddies and lasses of the Old Sod and Gomorrah persuasion—with this sensational big mother headline announcing that there are hustlers on Second Avenue at 53rd Street—a fact that every two- or four-legged sodomite has known since Cain set up shop on the northeast corner. Talk about your phenomenal scoop, right? Yeah, scoop of dog shit. Somehow it all comes down to Ireland. I used to like Ireland. Used to think the IRA was a righteous club, a kind of Black Panther Party with red hair and freckles.

In London, once upon a time, before Ralph was dead or I'd ever fucked a man to sleep, I met a drunk in Russell Square, a beggar: Irish, beard/mustache, fingers stained yellow from unfiltered cigarettes, Turkish when he could get them—and I bought him a whole pack near the poetry bookstore and the School of Economics. "Watch out for Ireland," he said, as broad in the blarney, I thought, as he was in the brogue. "Another Vietnam, my son, as sure as I'm standing." And he was, still standing, breathing the most fetid breath I'd ever smelled, being young. I was "Up the Irish" for years after—Yeats, O'Casey, Behan. Now I'm sick of it. Sick of blowing up the English just because they shop in Harrod's.

Sick of the prig English, their stiff lips and limp dicks, but mostly sick of every Roman Catholic country on earth.

Fuckin' Ireland. The country's about as big as Staten Island and they can't even figure out how to have two religions without killing each other (a lot like Israel, but don't get me started). No doubt about it, religion has caused more evil in the world than every hooker put together. Religion is the process by which God is eliminated from matters of the spirit and replaced by human will, the empirically fallible will of a self-protective priesthood. Simple as that. And isn't patriotism, like cannibalism, a form of religion, really?

So I just eat an overpriced ham sandwich at Jerry's on Prince and wonder if these really deep, shrewd news hounds at the *Post* know that black men sell dope in Washington Square or that there are rainbow-colored junkies in this city washing windshields for quarters to support minor children. I have a cousin who's missing an eye for refusing one of these overzealous spot-removers. An oft-wed black sheep (son of an oft-wed black sheep), he was once married to one of the Rockettes, who used to dress up like nuns for the Easter show at Radio City Music Hall and carry white lilies up to this stage-set altar to form a giant cross (for which spectacle we'd wait outside on 50th Street for hours, me mesmerized by the stark naked Art Deco cement men above the entrance to Rockefeller Center, the first men I ever coveted in my heart, and still do).

And I wonder if the *Post* boys know how heroic old Manhattan pissed on the potato-eaters who built the bridges and subways and City Hall, those same County Corkers who lynched escaped slaves from lampposts in the Village during the Civil War riots. Talk about casting a jaundiced eye. I guess that's why they call it "yellow" journalism. Because of the cowardice.

So I go to visit the folks on the Island, during the Gulf War, which turns out to be the usual mistake, and of course, masters of the mundane, they have a yellow ribbon tied around the trunk of a tree I grew up with and got to know fairly well. I even sat in that tree, and here it is hung with this hate-thing. Oh, the next-door neighbors have a bigger one, the Irish neighbors (no one's speaking to the Polish neighbors because the old man, who used to sell Wise Potato Chips, has gone completely dotty), and a flag in the picture window that says *These Colors Never Fade*. Sweet, sweet as new corn. Catholics and politics. So this friend of mine in California, not, to be sure, a bastion of rigid news sourcing, tells me this rumor that's being investigated in Europe that the pope, the Polish one, was in fact a collaborator with the Nazis during World War II, that he actually turned over the names of Jews to save his own skinless kielbasa. I believe it. Popes have been helping Nazis all along—take Pius XII, please! It is said, and by Roman Catholics themselves, mind you, that Pope John Paul I, whose pontificate was shorter than the Gulf War, that Johnny Paul Uno was actually murdered right there in the Vatican by an opposition claque of Machiavellian minions.

Chris (for Christian, not Christopher) says he doesn't believe any of it, but then Chris goes to Georgetown were Jesuits teach Skepticism 101 no matter what the curriculum is called. He admits, though, that the whole clergy is queer, including New York's reigning necrophilic, Cardinal O'Connor (who likes his cock-swallowing acolytes dead, you see), that "We're not in the business of saving lives, but of saving souls" anticondom pro-lifer, that genocidal bog-hopper with a piss-shooter the size of a leprechaun's. "Why didn't someone try to kill him?" I can remember asking about Hitler, since he was so obviously evil. Same goes for O'Connor. How come he's still alive?

So somebody pistol-whipped a priest in Queens or Brooklyn or someplace to feed a wicked jones with the parish lucre and everybody's all shocked and alarmed. Right. Fucking priests been pistol-whipping faggots for centuries. Kill 'em all, that's what I say. Like cockroaches.

So it's Easter, and Passover, but I don't miss chocolate bunnies under yellow and lilac cellophane. You know what I miss? Rubberless fucking, since fucking with a glove on is no fucking at all, as any man who has ever done both will tell you. Oh, it might be worth giving up "unprotected" sex to save a life, but what's a life that only has protected sex in it? Rhetorical question. It's like a bullfight where the sword stays in its sheath.

Bullfights. They make me weep, they're so inaccessibly beautiful. They are, of course, the ultimate *symbolic* entertainment: Either the matador will fuck the bull (with his sword), or *el toro* will fuck the *toreador* (goring him with one or more horns). It is, Carlos Fuentes assures us, the ritual of man's supremacy over nature. But it's really about fucking, which is to say about man's total abandonment to, and submissiveness in the face of, nature.

The bullfighter is dressed magnificently in second-skin topaz satin, his asscheeks clenched tighter than fetal fists, his bundle of genitalia casting harsh shadows on his hard thighs. The bull comes equipped with a prick the size of the man's arm, two horns, and a lolling tongue that looks like a dick and a tongue combined—one of those giant mollusks on display in Chinatown fish shops. Of course, the bull will die even if he manages to take down his tormentor in the process, immortality, like justice, being a fantasy.

Two men fucking is like a bullfight, too, a ritual of man's confrontation with the nature in himself. No illusions of sanctioned procreation to dilute the event, no easy retreat into the uncomprehending "otherness" of opposites, just man as he is, man doing to himself—and having done to himself—the thing the world has taught him will most surely damn him for all eternity. So, the bull dies, fucker or fuckee. And blood glistens in the parched sand of the arena. A man fucking a woman is beautiful, too, in its way, I suppose. But there is no mortality in it. It is, if ritual at all, an enactment of the myth of life. Queer sex is nature in the service of itself in the present, not the future.

The greatest of all mysteries, *The Mahabarata* tells us, is that every man must die, and yet each day lives his life as if he is immortal. In the face of such wisdom, such clarity, it hardly seems to matter if there is an eternity at all.

Once upon a time when Easter and Passover happened on the same day, I was sitting in the administration building of the college I went to by mistake, along with a third of the student body, in protest over fraternity exclusion of Blacks and Jews. I remember a chevron of geese flying overhead and a balmy, spongy-earth day with daffodils blooming wild on green hills, and I remember hope. (That's why preserving the hope of the young is so important, so it can be remembered later in life.)

The upstate May-time sky was clear and blue, like Chip's eyes as he veils his hair now over me and puts his tongue onto my tongue like the Host. The body and blood of Chip. As often as I do this...I remember all kinds of men. Most of them dead. Like the reed-thin corpses of the Holocaust (their exposed genitalia the first human penises I ever saw, enormous-looking, enticing even attached to dead men). Like the saints and disciples. Horrible deaths, most of them. Crucified, stoned, burned, quartered, fed to wild beasts—just the sort of thing the church has been doing to fairies forever.

Now Magic Johnson has AIDS, which is sad I guess, but I can't get all broken up about it. Arthur Asch has been dropped as a crossword clue in the *New York Times,* so there's some real impact on my life there. "Isn't it awful about Arthur Asch?" some twinkie in Lycra biker shorts gushed at the gym right after that news became public. To tell the truth, I didn't actually give a shit about Arthur Asch. Or any other heterosexual. They've had their millennia, and they've blown it (up). The world is better off without them. There are too many people anyway. Too many people who hate. So I guess the world would be better off without me, too, since I have learned to hate so purely. But then, the world won't have long to wait for that. I'll be going one of these days, one of the ways we're dying: bad blood, tainted blood, spilled blood. We're all dying of the yellow anyway, of the Empire State Building piss yellow of religious holidays and patriotism, an oily yellow lost in a mist that looks like it should smell of subways, that bum-urine and burnt electric cordite smell of blue-white sparks on gleaming tracks. Instead it smells sweet. Like the licorice jelly beans my Polish Catholic godmother picked out of the Easter baskets she gave me before she died and went to burn in hell forever for marrying a Lutheran and loving her queer nephew without condition.

So it's late. The car alarm out front finally died after about six hours since the police don't have the authority to do anything but beat up faggots who have the temerity to hail a yellow cab outside the Stage Deli. My fingers still smell like Chip, like the scented massage lotion he rubbed on my body and I rubbed on his, of my own semen and his, of Obsession for Men, and large, luminous eyes, of views of the Empire State Building from the floor-level mattress of a part-time hustler who's moving south at the end of the month to pursue a career in music. It's Easter already by the digital Bulova on my desk. It's raining, which means the smeared diarrhetic dog shit is being washed from the sidewalk out front with the soot from chimneys a century old and more. The acid that turns copper green is washing out of the air onto the cobbled streets of lower Manhattan while a small rat forages under my sink for the poisoned oats an exterminator left there on Good Friday.

The rain falls onto the aluminum hood of the kitchen exhaust fan, reminding me of an intravenous drip and nickels. Some unkillable fungus grows under my toenails (I call it Cardinal O'Connor). But despite it all, despite the pot of coffee and a quart of Diet Pepsi I just ingested in lieu of the blood of Christ, I'll sleep soundly tonight, while junkies curl up in doorways and shoot tepid smack into their veins, grateful not to go to sleep sick. After all, it's a holiday.

I'll take an aspirin against the pains of holidays and age and sleep with memories of Chip in my mouth, of Joey Stefano (higher than a kite, his asshole open to accept the loneliness of the male world). I'll think of lovers who smelled of formaldehyde even before they died and jerk off wondering if Ralph was ever happy. And I'll drift off on clouds of beer-swilling Texican Daniel. He was a rose, all right, a yellow rose that I am dreaming of, of Danny Boy from Dallas, of hate in Irish eyes, and vengeance.

About the Authors

M. Christian lives, works, and plays in San Francisco (and is most of what that implies). He is proud to consider himself a literary street-walker with a heart of gold. As such, he can be many things to many people—but that costs extra. Known whereabouts: *Noirotica, Southern Comfort, Best American Erotica 1994, FutureSex* magazine, and other fine, and slutty, publications near you.

Mitch Cullin studies Creative Writing at the University of Houston. His short fiction has appeared in *The Santa Fe Literary Review, The Gilasolo, CTC Chronicle, The Bayou Review,* and *Christopher Street.* He won a 1995 Southwest Writers Workshop Award for his story "Ricochet."

Jameson Currier's writings about AIDS and the gay community have appeared in a variety of publications, including *The Washington Post, Newsday, The Philadelphia Inquirer, The Los Angeles Times, Ten Percent,* and *Body Positive.* He is the author of *Dancing on the Moon: Short Stories About AIDS* (Viking Penguin) and the creator of the documentary film *Living Proof: HIV and the Pursuit of Happiness.*

Mark David M. Fennell lives in New York City, where he is a freelance book designer and self-proclaimed computer geek who has thousands of CDs, about twelve of which he listens to. "Prime Real Estate" is from his yet-to-be-published collection of short stories, *Rampant.* He is currently working on a novel, *Letters from My Last Best Friend.*

Stephen Greco is a former senior editor of *Interview.* His story "Good with Words" appears in *The Penguin Book of Gay Short Stories* and was also included in *Flesh and the Word.*

Rick Jackson grew up in a small logging town in central Oregon. After learning all that lumberjacks had to teach him about love, Rick ran away to the Marine Corps. He now officially lives in Honolulu, but spends most of his time wherever the action is. Over the last decade, he has written more than five hundred stories for a variety of magazines, including *First Hand, Advocate Men, Drummer,* and *Inches.* His first book, *Horndog Squids and Cherry Marines,* made the Pentagon nervous. Two more books await publication.

A recovering Californian, **Alex Jeffers** lives with his two cats in Boston, where they listen to a great deal of Baroque music and read a lot about faraway places. *Safe as Houses,* his first novel, was published in 1995 by Faber and Faber. "The Voice of the Capon" is excerpted from "Dramma per Musica," a pseudo-autobiographical novella, the whole of which will be included in his pseudo-autobiographical second book, *Selected Letters: the Ethan stories.* Shorter work is forthcoming in *modern words* and *Happily Ever After: Erotic Fairy Tales for Men.*

Owen Keehnen resides in Chicago. His work has appeared in such anthologies as *Flesh and the Word 3* and *Ex-Lover Weird Shit,* and in numerous magazines, including *Forum, Christopher Street, Men's Style,* and *Holy Titclamps.*

Miodrag Kojadinović grew up in Serbia, which only abolished its sodomy law in the spring of 1995. He studied general linguistics in Belgrade, Yugoslavia, and did further work in language in Hasselt, Belgium and the Nijenrode Castle, Netherlands. His poetry has appeared in *Delo, Afterthoughts,* and *Prism International;* and his film, book, theater, and photography reviews, as well as political commentaries, in *Angles, Triangles, Steam,* and *Vreme.* He has translated the works of Gerard Reve and Timothy Findley into Serbian. He lives in Vancouver.

Michael Lassell is the author of two volumes of poetry—*Poems for Lost and Un-lost Boys* (Amelia) and *Decade Dance* (Alyson), winner of a Lambda Literary Award—and of *The Hard Way* (Richard Kasak Books), a collection of his poetry, fiction, and nonfiction. He is the editor of *The Name of Love* (St. Martin's Press) and *Eros in Boystown* (Crown), two small anthologies of poetry by gay men. His work is included in anthologies such as *Gay & Lesbian Poetry in Our Time, Men on Men 3, Hometowns, Flesh and the Word, New Worlds of Literature, Looking for Mr. Preston, The Badboy Book of Erotic Poetry,* and *Wanderlust.* His writing has appeared in scores of literary and not-so-literary journals from *Fag Rag, Torso, Lisp,* and the "Queer City" edition of *The Portable Lower East Side* to such publications as *The New York Times, Interview, Dance Magazine, Out, The Advocate,* and *Frontiers.* He lives in New York City.

Scott O'Hara is the editor of *Steam* magazine, and can be reached at P.O. Box 460292, San Francisco, CA 94146. He welcomes letters, filthy or otherwise.

Carol Queen is a San Francisco writer, activist, and sex educator. Her work appears frequently in sexzines and has been anthologized in *Leatherwomen, Dagger, The Erotic Impulse, Bi Any Other Name, Madonnarama, Once Upon a Time: Erotic Fairy Tales for Women,* and other collections of erotic writing and sex essays. "Ganged" is excerpted from the novel-in-progress *The Leather Daddy and the Femme.* For the first two chapters of the novel, see *Doing It for Daddy* (Alyson), edited by Pat Califia.

Matthew Rettenmund is the author of the books *Encyclopedia Madonnica* (St. Martin's Press) and *Totally Awesome '80s* (St. Martin's Press), and the novel *Boy Culture* (St. Martin's Press). His short story "I Am in Love with Prince Andrew, Duke of York" appears in *Mondo Royals,* and his erotic fiction has appeared in the anthologies *My Three Boys, Sportsmen, Switch Hitters, Wanderlust,* and *Southern Comfort,* and in *Badboy* and *Mandate* magazines. He is currently an associate editor for MMG Services, which publishes several gay erotic magazines.

Thomas Roche's writing has appeared in such magazines as *Black Sheets, Paramour, Boudoir Noir,* and *Slippery When Wet,* and in such anthologies as *Dark Angels, Ritual Sex, S/M Futures, Selling Venus, Razor Kiss,* and *Switch Hitters,* among others. He is the editor of *Noirotica* (Richard Kasak Books) and coeditor, with Michael Rowe, of the forthcoming *Sons of Darkness* (Cleis Press).

Michael Rowe is the author of *Writing Below The Belt: Conversations With Erotic Authors* (Richard Kasak Books) and the novel *Darkling I Listen* (Richard Kasak Books), and coeditor, with Thomas Roche, of the forthcoming *Sons of Darkness* (Cleis Press). His essays and journalism are widely anthologized, and his fiction appears most recently in *Flesh and The Word 3, Flashpoint,* and *Queer View Mirror.* He lives in Toronto with his life-partner, Brian, and their adopted nephew, Patrick.

D. Travers Scott studied writing and performance at the School of the Art Institute of Chicago. His work has appeared in publications such as

179

Harper's, Steam, Fruit, High Performance, wilde, New Art Examiner, numerous 'zines, and in the anthologies *Reclaiming the Heartland, Southern Comfort, Switch Hitters, Ritual Sex, Hard at Work,* and *The Object of My Affection.* A winner in *Steam* magazine's 1994 Porn Press Awards, he recently edited an issue of *P-form* on pornography and performance art. He lives and works in Portland, Oregon, and thanks Jase and the rec.arts.bodyart folks for their help with his story.

Simon Sheppard's work has appeared in publications ranging from *The James White Review* to *The Badboy Book of Erotic Poetry.* His erotic stories can be found in a growing number of anthologies, including *Ritual Sex, Noirotica, Stallions & Other Studs,* and *Switch Hitters.* He lives in San Francisco, where he is, among other things, a leather daddy.

180

ABOUT THE EDITORS

Scott Heim is the author of the novel *Mysterious Skin* (HarperCollins), the poetry collection *Saved from Drowning* (Chiron Press) and the forthcoming novel *In Awe* (HarperCollins). He holds degrees from the University of Kansas and Columbia University.

Michael Ford, series editor, is the author of numerous books, including *The World Out There: Becoming Part of the Lesbian and Gay Community* (The New Press). His articles and essays have appeared in magazines including *The Advocate, Lambda Book Report, Publishers Weekly, Current Biography, Music Alive,* and *QW,* and in the book *Generation Q: Inheriting Stonewall.* Writing as Tom Caffrey, he is the author of the erotic short story collections *Hitting Home & Other Stories* (BadBoy) and *Tales from the Men's Room* (BadBoy), and is the editor of *Happily Ever After: Erotic Fairy Tales for Men* (Richard Kasak Books). His stories have appeared in *Best American Erotica 1995, Flashpoint, Ritual Sex,* and *Sportsmen,* among others.

Books from Cleis Press

Sexual Politics

Forbidden Passages: Writings Banned in Canada introductions by Pat Califia and Janine Fuller.
ISBN: 1-57344-020-5 24.95 cloth;
ISBN: 1-57344-019-1 14.95 paper.

Good Sex: Real Stories from Real People, second edition, by Julia Hutton.
ISBN: 1-57344-001-9 29.95 cloth;
ISBN: 1-57344-000-0 14.95 paper.

The Good Vibrations Guide to Sex: How to Have Safe, Fun Sex in the '90s by Cathy Winks and Anne Semans.
ISBN: 0-939416-83-2 29.95 cloth;
ISBN: 0-939416-84-0 16.95 paper.

I Am My Own Woman: The Outlaw Life of Charlotte von Mahlsdorf translated by Jean Hollander.
ISBN: 1-57344-011-6 24.95 cloth;
ISBN: 1-57344-010-8 12.95 paper.

Madonnarama: Essays on Sex and Popular Culture edited by Lisa Frank and Paul Smith.
ISBN: 0-939416-72-7 24.95 cloth;
ISBN: 0-939416-71-9 9.95 paper.

Public Sex: The Culture of Radical Sex by Pat Califia.
ISBN: 0-939416-88-3 29.95 cloth;
ISBN: 0-939416-89-1 12.95 paper.

Sex Work: Writings by Women in the Sex Industry edited by Frédérique Delacoste and Priscilla Alexander.
ISBN: 0-939416-10-7 24.95 cloth;
ISBN: 0-939416-11-5 16.95 paper.

Susie Bright's Sexual Reality: A Virtual Sex World Reader by Susie Bright.
ISBN: 0-939416-58-1 24.95 cloth;
ISBN: 0-939416-59-X 9.95 paper.

Susie Bright's Sexwise by Susie Bright.
ISBN: 1-57344-003-5 24.95 cloth;
ISBN: 1-57344-002-7 10.95 paper.

Susie Sexpert's Lesbian Sex World by Susie Bright.
ISBN: 0-939416-34-4 24.95 cloth;
ISBN: 0-939416-35-2 9.95 paper.

Lesbian and Gay Studies

Best Gay Erotica 1996 selected by Scott Heim, edited by Michael Ford.
ISBN: 1-57344-053-1 24.95 cloth;
ISBN: 1-57344-052-3 12.95 paper.

Best Lesbian Erotica 1996 selected by Heather Lewis, edited by Tristan Taormino.
ISBN: 1-57344-055-8 24.95 cloth;
ISBN: 1-57344-054-X 12.95 paper.

Boomer: Railroad Memoirs by Linda Niemann.
ISBN: 0-939416-55-7 12.95 paper.

The Case of the Good-For-Nothing Girlfriend by Mabel Maney.
ISBN: 0-939416-90-5 24.95 cloth;
ISBN: 0-939416-91-3 10.95 paper.

The Case of the Not-So-Nice Nurse by Mabel Maney.
ISBN: 0-939416-75-1 24.95 cloth;
ISBN: 0-939416-76-X 9.95 paper.

Dagger: On Butch Women edited by Roxxie, Lily Burana, Linnea Due.
ISBN: 0-939416-81-6 29.95 cloth;
ISBN: 0-939416-82-4 14.95 paper.

Dark Angels: Lesbian Vampire Stories edited by Pam Keesey.
ISBN: 1-57344-015-9 24.95 cloth;
ISBN 1-7344-014-0 10.95 paper.

Daughters of Darkness: Lesbian Vampire Stories edited by Pam Keesey.
ISBN: 0-939416-77-8 24.95 cloth;
ISBN: 0-939416-78-6 9.95 paper.

Different Daughters: A Book by Mothers of Lesbians, second edition, edited by Louise Rafkin.
ISBN: 1-57344-051-5 24.95 cloth;
ISBN: 1-57344-050-7 12.95 paper.

Different Mothers: Sons & Daughters of Lesbians Talk About Their Lives edited by Louise Rafkin.
ISBN: 0-939416-40-9 24.95 cloth;
ISBN: 0-939416-41-7 9.95 paper.

Dyke Strippers: Lesbian Cartoonists A to Z edited by Roz Warren.
ISBN: 1-57344-009-4 29.95 cloth;
ISBN: 1-57344-008-6 16.95 paper.

Girlfriend Number One: Lesbian Life in the '90s edited by Robin Stevens.
ISBN: 0-939416-79-4 29.95 cloth;
ISBN: 0-939416-8 12.95 paper.

Hothead Paisan: Homicidal Lesbian Terrorist by Diane DiMassa.
ISBN: 0-939416-73-5 14.95 paper.

A Lesbian Love Advisor by Celeste West.
ISBN: 0-939416-27-1 24.95 cloth;
ISBN: 0-939416-26-3 9.95 paper.

More Serious Pleasure: Lesbian Erotic Stories and Poetry edited by the Sheba Collective.
ISBN: 0-939416-48-4 24.95 cloth;
ISBN: 0-939416-47-6 9.95 paper.

Nancy Clue and the Hardly Boys in A Ghost in the Closet by Mabel Maney.
ISBN: 1-57344-013-2 24.95 cloth;
ISBN: 1-57344-012-4 10.95 paper.

The Night Audrey's Vibrator Spoke: A Stonewall Riots Collection by Andrea Natalie.
ISBN: 0-939416-64-6 8.95 paper.

Queer and Pleasant Danger: Writing Out My Life by Louise Rafkin.
ISBN: 0-939416-60-3 24.95 cloth;
ISBN: 0-939416-61-1 9.95 paper.

Revenge of Hothead Paisan: Homicidal Lesbian Terrorist by Diane DiMassa.
ISBN: 1-57344-016-7 16.95 paper.

Rubyfruit Mountain: A Stonewall Riots Collection by Andrea Natalie.
ISBN: 0-939416-74-3 9.95 paper.

Serious Pleasure: Lesbian Erotic Stories and Poetry edited by the Sheba Collective.
ISBN: 0-939416-46-8 24.95 cloth;
ISBN: 0-939416-45-X 9.95 paper.

Switch Hitters: Lesbians Write Gay Male Erotica and Gay Men Write Lesbian Erotica edited by Carol Queen and Lawrence Schimel.
ISBN: 1-57344-022-1 24.95 cloth;
ISBN: 1-57344-021-3 12.95 paper.

Politics of Health

The Absence of the Dead Is Their Way of Appearing by Mary Winfrey Trautmann.
ISBN: 0-939416-04-2 8.95 paper.

Don't: A Woman's Word by Elly Danica.
ISBN: 0-939416-23-9 21.95 cloth;
ISBN: 0-939416-22-0 8.95 paper

1 in 3: Women with Cancer Confront an Epidemic edited by Judith Brady.
ISBN: 0-939416-50-6 24.95 cloth;
ISBN: 0-939416-49-2 10.95 paper.

Voices in the Night: Women Speaking About Incest edited by Toni A.H. McNaron and Yarrow Morgan.
ISBN: 0-939416-02-6 9.95 paper.

With the Power of Each Breath: A Disabled Women's Anthology edited by Susan Browne, Debra Connors and Nanci Stern.
ISBN: 0-939416-09-3 24.95 cloth;
ISBN: 0-939416-06-9 10.95 paper.

Woman-Centered Pregnancy and Birth by the Federation of Feminist Women's Health Centers.
ISBN: 0-939416-03-4 11.95 paper.

Reference

Putting Out: The Essential Publishing Resource Guide For Gay and Lesbian Writers, third edition, by Edisol W. Dotson.
ISBN: 0-939416-86-7 29.95 cloth;
ISBN: 0-939416-87-5 12.95 paper.

Fiction

Cosmopolis: Urban Stories by Women edited by Ines Rieder.
ISBN: 0-939416-36-0 24.95 cloth;
ISBN: 0-939416-37-9 9.95 paper.

Dirty Weekend: A Novel of Revenge by Helen Zahavi.
ISBN: 0-939416-85-9 10.95 paper.

A Forbidden Passion by Cristina Peri Rossi.
ISBN: 0-939416-64-0 24.95 cloth;
ISBN: 0-939416-68-9 9.95 paper.

Half a Revolution: Contemporary Fiction by Russian Women edited by Masha Gessen.
ISBN 1-57344-007-8 $29.95 cloth;
ISBN 1-57344-006-X $12.95 paper.

In the Garden of Dead Cars by Sybil Claiborne.
ISBN: 0-939416-65-2 24.95 cloth;
ISBN: 0-939416-66-2 9.95 paper.

Night Train To Mother by Ronit Lentin.
ISBN: 0-939416-29-8 24.95 cloth;
ISBN: 0-939416-28-X 9.95 paper.

The One You Call Sister: New Women's Fiction edited by Paula Martinac.
ISBN: 0-939416-30-1 24.95 cloth;
ISBN: 0-9394l6031-X 9.95 paper.

Only Lawyers Dancing by Jan McKemmish.
ISBN: 0-939416-70-0 24.95 cloth;
ISBN: 0-939416-69-7 9.95 paper.

Seeing Dell by Carol Guess
ISBN: 1-57344-024-8 24.95 cloth;
ISBN: 1-57344-023-X 12.95 paper.

Unholy Alliances: New Women's Fiction edited by Louise Rafkin.
ISBN: 0-939416-14-X 21.95 cloth;
ISBN: 0-939416-15-8 9.95 paper.

The Wall by Marlen Haushofer.
ISBN: 0-939416-53-0 24.95 cloth;
ISBN: 0-939416-54-9 paper.

We Came All The Way from Cuba So You Could Dress Like This?: Stories by Achy Obejas.
ISBN: 0-939416-92-1 24.95 cloth;
ISBN: 0-939416-93-X 10.95 paper.

Latin America

Beyond the Border: A New Age in Latin American Women's Fiction edited by Nora Erro-Peralta and Caridad Silva-Núñez.
ISBN: 0-939416-42-5 24.95 cloth;
ISBN: 0-939416-43-3 12.95 paper.

The Little School: Tales of Disappearance and Survival in Argentina by Alicia Partnoy.
ISBN: 0-939416-08-5 21.95 cloth;
ISBN: 0-939416-07-7 9.95 paper.

Revenge of the Apple by Alicia Partnoy.
ISBN: 0-939416-62-X 24.95 cloth;
ISBN: 0-939416-63-8 8.95 paper.

Autobiography, Biography, Letters

Peggy Deery: An Irish Family at War by Nell McCafferty.
ISBN: 0-939416-38-7 24.95 cloth;
ISBN: 0-939416-39-5 9.95 paper.

The Shape of Red: Insider/Outsider Reflections by Ruth Hubbard and Margaret Randall.
ISBN: 0-939416-19-0 24.95 cloth;
ISBN: 0-939416-18-2 9.95 paper.

Women & Honor: Some Notes on Lying by Adrienne Rich.
ISBN: 0-939416-44-1 3.95 paper.

Animal Rights

And a Deer's Ear, Eagle's Song and Bear's Grace: Relationships Between Animals and Women edited by Theresa Corrigan and Stephanie T. Hoppe.
ISBN: 0-939416-38-7 24.95 cloth;
ISBN: 0-939416-39-5 9.95 paper.

With a Fly's Eye, Whale's Wit and Woman's Heart: Relationships Between Animals and Women edited by Theresa Corrigan and Stephanie T. Hoppe.
ISBN: 0-939416-24-7 24.95 cloth;
ISBN: 0-939416-25-5 9.95 paper.

Ordering information

Since 1980, Cleis Press has published progressive books by women. We welcome your order and will ship your books as quickly as possible. Individual orders must be prepaid (U.S. dollars only). Please add 15% shipping. PA residents add 6% sales tax. Mail orders: Cleis Press, PO Box 8933, Pittsburgh PA 15221. MasterCard and Visa orders: include account number, exp. date, and signature. FAX your credit card order: (412) 937-1567. Or, phone us Mon–Fri, 9 am–5 pm EST: (412) 937-1555.